I0687432

The Devil You Know

Alex Breck

Seilachan Fort

Published by Seilachan Fort

Copyright © Alex Breck 2016

www.alexbreckbooks.com

All rights reserved. No part of this
publication may be reproduced, stored or
transmitted in any form, or by any means
electronic, mechanical, including photocopy,
recording or otherwise, without the prior
permission of the copyright owner.

This book is a work of fiction. Names,
characters, places and incidents are either a
product of the author's imagination or are
used fictitiously. Any resemblance to actual
events, locales or persons, living or dead is
purely coincidental.

ISBN: 978-0-9933887-1-2

To my beautiful family as always for their love, support and endless patience.

"Fancy thinking the Beast was something you could hurt and kill!" said the head.
William Golding, *Lord Of The Flies*

Chapter 1

'So what's it mean anyway pal?
Kinda like a gang motto, aye?'

Silence…

'Then you're some sort a' soldier, eh?
Come on, am I right or no?'

The lad was only making chat, Lachie
knew that. He tried to mask his irritation, slowly
clenching and releasing the muscles in his jaw.
He toyed with the idea of explaining the
meaning of the Latin text. But on looking into
the acne-ridden face hovering in front of him,
the clumsy features which looked as if they had
been put together in a hurry, he decided not to
waste his breath. The puffy eyes were too
closely arranged and still encrusted with sleep
despite it being well after lunch-time. The
clammy air shifted a little each time the boy
moved around him and Lachie's nose wrinkled
in disdain as he detected yet another waft of
musty body odour.

His own darling parents would have
instantly condemned the lad to one of the lowest
strata of polite society by saying he had a
'Catholic' face. Lachie detested any brand of
bigoted attitude although he could never have
been described as the overly tolerant type. He
held no allegiances and felt no trace of love for
any part of humanity. Blind discrimination and

1

constant rejection had been the central pillars of his miserable life.

But all that was about to change.

Taking a swig of Red Bull, the boy swung back around to face his customer and Lachie closed his eyes, counting backwards from ten, as a syrupy burp washed across his face.

'It's a song lyric then? Some old-school heavy-metal band stuff?
Mind, you look mair like a rap dude, no offence like.'

Lachie grimaced and thought comfortingly of the 9mm pistol sitting only feet away in his prized San Francisco Giants jacket. This would be his second unplanned kill of the week.

He didn't want to think about killing people right now. He was there to cheer himself up, which had been the whole point of getting another tattoo; to reassert his masculinity, to rebuild his confidence and redefine his purpose after the debacle of the first outing of The Project.

He took a long, slow, deep breath and let it all go.

'No... It's *none* of those things.
It's an old Roman battle text.
Alea iacta est.
It means 'The die is cast.''

2

'Like Caesar and all that?'

'Precisely. Very good.
It was attributed to Julius Caesar at a defining moment in his career as he led his army across the Rubicon river into Northern Italy.'

'Cool! So I was right an' all. Soldier stuff.'

Lachie just smiled thinly and closed his eyes again.

Chapter 2

He continued to sit there with his eyes shut; listening to the quiet hum of the equipment at his side as Crud Face deftly completed the ornate wording.

The die is cast.

He felt his heart beat faster as he considered the next phase of the operation. This time he would get it right. It would take longer than originally planned but perhaps he'd gone off too quick before and if the weather up there had been half as bad as down here, it might have posed him a considerable problem. Admittedly, the weather would always be out of his control but still he had to ensure as many elements of The Project as possible were nailed down tight. He liked to think of it as a project. It made it sound like it had some sense of cold reason behind it instead of 'by reason of insanity.'

The die is cast.

There was truly no way to turn back now. He had killed. He couldn't change that, even if he wanted to. Deep down, of course he regretted what had happened. But in no way would he let the death of one miserable brat interfere with his grand plan. As he sat in the tattoo parlour, trying to ignore the inane jarring conversations from the gents barbers on the other side of the greasy partition, he wondered what the response would be if he gave these men an inkling of what lurked in this odd looking head of his. Ha!

Inkling. In a tattoo parlour. He laughed inwardly and thought again of his pistol nearby.

It had always been like this for Lachlan Hector Struan Maclean. Born on a cold winter's night in 1988, his traumatic birth had been marked down in history with the scarring of the beautiful Scottish countryside by a burning American airliner. As if the devil himself had flown over Scotland that black night. The world had been irrevocably changed in one moment of evil yet the private anguish of the Clan Maclean had little to do with the tragedy of a plane crash. His mother had produced her third child, a tiny pale hairless creature with violet coloured eyes. An albino boy.

Of course his mother had tried to love him. To her, he was still her son, her only boy. But it could have been no coincidence they had decided not to try for any more children shortly after his arrival.

His father had always been a remote influence, featuring only occasionally on the family radar. Lachie remembered him as always having been away from home, working abroad on one lucrative oil geology contract after another, mostly in Africa. But the distance had not been just geographical. No-one would have described him as a 'family man' but he had been particularly absent in the life of his young son, whom he'd considered to be a runt, a hideous aberration who in previous times would have been drowned at birth.

Lachie grew up knowing his two older sisters despised him for his ugliness and he saw how they were embarrassed by him in front of their friends even before he developed his anti-social habits such as his perpetual scratching and chronic wheezing. His allergy-related asthma had all but disappeared now but in those days he'd been tortured by the strong perfumes his elder siblings doused themselves with at every opportunity as if somehow they had been aware of the additional suffering this caused him.

The family were all privately educated and so young Lachlan had been despatched to an exclusive boy's school in the rolling Perthshire hills where all but his mother could effectively forget about him.

He had little doubt those terrible schooldays had made him into the monster he had now become. It made him feel better to have something to blame apart from himself. He had eventually hauled himself up to barely average height as an adult but during his childhood he had been far smaller than his contemporaries, the steroid asthma inhalers helping to stunt his growth in an unnecessarily cruel twist of fate. Vomited into the perfect gene pool of upper class British youth it came as no surprise the other boys looked upon him as some kind of macabre curiosity.

Even at that moment, sitting there in the tattoo parlour, Lachie could hear the torments from those cruel faces looking down upon him.

'What kind of lab rat are you supposed to be then?'
'Were you grown in one of our Petri dishes?'
'How come your eyes are so *red* all the time?'
'Are you a *vampire*?'
'Why are you so white and skinny?'
'Where's your hair? It's like an old man's.'

He learned at school how the Nazis had considered albinos to be subhuman and that's how he was made to feel. His peers had voted him their Pope of Fools, their Quasimodo - the ugliest boy in the school.

Hopeless in all sports, this additional disability simply compounded matters and so mostly, they left him to his own devices and he developed a lifelong addiction for violent computer games. Online, he found his sanctuary, where he could leave his physical body behind. But he also read voraciously, including Hugo's *The Hunchback of Notre-Dame*, which helped him come out of school top of his class at the earliest opportunity. Despite the protestations of his headmaster who had foreseen a glittering academic career after university, Lachie signed up for the same army regiment as his paternal grandfather had done before him, although in different circumstances.

Lachie squirmed in the chair unable to relieve the persistent itching around his groin as his arm continued to be worked upon. *Who was it*, he thought for a moment. Then he remembered who had said it.

Samuel Johnson.

Patriotism is the last refuge of a scoundrel.

He hadn't thought like that at the time, but in the end the army had been little better than school. He had enlisted in the Royal Scots Fusiliers, still optimistic he could make his father proud of him. His family had a long connection with the Fusiliers and his grandpa had received the George Cross for bravery from his campaign in Sicily in '43. Lachie's father had been overjoyed the world might actually have a pigeonhole for his mutant offspring and so the family breathed a collective sigh of relief and considered him as case closed.

Unfortunately he became once again an innocent victim of the gods of Time as shortly after his arrival, financial constraints left his regiment disbanded and amalgamated into the vastly unpopular generic Royal Regiment of Scotland. Considered a Jonah by many of his peers he still managed to rise swiftly through the ranks to become a Captain, largely through old family influence, but even so he faced constant bullying and universal dislike. His appearance had destined him for perpetual virginity by the unanimous decree of his peers. Together with his predilection for masturbation and his equally strange teetotal behaviour, he had little in common with the other men.

He wriggled awkwardly in his chair. *Like I gave a fuck by that point.* The creeping corporatisation of the army allowed him to move into the I.T. side of things which he genuinely enjoyed and also seemed to have an aptitude for.

Then one day soon after, he received the tearful call from his mother.

'It's Daddy…
He's been killed in E.G.
Please come home.'

Lachie still remembered exactly how he had felt as if it had been this very day. He had placed the phone gently down and smiled, before raising a fist in the air in a silent salute to the rebel forces of Equatorial Guinea. He then collected his personal papers from his quarters and walked out, never to return.

Of course, he'd gleefully killed his father many times by then.

Gods of War II.
Manhunt.
Grand Theft Auto.
Call of Duty Black Ops.

But in an exceptional twist of unexpected good fortune, this time 'Real Life Inc' had gone one better, with bells on. Old Pops had got himself snuffed out in the line of duty. In addition, the oil company were found to be negligent and so under the harsh glare of worldwide media scorn they had admitted full culpability. The upshot for Lachie meant he'd become independently wealthy beyond his wildest dreams.

Those dreams had also become pretty wild too. He'd been given the ultimate reboot program. *Add To Cart* with free checkout – a strictly unlimited offer. His new found independence, for the first time in his miserable life, was something he'd been determined to grab with both of his trembling hands and never let go. Despite all the negativity of his past life he had fervently hoped maybe now things would look up for him.

The first thing he'd done was have the most outrageously expensive eye surgery to try and mitigate his poor eyesight. There had been no Specsavers for this boy, not this time. He still didn't know if it had been totally successful and at best it would only ever make a slight improvement rather than eliminate his myopia. For the next few months he had been advised to continue shielding his eyes from direct sunlight as he'd been doing his entire life. So for the time being he still hid behind his trademark rapper sunglasses which he wore with his second-skin Giants jacket and matching cap.

He'd moved out of the ancestral home with indecent haste and bought a nice house in Bearsden, an upmarket area of Glasgow close to the countryside. He told his neighbours he was studying for an I.T. Masters but neglected to mention his specialism was in the field of chronic masturbation. Naturally, his next important step concerned the loss of his virginity and so he'd abstained for almost an entire week before flying out to Berlin for a romantic assignation.

Lachie scratched impatiently as the memories of his doomed encounter flooded back. Crud Face lifted his hands in mock surrender as he was subjected to a pair of malevolent red eyes.

'OK pal, I'm nearly done, honest! Be finished in just a wee sec!'

Of course the 'date' in Berlin had been bought and paid for. Yet now with his new found freedom, he felt anything might be possible. He thought if he went somewhere different, alien even, then perhaps his psychoses might be left behind. He'd been cajoled into visiting prostitutes a couple of times in the army, but each encounter had been a gut-wrenchingly awful experience.

Despite his sordid personal habits and his addiction to mind-numbingly violent computer games, deep down he still thought sex should have some modicum of romance even for an odious creature like himself. Both of the experiences in Glasgow had been with women he wouldn't have looked twice at outside a brothel and he found their coarse language and common backgrounds to be a complete turn-off.

Of course, deep down he knew he was making pathetic excuses for himself and a 'real man' would have just got on with it and so this provoked his inner demons further and pushed him deeper along the dark path he had now embarked upon this spring.

It never occurred to him even for a moment that his feelings had been entirely natural and the vast majority of everyday fully functioning 'normal' males would have felt exactly the same way and very few of them would ever have contemplated buying the services of a prostitute.

However, it had been the usual story with Lachie and he couldn't raise any more than a smile with either of the two women who each belied the myth of the warm-hearted prostitute. Previously availed of the monetary aspects of the transaction they wasted little time on the hideous looking boy who couldn't get it on. Any last sentimental notions Lachie may have harboured about the fairer sex had been dashed and his resentment and paranoia only increased exponentially.

But this 'affair' in Berlin should have been different. He had booked a suite in a top hotel and arranged to take Ekaterina to a top show followed by a sumptuous meal. The plan then had been for the amorous couple to retire with the finest champagne to their enormous Jacuzzi bath.

He needn't have bothered. The fleeting look of abject horror on her face as he opened his hotel room door had said it all. He'd seen pictures of her of course, but still, she stopped his heart for a second. Six feet of absolute perfection wrapped in a skin tight chain mail dress and draped with gorgeous jewellery. She took a small step backwards and her practiced smile faltered just long enough for Lachie to notice and so that was it as far as he was concerned. The two of them went through the motions of a date but his feelings of dread about the later events only grew stronger as the evening progressed. There was no doubt she was vivacious and intelligent and a different animal to the vicious and hard women he had consorted with back home.

He imagined in an alternate universe she would have been a dream date for any man and so he decided to keep it just like a traditional 'first date' and he ordered her a taxi after the meal. The look of unabashed relief on her fresh young face would stay with him for ever.

Back in Scotland, Lachie went into a self-imposed hibernation and it was during this dark winter of self-loathing and bitter recriminations when the twisted tendrils of The Project began to insinuate their way into the black recesses of his damaged mind.

Chapter 3

His tattoo finally completed, Lachie chose to walk back to the city centre rather than indulge his latest bad habit – excessive taxi consumption. Besides, he felt restless and claustrophobic after being cooped up with the bath-shy fool and he thought it looked like it could turn out to be a bright and optimistic day even for a depressive like himself.

As he strode purposefully down the shaded side of the busy street, he must have looked to the world as just another US obsessed young student. Still wearing his customary San Francisco Giants baseball jacket, he had worried if this might have been an unnecessary risk after the shambolic events of the last 24 hours, but as he glanced around him, his red eyes hidden behind black 'rehab' glasses, he could see countless other twats dressed like him. Besides, the look suited him, the shades and the baseball cap covering his head and protecting his eyes from the glare. But all the same, he couldn't fathom the obsession of his contemporaries for aping the dress code of uneducated morons from some no-go housing project in Detroit or wherever.

One of the peculiar repercussions of his many disastrous experiences with the rest of the human race meant despite not wanting to be like anyone else on the planet, he categorically did not want to be himself. He'd picked on baseball as a sport to be interested in when he'd been at school, partly because it would upset the traditionalists but mainly because he knew there'd be little chance of him ever being expected to try and participate in it. But he loved his jacket, its orange sleeves proudly displaying the past glories of six World Series wins before the triumphant seventh win in 2012. The commemoration jacket he wore wasn't just any old run of the mill effort. The body was pure leather with a matching price tag of more than £1,000. He had an optional extra too – an inner sleeved pocket sized perfectly for his automatic pistol.

Despite the bright day, a gloomy cloud latched on to Lachie from a safe distance and his mind began racing as to how he could perfect The Project so as to avoid the problems of the previous day. He could not do *that* again, he knew, so there had to be another way.

Crossing the road by the ornate frontage of a plush modern hotel he decided to go on a detour and work out for a few hours, another of his latest obsessions. He stepped through the traffic, absentmindedly looking around for a cab and then jumped backwards as a ridiculous looking stretch Cadillac limousine nearly took him out as it pulled away imperiously into the traffic.

He'd discovered that exercising fiercely in his new health club often sparked some of his best and most imaginative ideas and his heart had begun beating faster with the fresh kernel of one coming to life as he sat scratching furiously in the back of the taxi.

The gym was in the latest style of stripped down no-frills packages and it fitted Lachie like a glove. Struggling with its location amongst the more 'country club' clientele, it nevertheless was ideal for someone like him; few staff and even fewer members. Most who did attend left the freaky looking guy to his own devices. Wearing shades *inside* a gym? Plain weird. However, he'd soon earned the grudging respect of the few die-hard Cro-Magnon guys as he efficiently sculpted his skinny alabaster white body into a passing resemblance of a grown man.

Today, he would nearly break his body into pieces as he desperately tried to forget the disastrous first phase of his mission.

It always came down to planning. He knew it. He was a highly trained army officer for crying out loud. Yet he had jumped in, half-cocked. He knew *that* too. After spending the whole winter preparing for direct action, setting the scene and spending an obscene amount of money, he had worked himself into such a frenzy he'd almost jeopardised the entire mission. He cranked the treadmill up to 8.5 mph in an effort to displace his negative thoughts. But it made no difference.

He'd researched the geography meticulously and he had been in Zone A at the allotted time as per the plan. The weather had played its role perfectly and the rain had been tipping down. In fact his wipers were struggling to cope with the volume of water being dumped on his windscreen and his biggest worry had been his lamentably poor eyesight. But rain had always been his preferred choice as it would enable the pick-up to be easy, or so he had thought. His one fatal flaw had been he didn't really know how to speak to girls and he lacked the fundamental knowledge of how they act in any given situation.

Therefore when he stopped and offered the two schoolgirls a lift in his car Lachie didn't anticipate that they would look at each other and think with one mind – child molester!

His subsequent panic and ham-fisted grabbing at the nearest one didn't help much either. As the small girl, greasy with rain, slipped out of his grasp, the other one screamed and ran off. He'd instinctively let the first girl go but then as the sickening realisation hit him that he was suddenly faced with his whole scheme unravelling in an instant, he'd then pulled out his gun and shot the running girl in the back of the head from a hundred feet. The closer girl fell to the ground howling and bunched her skinny body up into a foetal position on the wet pavement.

Horrified at what he'd done, he stood paralysed in the rain for what couldn't have been more than a brief second but there had been no more time to think. He heard the roar of angry men running towards him so he'd thrown himself back into the car and gunned it down the puddle-strewn road.

Chapter 4

'Will some bastard go and get me some *real* fags, for Christ sake?'

DI James Boyle was having a crap day and he hadn't even made it to nine in the morning yet. Bad enough the electric had run out in his rented flat during the night meaning his electronic cigarette charger hadn't charged up, then he comes in to find The Boss has dumped another murder case on his desk. No, what had really wound him up was that in the ten minutes he'd been there, some swine had unplugged his charger in favour of their poofy Blackberry. He had now been awake for a full two hours without a smoke! No wonder they called this new brand, *or was it called a flavour*, Bull Smoke.

'Bull Smoke? Bull *Shit* more like. I've really had it with this crap.
Steel..?
Where the hell have you got to now?'

He was definitely raging like one, thought DC Gary Steel morosely as he manoeuvred his rotund body expertly through the chaotic desks of the Ops Room.

'Morning sir! Take it you've seen the missives from on high, sir?'

'Aye. Yet another nasty wee shite out there.
Give me the latest will you?
And find Mackie. Tell him to get me 20 Regal and be fuckin' nippy about it. Can never find either of you these days.'

Steel gulped and spoke quietly.

'Sir…, DC Mackie is on an ethnic awareness workshop today *and* the morra', sir.'

'That's put the fucking tin lid on it, so it has!
Some nut-job's out there, killing wee lassies and half the team's away learning bastarding Urdu! Give me strength!

'Yes sir,' said Steel.

'Right! Grab the file. You're driving. Let's get over there before she can dump any more crap on to us. First stop the fag shop mind. Or so help me, it'll be me up on a murder charge before tea-break…'

Boyle wasn't just grumpy because he was nicotine-deprived. He knew this case would get to him because the dead girl so happened to be the same age as his own wee girl, Jenny, whom he hadn't seen in weeks. It wasn't entirely down to Marie being an awkward cow; she'd been pretty good most of the time. It was the bloody job…as per usual. He'd missed a couple of allotted weekends due to some carnage or other and now with their eighteen year old John in trouble himself, the pressure was on him.

The car ploughed through the narrow city streets, headlights on full stun as daylight struggled to penetrate to ground level. Steel piloted them with skilfully controlled aggression as Boyle urged him to drive ever faster. He might be a lazy twat most of the time but Boyle had to admit to a grudging respect for his driving prowess; one of the more useful outcomes of yet another police course.

Leafing through the file, Boyle read out the gist of another depressing gun crime statistic. In his twenty years policing the streets of Glasgow, he'd have to agree that serious crime hadn't got a hell of a lot better in the Mean City. But they'd all been relieved at the reduction in overall shenanigans amongst the general population and he'd never had to deal with half as much fucking about between the traditional gangs as his predecessors' had endured back in the halcyon days of his namesake Jimmy Boyle.

Now approaching forty, a brutal fact he hated to be reminded of, during the early years of his police career he'd cursed his parents often and loudly as he'd tried to shake off the jokes referring to his connection to the notorious gangster who had shared his name. This only intensified when the media had a collective orgasm on the day the 'other' Jimmy left the special prison at Barlinnie as an internationally feted 'misunderstood' artist. Of course, your average beat cop had thought the societal resurrection of Mr Boyle from a man more used to dabbling in other men's blood than acrylic paint or sculptors' clay had been a complete crock.

Surprisingly, *this* Jimmy Boyle didn't agree. Sure, in his youth he didn't argue with the established police view, but over the years he began to feel if he heard the opinion 'piss-artist mair like,' once more, he would jump in the river Clyde. The other less surprising product of this 'art as saviour' theme had been every other nasty wee thug in Glasgow would try and claim that they too were 'tortured' artists after being apprehended tormenting some other poor scrote.

No, as he got older and steadily more jaded by the relentless tide of filth, he began to think he too might have been in the wrong line of work. He noticed he'd begun to take more interest in any art-related crime cases. He routinely found himself reading the arty supplements of the Sunday papers even *before* the football pages and he would often be dithering outside art shops trying to find a strong enough reason to go in. He never did.

Looking back, he could have blamed his old da' easily enough if he had been that type of man. A Ravenscraig man back in its heyday when thousands were employed within the factory walls, his father had been smart enough to see the end of heavy industry in Scotland even as the Thatcher era had begun to rip the heart out of the central belt. *Get a government job, son. There will always be work for the polis.*

In his way he had been right, Boyle thought darkly as the car approached the crime scene. He thrust an unlit cigarette in his mouth, willing the wheels to stop. There will always be fresh supplies of scum to keep him occupied. What was the song again? Oh aye. *The woodwork squeaks and out come the freaks…*

'Alright, what have we got here?'

'Morning sir. Girl was shot just there on the pavement, back of the head, looks like a professional job sir.'

'I've read the file son. Tell me when did *you* join CID, eh?
If it *was* a professional job why the fuck did he do it at peak fucking traffic hours in front of witnesses and then leave the other wee girl alive?

'Sorry sir…I just, what I mean is…' The young constable stammered and fidgeted as if trying to complete the sentence in sign language.

'Aye well…Just give me an update on the specifics.
Who saw anything?
What are their names?
Where are they now?

Steel…? I want you to organise this rabble to take statements before lunchtime, while I speak to the lucky lass who survived.'

Boyle strode off, puffing furiously. It would be a good ten minutes walk to the girl's house. He should get three fags in by then at least.

'Oh and Steel! I want you to bell me the second you get a bead on that gun,' he yelled over his shoulder.

As he walked across the potholed road, the first glimmers of sun began to dry up the rough tarmac leaving isolated oily pools. Boyle glanced up at the tired looking houses, each one black with mould and decay, uglier than a row of junkie's teeth. The corner house, vulnerable to the harsh elements on this exposed estate had been boarded up, presumably empty. Every square foot was adorned with graffiti and the 'garden' had mysteriously accumulated the rubbish of several years piled in the nettle strewn front grass. *Nice neighbours*, he snorted, lighting the third cigarette as he opened the rusty gate of numbers 17 to 20 Dalhousie Avenue.

It was a waif-like wee girl who eventually answered the door. *Could have smoked another one by now*, he grumbled to himself as the half-dressed child ushered him in, her eyes red-rimmed and tired looking. Boyle reeled as he entered a living room as warm as a sauna. He noted the three bar electric giving it big licks underneath a chrome framed picture of a bunch of flowers which could have easily been the product of a drunken hurl on a Friday night. Judging by the stench in the room, he guessed the occupants were not unused to a wee 'over indulgence' every now and then. Choking on the stale alcohol smell, he hastily fought to loosen his collar before he passed out.

'Morning...Mrs Meekin is it?
My name is Detective Inspector James Boyle.
If you don't mind I'd like to ask you and your daughter Emily a few questions?'

The unkempt woman on the sofa stared up at him, her face devoid of emotion. *Pissed as a fart*, Boyle decided immediately. Her upper body swayed precariously with the effort of having to speak. The words came out slurred and loaded with the venom of the aggrieved.

'Bit fuckin' late... is it no' like? Ah said tae yon other cunt..., ah sez tae her like- Wait, who ur ye again? Polis?'

'Mrs Meekin, is your husband available? I only need a couple of minutes-'

'Aye! Ah could dae with a few minutes wi' him an' all.

25

Banged up in Greenock, so he is… nae thanks tae your lot, the basturt.'

'I do apologize, Mrs Meekin, eh…, Donna. It says on my report that your husband-'

A plaintive voice cut through the fetid air, like a bird in a cage.

'Inspector! He's no ma real da' he just stays wi' mum and me but. An' he's gaun an' fucked off 'cos of yous polis like.
Ah'm Emily.
It was me who seen it, so it was.'

Boyle loosened his collar further. The poor wee wretch! Nobody to look after her after a near death experience. He made a mental note to call social services as soon as he was done here. Bloody cutbacks – she would possibly have got two or three hours yesterday afternoon and that's it. Meanwhile she's been left with 2016 Mother of The Year.

He leant down and tried to soften his voice as much as possible.

'Here lass, let's talk out there in the fresh air eh?' He herded the girl out the door before the mum could formulate a response and the two of them sat down side by side on the front step.

26

'Are you alright hen? Do you want someone over to watch you?' Boyle elbowed her unintentionally as he searched in his jacket for cigarettes. Emily jumped up and turned on him, her eyes like small black pinpricks in the bright sunshine.

'We're fine, so we are! Can ye no' jist leave us alone? Yous'll only make it worse and then he'll *never* come back. Then what the fuck will we do?'

'All right then. Just tell me as much as you can remember.
Any wee thing. It might sound daft to you but it might help us catch this man.'

'Wise up pal! You'll no catch him, like. He'd be wan o' Rocky's boys, sent after me tae put the fear o' God intae Tam, ma step-dad.
Mind you, he wisnae frae aboot here mind.
No many pure white rapper dudes workin' wi' Rocky like.'

'So you're sure he was a white guy? My file says you were upset about his dark eyes yesterday?'

'So I was an' all, by the way. The radge had pure mental *red* eyes, man. Red eyes! Pure *wasted* he was, off his face!'

Later, after a visit with the dead girl's parents which sadly had been even more depressing than his prior appointment, Steel gave Boyle a breakdown on the small scale turf war which had seemingly escalated in recent months.

'All under control according to Drug Squad sir. Told me to give it a complete body swerve.'

'Under control!

Boyle choked on his sausage roll, pastry shrapnel flying over the dashboard and windscreen.

'Easy for them to say. They've no got a wee girl down in the morgue.'

Back at the Pitt Street HQ, Boyle reviewed the case over a Styrofoam coffee and one of his newly operational plastic cigarettes. Not too bad, he considered, especially when you still had that real fag smell off the fingers to give it that authentic tang.

But he wasn't so sure about the authenticity of the story he had been spun that morning. He had little time for philosophising. You go with the facts or listen to your gut – deal or no deal. There was a backlog lurking since they'd left and Baxter had also requested a 'chat' at 5pm in her office. He hated these so-called informal meetings where she expected him to keep the details of up to a dozen cases in his head while she casually fired off volley after volley from her notes. She was a legend in policing, not only because she'd made DCI in record time but because she could pick a hole in a story through the eye of a needle at a hundred paces.

Boyle had another good reason for trying to avoid Barbara Baxter. He quite liked her, not so much in a romantic way, but more in the 'kindred spirits along the road of life' sense. She was similarly aged to him and also *sans* marriage partner; her prick of a husband having flown the coop with some wee hairdresser, reputedly because his masculinity couldn't square off the fact his wife might be more successful than him. And so the pair of them had put the world to rights on several occasions, always strictly above board, helped in no small way by the fact neither of them was partial to the demon drink.

No. He was dodging Baxter because, as his superior officer, he was duty-bound to inform her of the latest shit storm in his own beleaguered private life. He had been getting enough grief from Marie about their son and he could only expect similar pelters from DCI Baxter.

His son and heir had recently been arrested for fighting outside a pub on holiday and when searched by police, a small lump of cannabis had been found. He'd sworn to both parents that it had been a one-off holiday thing but Marie had laid the blame firmly at Jim's door. His lack of parental control, a weak fatherly influence and the boy's insecurities resulting from his parent's impending divorce and so forth.

He felt his face grow hotter as he remembered the incident which resulted in his expulsion from the matrimonial nest. Bizarrely, at that time it had been his excessive and 'domineering' fathering which had sparked the final showdown.

If there was one thing in life that really bugged James Boyle and there were *plenty* of candidates to choose from, top of the list had to be violent computer games. So when he'd come home from work on a Saturday evening to see John still welded to his Xbox, not having moved a muscle since he'd left first thing in the morning, he'd feel the life inexorably sap out of him. He genuinely tried to be part of it in the early days but as the game themes became ever more violent and debased Boyle couldn't help being reminded of real life cases which he had had to deal with and all the psychological traumas that accompanied them.

For a long time he'd fought an internal battle with himself about waking his son up to the harsh realities of the real world and then he and Marie would spar endlessly over many a long night. In her eyes, her baby boy could do no wrong and she told Jim it was a phase all young boys go through nowadays and he shouldn't be so 'selfish' as to bring his work home with him. In the end he'd chosen to let the fates decree and so 'bring his work home' had been exactly what he'd done.

There had been a particularly horrible Glasgow case of a youngster being kidnapped and subsequently stabbed and burned alive purely due to his ethnic background. Jim had walked in on his son playing his favourite new game in the same week, Grand Theft Auto, around the point where John had been gleefully barbecuing prostitutes with a flamethrower. So he casually dropped a file onto the lounge table as he went upstairs for a shower, saying something along the lines of, 'Promise me you'll not look in that file son, it's a horrible murder case I'm working on'. His son, being a curious sixteen year old, had it open before his father had time to pull a sock off and the upshot was the 'poor wee boy' had nightmares for weeks. Marie had gone thermonuclear when their son grassed him up and the subsequent fallout for his parents' marriage, inevitably, proved to be total and utter devastation.

But Baxter had been a total gem.

'Och Jim, honestly, it's a fuss about nothing really. I'll have a wee word with Ayr branch and we'll have this one dropped quicker than a *Jim'll Fix It* badge…

Now, what's this you've given me here about the Garthamlow shooting yesterday? You don't think it's drug related? Come on, I want to hear what that famous gut of yours is telling you.'

Chapter 5

The 'Bottom Line' was about as subtle and as classy as you would expect a Glasgow lap dancing club to look like in the unflattering brightness of a spring afternoon. Lachie had been there once before on an Army stag night although he had remembered it as being far more cosmopolitan at the time. He was having serious second thoughts about this repeat visit.

But that had been the sole reason he'd chosen this tip rather than one of the three or four other locations he'd been offered by his online porn broker. The very fact he'd been there before, therefore proving it must be, by virtue of his innate class and breeding, a safer and more respectable outlet than some skanky tenement close or the like.

Lachie surveyed the building for the third time, fully aware he would start attracting the wrong kind of attention if he loitered any further. The grimy windows had been blacked out from the outside with the entire face of the club painted over with a drab matt grey which would have looked overly utilitarian even on a battleship. Over this uninspiring façade a small child must have been recruited to paint an abysmal series of female posteriors which were about as appealing as haemorrhoids. Doesn't really *need* to market itself, Lachie told himself, as long as there's naked women inside they will always have a steady stream of sad bastard customers, just like me.

Taking a deep breath, Lachie approached the two doors. The bigger left hand door was obviously for the main club and looked locked.

Go through the right hand door and down the stairs, he had been told. *Straight on to the private bar on the left hand side of the room before the 'dance' studio.* He tried to peer through the filthy window but the inside had been obscured by lurid flyers and adverts for 'private sitting' portrait painting classes. Yeah right. His contact had stressed the importance of not going into any other rooms or speaking to anyone apart from the bar guy who would be expecting him.

The flight of stairs looked perilously steep and barely wide enough for one. Ditching the shades before he became airborne, Lachie switched on his well practiced air of nonchalance and strolled into the grubby lounge area. The bar was devoid of customers. Loud music blasted through from the next room and as Lachie kept walking towards the noise he suddenly jumped as he saw a heavily built, oily faced man appear from underneath the bar with the makings of a sandwich in one hand and a phone cradled in the generous folds of his neck.

The man nodded and Lachie approached the bar, mentally rehearsing his lines. But the guy didn't look like he was in a hurry to get off the phone anytime soon. His accent sounded Polish or some other East European country. Being a social recluse, Lachie hadn't mixed with many of the substantial influx from the region who'd become an integral part of the fabric of 21st century Scotland and so he couldn't get a fix on the exact nationality. Wherever the fuck he hailed from, the guy must have seen a hundred pound note before as the call was instantly curtailed as an impatient Lachie casually placed one on the bartop and slid it over.

'I've come about your 'catering' order for next week.
Have you got the list for me?'

The man snatched the cash and smiled.

'You got the money, my friend?'

Lachie opened his wallet and flicked out a further two pink bank notes towards the man who in return reached under the bar and without taking his eyes off Lachie's wallet, brought out a small brown paper bag and tossed it over.

'You need more, my friend…call direct next time.
Is much cheaper, you know. Here my card. I am Tomas.'

'I will remember that, Tomas. Thank you. What's going on next door?'

It had only been a casual throwaway remark, Lachie had thought later. Why couldn't he have kept his mouth shut?

'Is special…private party.
VIP invitation only…'

'Here's my ticket.' Still giddy from the
success of his transaction, Lachie dropped
another hundred on impulse.

'Okay dokey my friend!
You can go but maybe only watch for
one minute.'

He found himself looking onto a stage
'set' mocked up to look like a school classroom
but Lachie remained oblivious to anything else
around him except the grotesque scenario
directly under the baking hot glare of the studio
lights. Eighties rock was pounding and it would
have been impossible to make yourself heard
even if you had wanted to. He pulled off his
Giants cap and rubbed his damp face
uncomprehendingly.

Centre stage he could see two men with a
small boy who might have been perhaps six or
seven. Another two men were operating the
cameras, one of whom cast an alarmed glance
towards Tomas who remained half way in the
door. Out of the corner of his eye Lachie saw
him pat his breast pocket conspiratorially and the
man nodded, turning his attention back to the
action.

The boy had been forced to bend over a
small desk and one of the men appeared to be

having anal intercourse with him whilst the other man seemed to be preoccupied with forcing his groin towards the boy's face. Lachie stumbled forward unintentionally and he caught the eye of the plainly terrified boy who'd been made to wear a sick pastiche of an old style schoolboy cap held askew on his head by an adult hand.

He couldn't bear to watch for another second so suddenly Lachie found himself leaping forward, his screaming voice lost in the madness. He tripped headlong over one of the tripod legs of a studio light and the whole bizarre spectacle erupted into chaos as the blistering hot lamp toppled heavily across the set, knocking a cameraman flying.

The furious men, furtively pulling up their trousers, gesticulated madly as they cursed Lachie for this unforgivable intrusion. They turned away equally sharpish as Lachie pulled out his pistol, his arms out straight and pointing first at one then another. The older of the two 'stars,' who had only moments earlier been buggering a small child, stopped to pick up a monkey wrench and launched it past Lachie's head. His instant reward was a bullet through the centre of his forehead, silent but deadly, and he dropped to his knees as the music continued to blast out its macabre accompaniment.

The others then started to climb over each other in their frantic haste for the door with Lachie being directly in the path of the fellatio guy who had grabbed the boy to use as a human shield. Lachie had tensed his arms for the shot

when the boy heel-stamped the man causing him
to drop forwards but still enough to feel the hot
breath of a 9mm round caressing his scalp.
Taking his chance, the man threw the boy aside
and launched himself at Lachie and in a brief
tussle the two of them destroyed the rest of the
set before the man somehow found his way out
the door with the boy obscuring any chances of a
clear shot.

Within a few seconds there were only the
two of them left and Lachie hastily shooed the
boy out into the bar area. He'd no doubt the men
had fled, but for how long?

'Thanks mister…What happen now? I go
with you, yes?' the boy sobbed. Again there was
the unmistakable sound of an East European
accent.

'No! You're fine sonny.
Sit here while I work out what to do
for a second or two will you?'

Lachie got him a can of coke from
behind the bar and grabbed the phone. Although
he'd strayed far into uncharted territory he could
still see the boy would obviously be toast if he
stayed around the club for too much longer.
Same applied to him, for that matter. His head
spun as he punched 999 for the first time in his
life. It had all got too complicated too fast. He
took a long slow breath and allowed his military
training to take control of the situation.

'Get here quick will you – a wee boy has just been fucked both ways on Candid Camera and we are totally surrounded by guys with guns…'

Chapter 6

'Seven…eight…nine…*ten*! He grunted loudly like every other wanker who forgets he's got his earplugs in and has his music up way too high. He pumped his fist in the air as the last echoes of Queen's *We Are The Champions* faded inside his skull. He'd successfully bench-pressed his own bodyweight ten times – when he first walked into this building a couple of months ago, he couldn't have moved it off the rack. Even better, he now knew exactly what he had to do next to advance his plans! This meant he'd need to wheel out *Laxxxx88* and get smoking once more.

Later, as he fired up one of his state-of-the-art laptops back at the house, he had to laugh at himself a little. Working in IT for the army he had been given access to the logins, email addresses and even passwords of hundreds of service personnel and it continually amazed him how many people used obvious numbers like the number of their house or the date of their birth. For fun he had hacked into the personal bank accounts of colleagues using information unwittingly supplied by them. And now here he sat, with a username based on, let's see now…, oh yes, the year of his birth! But, no-one would be getting anywhere near *his* data though; he had NATO level encryption across all his systems. If those sick bastards he bought the dope from ever tried to trace him through his recent ill-fated purchase then they would be led a merry dance all the way through the alphabet from Alcatraz to Zimbabwe. Judging from the TV news reports, he guessed they would be a tad preoccupied themselves right about now.

But now to serious business, he told himself, as the blinds were pulled down and the room became dark. In fact it would be several days before Lachie would roll them back up, his sensitive eyes blinking against the harsh spring sunlight and a wide grin softening the rough features of his stubbled face.

And in the end, it had all been so easy, *even easier than getting the island.* Mind you, he scolded himself, I've set myself up for a good bit of hard graft, and this might not prove to be such a breeze.

So! He was now the proud owner of the long established and award winning stretch limo hire business, Castaway Island! Technically speaking, the 'award' bit had been made up; he had simply awarded himself the 'nationally recognised' accolade. Oh, and the actual business itself had been fabricated too. By 'long established,' read the day before yesterday. Any nosey types who made a concerted effort to contact the names on his long list of customer testimonials would possibly be surprised to find they all worked on the catering squads at Camp Bastion. He didn't imagine there'd be many calls for stretch limos in Helmand Province these days.

He knew the daft name for the limo business and then using real army names had been ill advised but after surviving the calamitous drug buying escapade, Lachie felt nothing could touch him. He'd even experienced a small taste of a hitherto unknown frisson of redemption, of doing something for the common good for a change. The little white devil with the red eyes would usually prick him at this stage and say something like' *Yeah? You did okay. We'll chalk that one up against the girl child you murdered a fortnight ago.*

There would be a little work to do before he could take on his first job. He needed to spend a day or so applying the fake tan with a trowel to try and get rid of his blue-white complexion and he thought he might as well dye his white hair blond at the same time. His customers would be expecting to see the beach-blond rapper style owner of Castaway Island, DJ Hektor, and not an out of work actor from last year's vampire sequel. He thought he might as well get into character today as this would be the first test drive of the car without the distraction of customers.

He'd booked it for the afternoon and been happy to pay over the odds in order to be allowed to supply his own chauffeur. The fake driving licence, fake local council accreditation and the copy and paste enhanced disclosure for his driver were accepted without question as Lachie explained the booking would be the first of a series while his master travelled around the local area working on his latest Hollywood blockbuster. *Top secret mind* – if they told a soul before the hire period ended then the movie company would sue them to hell and back. He even got them to sign a confidentiality agreement!

Sparkling in the sunshine like an over-accessorized actress from a past era trying to recreate her golden years, the car still exuded a certain beauty – if you liked that sort of thing. Personally, Lachie thought it represented another unfortunate slip in our collective bad taste and symptomatic of the sickness of our US-obsessed media hype culture, but he congratulated himself on at least having a modicum of self-control in not going for the three-axle Hummer. There was no need to go that far.

He walked around the car a couple of times to make sure there were no flaws in his plan and his heart thumped as he imagined taking it out onto the open road. In a way they were ridiculous; like someone had photoshopped your vision and literally stretched the picture. Clothed in a pearlescent white with the customary blacked out windows and ultra shiny alloys, the Lincoln had to be at least 25 feet long. Comparing it to a couple of standard sized staff cars in the dusty car park he realised with a little trepidation that it would take some time to get used to driving it on the narrow Scottish roads.

Lachie pulled open a door and peered in. Whoever designed the interior décor had exercised none of the restraint shown by the vehicle builder. Decked out in lavish full length leather seating down one side, facing onto a garish neon lit bar and music system, it was like all your kitsch 70's Saturday Night Fever nightmares rolled into one. A tacky neon New York skyline had been sprayed across the wall at least eight feet wide over a sparkling fibre-optic encrusted bar. Barely an inch of uncluttered space remained around the cabin walls between the liberal splashing of plasma TV's and backlit mirrors.

Maybe they will be able to watch themselves on TV's like this, *if they survive the summer*, he thought as a current of anticipation travelled up his spine. He reclined on the vast chaise longue and stared up at his reflection in the mirrored ceiling. He decided he looked out of place in this candy-coated hell, like a cross between Willy Wonka and The Mad Hatter. But he *was* mad, wasn't he? The enormity of what he had set out to do hit him like a baseball bat wrapped in gaudy cover shots from Hello magazine. *Can I pull this off?* 'Course you can Maclean' he heard himself saying, in a confident voice. Confident and educated, he thought as he checked the workings of the intercom, the privacy window and the climate control air conditioning. It was the sort of voice which sounded good through an intercom. *This is your Captain speaking...* He had the voice for radio, he had once been told. But I have the face for radio too, he heard himself whisper.

But, at the end of the day, he reminded himself, these cars, these hundred-grand boxes; what were they really for? Apart from the odd wedding or business meeting, they had only one main function; to allow various tribes of pissed up Neanderthals to be transported on a pointless journey going precisely nowhere but still allowing them to advertise their level of shallow idiocy / achievement to other similarly infected scum from the poisonous depths of the gene pool. But no amount of pine tree car fresheners could ever totally mask the underlying whiff of hypocrisy and pop-tart perfume. Or maybe it was the stale stench of vomit?

He started the engine and his inner-child couldn't help revelling in the subdued roar of the powerful engine. Panic replaced delight within minutes as he encountered his first navigational issue and used up several lifetimes of embarrassment to overcome a typically acute Scottish corner. Stuck for what seemed like forever, he realised he might need a little more practice than anticipated. As he held up the clamouring traffic, his heart raced with the implications of such an attention grabbing situation when the mission had gone live.

But then, as the limousine calmly purred safely onwards, he looked around him and it hit him like a punch on the jaw. Out there, he saw the rest of the world getting on with their drab lives, trying not to give the show-off wankers behind the strobe lights and smoked glass the remotest notion of smug satisfaction by looking at them. A broad smile broke through Lachie's frustration as he became instantly seduced by the beauty and the logic of his plan. He had a modern version of the 'Emperor's new clothes' on wheels. People had become so inured to the inane behaviour of passengers in stretch limos, he could as likely as not drape dead bodies out the windows and nobody would notice or even care.

But now he had to attend to the details. He'd taken the limo to Strathclyde Country Park to give himself a breather from the traffic knowing any onlookers would assume it to be just another wedding party. Waiting for the dismal weather to pick up so the bride can 'capture that special moment' for evermore whilst inside she has the niggling feeling they might have lost that essence somewhere along the road. Knowing deep inside that despite the Hollywood glamour of their conveyance, her fat hairy husband will still end up puking his guts in their ensuite that evening and would never talk to her like those charming men from her erotic paperbacks.

The wind whipped smartly across the man-made loch and Lachie glanced up at the darkening sky. He knew there would be no fairytale wedding for him, no honeymoon but no messy divorce either. He had the Island Castaway decals rolled up under his arm and he needed to check how quickly and easily he could get them on and off again. They were not the cheapest and were bought specifically for the purpose but it was vital he could front up this pretend business to the world for a few hours at a time but then dispense with it as if it had never existed. As indeed it never had.

He booked the car again for the whole of the following weekend having satisfied himself that the air-con would be fit for purpose and the stickers were easily transferable. Equally as importantly, he had the dim-witted girl at the limo company on the hook as she shyly asked him for the autograph of whoever would be a passenger on his next trip. Lachie had said he would see but told her she would never have heard of the guy before, an old music producer from the sixties, went by the name of Manson, a friend of the Beatles but he'd been out of the game for a long time.

Parking up on the partly developed but still bleak and desolate site of the old Ravenscraig works, Lachie readied himself to instigate the next part of The Project. If I am to die then this would be a fitting place, he thought broodingly, his mind still in Hollywood mode. *Wise up*, his anaemic devil rasped, '*if you die, your vision dies with you – no movie, no legacy.*'

That was it.

He wanted the legacy. This diabolical plan hadn't been about his pleasure or gratification, vicarious or otherwise. His life up until recently hadn't gone as he would have liked, there was no disputing that. But surely, he could still walk away from all of this? Newly enriched at only 28 years old, why couldn't he start over again? Only someone who had never experienced his abject and prolonged suffering, the absence of love and the mind warping all-encompassing rejection could ask such a question.

His life had broken him. Damaged beyond any serviceable repair. If he had been a piece of hardware he would have been skipped long ago. As software then a complete re-installation would be required and so far as he knew, no amount of money could give him a soul transplant. So what if he died then? A life unfulfilled. But if he could last another six months or so then fine, there would be a marker left, a fitting totem for his tortured existence and a damning indictment on the way we all live.

Lachie poured himself a coke and carefully unscrewed the measured vial of the drug and tipped it into the pretentious faux-crystal champagne flute. It should take around twenty to thirty minutes he'd calculated. It would be far quicker with them, he knew, so he'd purposely starved himself today so as to speed up the process. He flicked on some music channel and jumped as the surround system boomed into life. Once he'd acclimatised himself to the volume and found a channel he liked he found himself getting into it; a good mixture of his favourite power ballads and some soft porn rap shit. He imagined the limo full of writhing black women and his heart began to beat in synch with the pulsating bass lines.

Enjoying himself far more than he would have ever anticipated, he thought he'd better try the other stuff too or else he'd be boogieing there all day. He staggered around to the drivers cab and flicked the dial secreted underneath the dash which switched the air conditioning unit from the standard one to the device he had installed the day before. So far, he hadn't noticed anything too different and he felt vaguely euphoric despite the fact this would count as a failure if it didn't do the business. Back in disco heaven he lost himself in the onscreen gyrations and remembered thinking if nothing else he would have to chalk this one down to first rehearsal.

What seemed like only the next moment or so, he found himself lying on the stained carpet shivering with cold. He knew immediately his trousers were at his ankles. He must have fallen off the seat. As he tried to stand, pulling up his jeans as he did so, someone smacked the back of his skull with an iron bar. Or that was how it felt. He lurched forwards clutching his head in both hands and threw up spectacularly across the leather seats narrowly missing the racks of pristine glasses.

He moaned in pain and scrabbled for the volume remote. Next he staggered to the drinks bar, tearing the top off a sparkling mineral water and pouring it down his throat, over his head and across his screwed up face. His throat burned like molten lava. Lachie didn't drink alcohol. The last time he tried it at a family Hogmanay bash around fifteen years old he'd tried to chat up a cousin and then fallen down the stairs, breaking his nose. His father who had miraculously been at home had to get someone to drive them both to the local hospital, over forty miles away, upon where the driver left them to rejoin the festivities. His doting dad spent the rest of the night laughing and joking at the nurses' station while he lay on his side puking into a cardboard piss pot until he fell asleep.

But this, if anything, felt worse. He cursed himself silently for not having any painkillers. The back of his throat felt like sandpaper and he pulled himself up into the foetal position and rocked manically until the throbbing subsided. Only then did he think to look at his army watch. He'd been out cold for a whole seven hours. He couldn't remember much before he'd blacked out. Despite the pain, the cold and the all pervading smell of fresh sick, he smiled broadly.

It had worked! The Project would go ahead...

Game on!

Chapter 7

Situation normal Boyle decided, as his day just got steadily worse. He'd been in with DCI Baxter again and she'd definitely lived up to her nickname of U.X.B., only this time the bomb had gone off. Her wrath hadn't been so much directed at him, but at his department as a whole. The bodies were piling up, she had told him quietly, and *this is not Taggart you know*, she said, referring to the bane of all Scots' police officers' lives, the mainstream cop series which had been playing weekly since he joined the force. Boyle had vented some of his shared frustrations at the way things had been going of late but even to him they sounded like a string of excuses. Baxter intimated she had held him in higher regard than that.

> 'I know you're under pressure Jim what with the family issues, and I do appreciate your input and your dedication. But why does it always seem to be *you* alone here late into the evening, doing all the work? Where's the rest of your team on these murders? I haven't seen Steel this week, is he on another course?'

Boyle swallowed hard and focussed his eyes on a tiny piece of tape, yellowed with age, which had gradually peeled away from the edge of Baxter's grimy desk, leaving a small triangle of as yet unblemished purity. He felt his toes curling in weary frustration as he covered for his colleague.

> 'No Ma'am. It's not like him to be off sick Ma'am. He was apparently the victim of an unprovoked assault a couple of nights ago outside his squash club. Uniform are on it but there were no witnesses and they reckon it's a grudge for some collar in the past.
> He's assured me he'll be back on duty tomorrow and I'll have a report on your desk on each of the unsolved murder cases by 5pm sharp.'

Baxter scraped her chair forwards and placed both hands flat on the desk and glared at him.

> 'Well that's all very well Jim, but I have to speak to the media before 5pm *today*. What have you got for me on the strip club incident, the one over on Maxwell Road?'

She let out a long sigh and Boyle didn't need to be a detective to note the panicky edge to her voice.

> 'Please don't tell me we have a new drugs war starting up...' she said, her voice fading away slightly before something lying on her desk seemed to re-animate her anger.

'The damned press have obviously got wind of some of the details and there's talk being bandied about of an armed vigilante and whatnot? What's the latest you have there?'

'It's a real can of worms Ma'am, to be frank. The club has been operating on the fringes for some time and there have been officers from Vice involved in the recent past. The word from them seems to be most of the troublemakers had already been banged up, if you excuse the expression, Ma'am...'

'Go on, Jim.'

'Well, they said if there's been renewed trafficking or porn activity then somehow it's escaped their attention and that of their best snouts, Ma'am. The truth is, whatever his actual motive might have been, the guy *has* gone and done us a favour, to be sure and we expect to get a significant number of convictions resulting from the incident.
I'm expect-'

'But you're no nearer on the actual *murder*, Jim? That's what I am interested in right now.'

'No, Ma'am. DC Steel and I will be
reviewing that aspect first thing
tomorrow morning.'

'So what, pray, should I tell that shower
of bastards tonight?
We are following several definite lines of
enquiry but we cannot comment further
for fear of jeopardising the
investigation…?'

Boyle slumped back into his seat and
grabbed a coffee flavoured cigarette. He'd
earlier made the daft decision to try and curb
both his worst vices in one fell swoop but Christ
knows how much longer he would be able to
keep a handle on everything. He flipped open the
notes on the two most perplexing murders on his
desk for some considerable time. If truth be
known they had precisely fuck all on either one
and Boyle did not like it one wee bit.
    The Garthamlow murder had been
painted by all and sundry as a local turf war
between two drugs gangs. They had easily
picked up the partner of wee Emily's mother
who'd even by his own admission, proved to be
a typically skanky wee bastard. However he'd
flatly denied being involved in any contre-temps
with Rocky's gang and in fact Boyle had the
distinct impression he was actually working for
Rocky. It seemed too much of a coincidence the
wee gobshite should have been picked up in the

harbour area of Aberdeen polluted with drink and still with three hundred quid in his pocket.

Boyle fancied he had been sent away either to set up some kind of deal or far more likely, given his IQ level, he'd been told to keep out of the way until the whole thing calmed down. If Rocky and his boys were on a war footing then his actions belied that, as far as Boyle could work out.

He glanced furtively around the empty office. It would be several hours before the cleaner arrived. Boyle deliberated for all of one second then grabbed his cigarettes out of his jacket and sparked up a heavenly Regal King Size. He inhaled deeply and as the smoke percolated through his body he was positive he could feel his synapses begin to fire more effectively. Tapping his ash contemplatively on the edge of the desk he knew should address the other obvious possibility; the murder might just be a botched abduction. It seemed an unlikely location for a case like that but who were they to question the motives of a sex monster?

The other interesting thing about the case had been the ballistics report which showed the gun used to shoot the girl was a British army registered automatic pistol which apart from being highly unusual also meant they should be able to trace its last known movements.

He grabbed the phone, singeing his hair in the process. Funny how soon you become unused to doing things, he mused as he put the cigarette between his lips and punched out a series of numbers. He'd an old buddy in the military who should be able to get him a quick trace on the gun. At least he would have something to beat Steel over the head with tomorrow morning.

After an embarrassingly insincere chat about meeting up 'for old times,' Boyle received the solemn promise he'd have a report before 9am the next morning which had been sweet music to his ears. He sat back in his chair and wondered if there could be something else going on. What were the chances of there being a new contract hire killer in town? He doubted it. But, if it the rumours were true and he was any good at his job, they would probably never hear about him again.

He looked at his watch. Despite the cigarette he could feel his stomach grumbling. It had been a long time since he'd eaten. It was a habit detectives like him often suffered from – forgetting to eat when your fast bastard partner wasn't around to nag you. But he'd give it another hour. He liked this time of day and he desperately needed a chance to sit in peace and try to make sense of things. *Some chance.* Boyle reached for another fag.

He'd been having alarm bells ringing in his head about the Maxwell strip-club shooting. Until the point at which he'd stopped breathing, the murder victim seemed to have been an ultra respectable middle class business-man, a real pillar of the community. Old family Newton Mearns, a Rotarian, a churchgoer and he'd played golf in the same four-ball every weekend without fail. Married with two children he had a clean record, not even a speeding fine. The only major blemish on his character was the fact, post-Savile, he had been well known for his work with children's charities, which with the benefit of hindsight now obviously singled him out as a raging paedophile.

There had been one other factor which also helped the sympathy factor with the red-tops to barely register above 'served the bastard right.' He'd been a banker with RBS.

Boyle banged his head gently off the desk a few times to see if it might help. Despite the cutbacks, the cock-a-mamie courses, and the relentless paperwork, his department had a pretty successful track record. His own team, though they could always do with a size 10 up the backside, were especially unused to letting a case get away from them. Baxter tended to give him the trickiest cases and he took pride in always getting a result.

He wondered if the two cases were *connected*. It was a random idea, granted, but they were getting nowhere as things stood. The first thing would be to check with Ballistics to identify any similarity in the weapons used. Maybe they were dealing with a tripped out ex-squaddie who'd gone PTSD after too many tours of Afghanistan. Or perhaps he'd decided to take his killing into the more lucrative private sector. He tapped out a short email for Steel to chase it up first crack. Another cause for concern which continued to irritate Boyle had been the complete lack of feedback from any of their more reliable snouts on either of these two murders. No-one seemed to know who might be responsible. He couldn't remember a case where they had so little to go on.

Glasgow had remained a small tight-knit city, crime-wise, and so this nearly always meant that someone in the community would know who did what to whom, where and also why they'd done it in the first place. Even in the 21st century, nothing much had radically changed in the game of catching bad guys or working out why they'd committed the heinous deed. Boyle had used to make fun of Gary Steel when he first joined CID on account of him being a 'fat bastard.' While he himself had never considering even spectating, never mind taking part, in the Commonwealth Games which had been hosted in his city a couple of years back, Boyle had wasted no time in picking out his new man's weak spots. He'd soon found Steel's most vulnerable area for attack was most definitely his overhanging belly and his attendant inability to climb more than a couple of stairs without wheezing like an asthmatic pit pony.

However Steel had obviously been similarly ridiculed throughout his climb up the ranks as he always had a quick fire retort. And if he was honest, Boyle could find little argument in the stinging rebukes he would get back in return.

'Sir!
With all due respect to your *advanced*
years, I would like to remind you I am
now a CID detective.
I don't *need* to run after the bad guys
anymore.
I only need to use my finely honed
detective's intelligence to deduce where
they are currently shacked up in this
delightful city and then tootle round in
the motor at stupid o'clock the next
morning to pick the wee bastards up.'

He sparked up another illicit cigarette.
Sure, there had been plenty chatter around the
pubs about the identity of the 'moral crusader'
with much of the hysteria being stoked, *plus ca
change*, by the local media. The Daily Recorder,
never knowingly under-sensationalised, had
even run a lurid photo series with what appeared
to be a ginger-haired Spiderman superhero who
actually had the Irn Bru logo on his chest.

As if that hadn't plumbed the depths
enough, they also had him spouting phrases like,
'Dinnae move pal or I'll *banjo* ye!' thereby
resurrecting an infamous word so lovingly
adopted by a proud nation several years
previously, after a local lad had allegedly used it
whilst foiling a bunch of inept terrorists intent on
blowing up Glasgow Airport. Footage of him
pulling a man from the burning wreckage of an
American SUV before decking him with a single

punch, in the aforementioned 'banjo' style, had gone viral.

Of course, the resultant security enhancements and lengthy queues each Fair Fortnight holiday, meant most sane Glaswegians had considered a similar explosive course of action ever since.

Boyle reached over and picked up today's rag, dumped on Steel's desk opposite him. He wondered how many times they would be able to include clever double-entendres for 'banker.' He found it remarkable that on pages 3, 4, 5 and 6 they could rant on about a new wave of 'tough love' washing away the tide of filth from the city streets due to the failings of the local police and then after that self righteous calumny, you'd turn over to page 7 to find a full frontal shot of the 'gorgeous Gina' practically falling out of her bikini for no apparent reason. Flick through a few more pages towards the back of the paper and there you'd find a full page of adverts for the telephone and internet wank lines. There were even some in Polish for fuck's sake.

But that gave him an idea.

He chucked the paper in the bin where it belonged and dug through his file notes on the *Bottom Line* shooting. The barman, who had mysteriously pitched up for duty a full three hours before his shift began and who'd 'never seen nothing,' hailed from Romania, as did the poor wee lad who'd been centre-stage. Too much of a coincidence clearly and the Vice boys hadn't wasted any time in stringing him up for various serious charges although they hadn't yet included accessory to murder.

He would get his opportunity to remedy that tomorrow, Boyle decided. Before Vice handed him over, he also thought it might be useful to get a more authentic feel for the situation as regards the Eastern European community. He remembered a very pretty Polish youth worker who had been helping the department recently with some translation work after some internecine fighting between groups of workers at a processing plant over on the eastern edges of the city. Sonia had seemed to take a shine to him and she'd a smile that would light up Hades. He would go and see her and try and work out if there could be an international angle to the situation. It would be a better start to his day than having to look at Steel's bruised coupon and that much he would put money on.

Boyle jumped as a loud voice startled him, thundering through the gloom like a fog horn.

'Oh, it's you! I should've kent. So there's nae need tae call the fire brigade then?'

Boyle swung round in his chair to see Lorna, the cleaner, wiping the sweat off her brow with a meaty forearm. He hadn't noticed how smoky the office had become.

'Sorry hen. It's been one of those days, know what I mean?'

'Aye…But it disnae mean I have tae breathe in a' your smoke does it? You can't do that these days, mind. I've got ma rights and that. I could sue you for giving me the big C and a' that. Have ye no got a hame tae go tae?'

'Aye okay, point taken Lorna. I'll make it up to you, I promise. But there's no bloody use in suing a man of my slender means, trust me.'

As he left the building, pulling up his collar against the freshening wind, he cursed furiously as he only just remembered he had left his electronic cigarette charger back in his office, eight floors up.

'Looks like we both lost then,' Boyle remarked caustically the next morning as an ashen faced DC Steel slipped into the driver's seat as unobtrusively as could be possible for a man of his bulk.

'Sir?'

'Well it can't have gone too well in your 'wee disagreement' looking at those bruises can it?

I, on the other hand, have just lost twenty
quid in the office sweepstake as I bet
your face couldn't be looking any uglier
than normal when you came in this
morning!'

'I love you too, Sir.'

'Come on then, let's go. I'm sure you'd
rather get the fuck out of here and then
you can tell me all about it. Swap your
phone with my fag charger just to be sure
you don't miss some important emails
we'll be getting before we get back with
a wee bit of luck.
I want you to drop me over at the
community centre at Bishopbriggs where
I have a date with a particularly bonnie
woman. Then you can go up and pay our
friend Ricky Bean an overdue visit. I
want you to find out just what is going on
over there and, with a coupon like yours;
today might be the best chance we've had
in a long time. Rocky will be that scared
just looking at you he might tell us the
truth for a change.'

It had been a short trip over to the east of
the city. A ten minute drive which Boyle would
replay in his mind over and over again in the
coming days. Despite the impressive facial
injuries, he had made DC Steel drive him as

usual, deciding on a whim, back in the office. He could easily have done the driving, dropped Steel off and done the whole trip in reverse. In some ways it would have suited him better as he wouldn't be leaving himself stranded but he felt that it would be better to throw his colleague back in the deep end but more than that; he wanted to be able to interrogate the man without any distractions. He had only realised when Steel had walked in earlier that one of the many niggles that had been irritating him for the last 2 days and nights was one very simple fact. He did not believe Steel's garbled story which he'd been fed on Monday morning when he'd called in sick.

He knew very little about the man. Certainly not the youngest DC by a long shot at 34 years old but his record had been good if a little unexciting. Unmarried, Gary had always been very reticent to talk about his personal life. The oldest of several brothers or sisters he'd stayed with his parents until his late twenties before moving into one of the ultra-modern apartments overlooking the Broomielaw. Police work and personal lives didn't usually go well together and if anyone could understand the difficulties of holding on to a long-term partner, it would be Boyle. He'd always felt comfortable with their working relationship and Steel seemed happy to keep a professional distance and he always showed just the right amount of deference when required. They never went to the pub together like many cops did because Boyle didn't really do that sort of thing and so after two years together Boyle realised he hadn't cemented any strong bonds of friendship with the man.

But he valued Steel as a partner and as they set off he began to feel genuine concern maybe the guy had got himself into some bother with a married woman or something of that nature. He wasn't gay, he knew that. Well…to be honest, he hadn't a clue. He had met lots of gay men and women through the job and apart from the obvious stereotypes it had become impossible to be sure. Did it make any difference? He remembered Big Joe. What a mountain of a bloke. He had biceps like pineapples and could lift two policemen off the ground, one in each hand and with his arms out straight. Boyle had been a naive young cop, not yet married when they had been required to go and see Joe one night. It had been the boyfriend who had answered the door, an older chap who looked like a college librarian. Apparently, they told Boyle later, his eyes had been as wide as saucers during the whole interview.

But over the years he'd developed one abiding aptitude; a hard-won talent he would stake his shirt on, every time. Call it copper's instinct or whatever, but he always knew when someone was lying to him. As long as he could see their face, he could tell. And right now, as Steel sat at the wheel, tapping nervously as he waited for the lights to change and talking even faster than the guy on the radio, Boyle felt his heart sink.

The man had lied to him.

It wasn't the end of the world. But for the first time in their working partnership, he knew he might not be able to trust his partner. Whatever happened to Gary Steel at the weekend to cause those injuries, it wasn't a fight outside a squash club.

Of that, Boyle was certain.

Chapter 8

I couldn't have chosen a better morning decided Leonard Tompkins of Tompkins Associates as he stood looking out across the bay re-evaluating his recent decision to head back down south, back to 'civilisation.' Balancing on the horizon he could clearly see the islands of Lewis and Harris and he remembered how it had been this sort of picture postcard scenery over at Luskentyre beach which had been one of the main reasons he and his wife had moved up here in the first place.

Today it was only early March but the sunshine shimmered across the water; the cold clear air allowing him to see literally for miles and miles. High above him he saw a buzzard circling, lazily surfing any available thermals. Unfortunately, in his personal and professional opinion, he would now cautiously advise you should always look at a location more than once before you buy, especially up here. His wife and he had visited three summers ago and fallen in love with the area immediately. But it had been a different situation when the weather changed for the worst and they were condemned to endure a dark, sodden and wind-lashed wilderness for months at a time.

Then there was the harsh economic climate to contend with. His wife had given up a highly paid professional job to come here and work; firstly as a cleaner, then a waitress with the pinnacle being a dead-end secretarial post in a stuffy architect's office.

After a frustrating year, he had left his own job in the local estate agent business and gone solo as he couldn't imagine in his worst nightmares being any worse off than they were. Through the turbulence of the housing crisis he had not only survived but thrived because he actually gave a shit about customer satisfaction which seemed to be as alien a concept to the locals as Gaelic language classes were to him. How many million pounds to make the road signs bi-lingual? Were there not more people in Scotland speaking Polish for goodness sake? That had been the last straw as far as they were concerned and the two of them were now desperate to rejoin the 21st century in only three weeks time.

This sale today, however, the greatest of his Scottish career, and the easiest, had been the icing on the cake. Who would argue a sweet 3.25% of over half a million pounds plus outgoings would be very tasty indeed for a few hours work.

The wind had become sharper as the sun vanished behind a cloud and Tompkins looked back along the coast road towards Laide. *Dammit to hell.* No sign of any approaching vehicles. He hoped the chap would get here soon and he was fervently praying the sun would stay out for the rest of the day. He didn't want to take any chances.

He saw old Archie the boatman glaring up at him from the pontoon, pointing repeatedly at his watch, as if the bugger had anything more important to be doing. Tompkins was still not speaking to him for insisting they took off from Little Gruinard as opposed to Mungasdale which sat only a mile or so further up the coast but more importantly made a far shorter boat trip. But Archie's croft was here and he obviously didn't see the point in going out of his way for the convenience of a couple of Englishmen. It would be a different story he thought, smirking like a naughty schoolboy, once everyone found out how much money this chap had. They would be all over him like nettle rash.

This last thought brought on a mild panic attack. He had, of course, downplayed any references to the island's chequered past in a manner worthy of an old school Tory Cabinet Minister. *Yes...*, he had said. The island *had been* used for anthrax testing way back over seventy years ago and a few sheep or cows may have been deliberately infected. But the whole island had been safely decontaminated a quarter of a century ago, he'd said glibly. *Why does that always sound far longer than twenty five years?*

Tompkins had glossy PR photos from 1990 of the Junior Defence Minister smiling nervously as he pulled up the anthrax safety warning signs. The buyer hadn't asked too many questions about the whole thing and so he had kept the information strictly minimal. The man seemed far more interested in the topography of the island, what were the indigenous species there and how easy would it be to land a boat. Tompkins got the impression he was some kind of aristocratic environmentalist type, possibly a lefty, so all the better to keep *schtum* whenever the conversation veered towards any possible controversy.

Of course, he knew the locals still avoided the place and regarded it as a dead place, a dark malevolent abscess reminding them of yet another unpleasant historical betrayal by those who wielded the rod of power. In the two years he and Diana had lived up here, it remained the only island they'd never visited in their little boat and to be honest he didn't feel overly happy about doing so today either. He had vowed to dispose of his clothing before he stepped back into the house and his wife had made sure he wore his oldest work clothes and left him strict instructions to use the shower by the utility room which they normally only used for hosing down their walking boots, gaiters and the like.

Their house lay over to the west near picturesque Gairloch where the fresh Atlantic breakers rolled in and Tompkins couldn't understand why anyone in their right mind would want to live over in this dark hole; it was depressing enough living up here most of the time.

Tompkins was dimly aware there had allegedly been a few prototype eco-warriors living in the area during the Thatcher era and it had reputedly been their protests that miraculously expedited the process of decontamination. It would be bloody typical for Archie to say something stupid about the hundreds of tonnes of formaldehyde dumped onto the island during their short boat trip.

He found himself continually looking down at his own watch now and he kept squinting his eyes to see if he could see any sign of a vehicle in the distance. Still nothing. A cold hand of dread began to wrap itself around his innards as he contemplated Diana's wrath when he'd have to tell her the Maldives trip would need to be cancelled. Then he heard Archie shouting something at him and he looked down at the man, holding his hand to his ear indicating that he couldn't possibly hear him from such a distance. The small man gave him a stony look and turned back towards the sea.

Lachie took one last look in the mirror and then smiled. I would be fooled myself if I didn't know better, he thought. It was just another uniform after all. First school, then army and in between all of that; this. The upper-class twat. He headed gratefully for the cottage door, too warm in his outdoor gear. Waxed Barbour jacket, check. Gieves and Hawkes tweed cap, check. Tatersall shirt, check. Silk cravat, check. Hunter boots, check.

Tompkins jumped in surprise as he saw and then heard the speeding rib roar up towards Archie's little boat causing it to wobble nervously. The man piloting the twin-engined craft waved over to Archie and then up towards Tompkins who was forced to scurry down the rabbit track from the road. He was certainly very well dressed, Tompkins noted, a little apprehensively. By the time he'd nervously pumped the chap's hand he'd bitterly regretted his own poor choice of clothing.

'Leonard Tompkins. Just call me Leo please.'

'Leo! Hector Watt, at your service! Sorry I'm late old chap, thought I'd never find my dashed sunglasses! Searched high and low but the new Range Rover is a complete tip inside! Devil of a hangover I'm afraid, the grape and the grain, we never learn do we? Archie…. Good to see you again! You don't mind if we take mine do you, I want to see how she'll be on the sand if that's okay with you?'

Leo looked from one face to the other like a nervous rabbit. They already knew each other! All sorts of desperate scenarios played out in his head as he gabbled on about what a nice boat Mr Watt had and how lucky they were with the weather and so on. But all too soon he found himself sitting at the back of the rib while Archie and Hector, stood up at the stern eagerly conversing like best friends. Shouting over the noise of the engines and the buffeting waves, Hector seemed to be asking about the timing of the tides and the fetch at certain points and other boating terms he wasn't entirely unfamiliar with himself but somehow he felt he'd been deemed irrelevant, superfluous almost.

Chapter 9

DC Steel walked out into the relief of the cool morning air which suddenly made him aware he was soaking with sweat, the moisture turning icy cold under his arms and down into the small of his back. The pasty faced big tosser must've had his heating turned up full, he thought, keen to vent his increasing frustration on somebody, anybody, apart from himself. He wouldn't be surprised if there were a couple of thousand cannabis plants growing in the loft. He briefly considered making the call but figured it wasn't worth the hassle and his lawyers seemed to have a permanent harassment suit filed against them without him pouring more fuel on the fire.

Today's confrontation had been predictably short but intense with no love lost from either side. Ricky Bean was a big bloke with the kind of unfeasibly broad shoulders and slim waist you used to only see in the Marvel comics. He hardly qualified for the superhero category though. Known to all as Rocky since his primary school days due to his love of the old Stallone movies and the fact his head bore all the sensitivity of a skip full of rocks, he was tougher than most and it was said the harder you hit him the better he seemed to like it.

Steel remembered an anecdotal story about the teenage Rocky where some of the local boys had changed his nickname to *Shaky* after he'd reputedly been caught nailing a poor lad's feet to a wooden floor before asking him to dance like Shakin' Stevens. Growing into his gangster role, he was often lampooned by the police for his laughable Alpha male posturing and ridiculous swaggering gait. Less comical was they were sure he was responsible for much of the crime north of the city centre, yet they had never yet pinned a single charge on to his fifty inch chest.

But there *was* something DC Steel knew about the big bastard that wasn't common knowledge around town. It wouldn't be something you'd tend to shout about either, not if you wanted to avoid breathing out of a tube for the rest of your life. It pertained to an area of his own life Steel would rather not draw attention to either. The fact of the matter was that big Rocky, one of Glasgow's most notorious tough guys, was as bent as a five bob note.

Not the only thing we have in common these days, he thought morosely as he picked his way expertly through the traffic on the way back to collect the boss. He'd just received an email from ballistics confirming that the gun used to shoot the wee lassie over at Garthamlow had been the same one which killed the 'porn actor' in the city centre last week. The shock had been too much to take in and in a panic he'd pressed delete and turned the engine on.

Finding himself speeding way above the limit and with other vehicles having to take evasive action to avoid colliding with him, he braked and gave himself a shake. Okay, this was a mess, but is still wasn't worth killing himself over. Not for the first time in the last few days, he wondered how his life had come to this point.

He'd never understood the attraction of the female of the species. He'd had a normal upbringing as far as he could remember. His mum had been the boss of the family. She'd worn the trousers in his parent's relationship that much had been evident from the start. But his dad had been a great traditional role model; taking him to football matches, roaring alongside him at rugby internationals and teaching him how to make a bow and arrow or how to build a proper glider and all the other 'dad' stuff they'd done together.

There had never been any great friction or confrontation that he could remember. He'd a younger brother and sister; both of them settled, married with children. So he had been the last one to leave home and there had never been any great pressure for him to do anything. Mum had her grand-weans now and at 34 he hadn't sent up any warning flares so far. Not until now.

He'd not been unpopular as a youngster. Crap at football admittedly but what God takes from one hand and so on meant he was a natural at snooker. To this day he would always be the first name on anyone's lips when they were putting together a police competition down at the Davis club on Gordon Street.

He'd gone out with countless girls, at least as many as his mates from school. But for him, it had only been going through the motions. He hadn't realised he was any different from his mates for a long time. He hadn't fancied boys either. It had simply been the fundamental problem in that he saw nothing at all enticing about a girl's body. He could be attracted to a beautiful face on a rare occasion and there had often been something in a girl's eyes which he would mistake for love or lust.

But when he had to get down to the mechanics of it all then the spirit would go out of him. In fact he would go as far as to say he found naked women quite nauseating to look at especially when they were trying, maybe trying too hard, to come over all alluring and sexy. He would look at a woman at this point, with her legs parted wide and her eyes beckoning him and he would see an open wound; a festering sore and he found it repulsive to go further unless it was dark or he'd had a skinful. But even in the dark however he couldn't escape his other main phobia about naked women. It was the *smell* of them. He couldn't understand how other blokes could be attracted to the musky aroma emanating from down there. It made him want to puke. There had been many a time when if a light had been switched on during a bout of lovemaking his unfortunate date would have been mortally offended at the look of distaste on his screwed up face.

It had been a slow progression from giving up on his unfulfilling sexual encounters with girls to the dark place he dwelt today. He had kept a diary of his feelings since he'd been in Primary Seven. At first they had been the innocent wonderings which almost all wee boys or girls would have had. Poetry almost. But as he grew older, these transcripts of his deepest and darkest longings became something else entirely. For a while he began to realise that what turned him on most, actually turned him on, as opposed to going through an act, was looking at his own self when in the act of arousal or even better when he would toss off in front of a mirror. He would find himself at a drunken lad's night out staring at what the bloke was doing rather than at the women in the porno films.

Back then, he had still never had any illicit entanglements, although he wrote about doing so in his increasingly lurid diary entries. But the fates decreed that his sordid imaginings would become public knowledge. His dad had been made redundant from the steel works and so had been skulking around the house a lot more during the day when no-one else would be in. Gary could never be sure but he suspected his dad had been looking at his diary; there were snide comments made and looks exchanged. His tattered old journal would sometimes be sitting a little too neatly under his bed.

A few months later, his dad had been found one night in the deserted car park of the working mens' club car park. By the time they'd turned off the ignition key it was far too late, the gaffer-taped hose had delivered the intended last rebuke. It had been a police colleague who had called him. They talked about the understandable mental pressures of redundancy. There would be as little upset as possible and the local papers were forbidden from reporting the death as a suicide.

The police interviewed the whole family with the utmost consideration when all Steel wanted them to do was barricade him into a small stone cell and beat him to death with iron bars.

Shortly after he moved out of the family home. He eventually succumbed to his deepest desires and learned how to pick up men through internet forums and gradually over time he found himself preferring younger and younger sexual partners. He found he didn't really like being screwed by men any more than he had liked screwing women and in fact the only thing which got him going involved pre-pubescent boys.

Admitting that to himself had been a pivotal moment in his life. With the death of his father, for which he took complete responsibility, he had effectively thrown himself off a moral cliff. He wasn't proud of the fact. In fact he loathed himself for it and before crossing that line of no return he had even gone without any sexual experience for several weeks in the forlorn hope the urges would pass. They didn't. He would find himself on a rollercoaster of surging emotions afterwards which would then smooth out to a dull, subdued almost sedated feeling for a few weeks until he would have another wild encounter and the whole adrenalin ride would begin again.

Then he happened to find himself in the Bottom Line that fateful day. It had been the first time he had done it – allow himself to be filmed. There had been strict rules. No head shots. No one could have been readily identified from the footage apart from the wee boy of course. He felt a twinge of sympathy for him but more from the knowledge his life wouldn't have improved much after that awful day. In fact, it might have ended up being considerably shorter too, knowing some of the people who had been involved.

As he had recuperated over the weekend he'd swithered over whether or not he should shop the whole bunch of them and try and paint the picture that it had been he who had been the 'vigilante superhero' who had blundered in by fortuitous accident. But there were too many problems associated with this. One being the fact he shouldn't have been walking around with a loaded gun. Why would he have been carrying it, for what purpose? He *did* own a gun and he was certainly keeping it close by him from now on, but at that point he would never have dreamt it would be necessary. Furthermore, the murder gun usually gets traced eventually, as unfortunately this one now had been and so the truth would have come out eventually. So the vigilante angle was blown.

But the other not inconsiderable factor against following the hero route was he would have the life expectancy of a Tesco lettuce once the news got out.

Now he was going to have to tell Boyle there was a definite connection between the two cases which was extremely problematic. He would love to catch the killer of the wee lassie in Garthamlow. But he knew when they did so, the best he could hope for would be his professional career would be in meltdown. He didn't remember reading anything specifically mentioning 'starring in illegal porn films' as breaking police codes of conduct but even if they turned a blind eye to that, it still left a slew of sexual crimes which would have the editor of the Daily Recorder spraying his Y-fronts.

The best outcome as far as he could see would be *heid the ba'* gets himself killed by someone else, which might not be so incredibly unlikely if he kept following the work ethic of recent weeks. Dead or gone –the most he could hope for. If he was a professional, a premise Steel didn't completely buy at this stage, then he may not even be in the city any longer. Tough luck for the family of the wee girl but nothing they could do would ever bring her back. Then he would be in the clear.

Or would he? If the assassin conveniently died or vanished, would those two murder investigations be closed? No. Only if he died. A promising possibility but how long would it take? It could be over in days. But and it was a big but, if he simply vanished, which was more likely, the investigation would continue. Not only that but it would narrow its focus when they realised the drugs war was simply not happening. If the killer left town then Steel himself would be far more likely to be uncovered as they probed deeper into the sexual aspect of the second murder. And they would never give up. These days a cold case never dies until they find an answer.

Then Steel remembered what the gaffer had said about little Emily Meekin and her delightful family and with a cold chill he realised what he must do to keep the enquiry team from dropping the turf war scenario. He looked at his watch. He had less than half an hour at best before Boyle would be champing at the bit. *I know*, he said to himself, *I need more time*. He fished his phone out of his pocket. Hopefully Boyle had plenty of cigarettes.

'Sir? Sorry sir, I've had a tyre slashed outside Rocky's gaff.
Yeah, I parked around the corner just like you said but one of the wee scrotes must have clocked me. It's only the one so I'll have it changed in a jiffy.
Yeah, I'm only just out, pretty chatty today for a change. Nothing earth-shattering sir, or believable either.
No nothing yet, my email is not picking up here for some reason. I'll pick them up back at the office later.
You'll get a taxi? You sure boss? OK then. Catch you back at HQ.'

He felt no compassion. For him to survive, it had to be done. The only thing which mattered. He had to trust his instincts.

Twelve minutes later, one of his lads motioned to Rocky to come across to the front window of the tenement flat. 'It's the shite, boss, they just pulled up the now…' Rocky pulled the net curtain carefully back in time to get a friendly wave from the uniformed driver before the car sped off towards town. 'Fuckin' harassment, that's what it is…' he muttered before turning to get his coat.

Chapter 10

'Steel? Boyle. Where are you?'

'Sir, just coming into town, traffic a bit mental, should be with you in five.'

'Fine.'

Fine was not the word Boyle wanted to use. He had another four-lettered one which also started with an 'F' in mind. Things were most definitely not fine, he thought as he walked down the back stairs to the underground car park. He would wait for Steel there. Whatever 'discussion' they were about to have was not for anyone else to hear.

He sparked up a real fag and breathed it in like a man drawing his first breath of freedom after a life stretch. His morning hadn't been totally fruitless. The lovely Sonia had shared her increasing worries about the Eastern European gangs making substantial inroads into Central Belt drug and sex-trafficking. She had unofficially given him a list of names he could check into but asked him not to pass them around publicly and for her own confidentiality to be maintained. He didn't need to ask her why.

She had an infectious laugh which had reminded him of Marie when they'd first met. They would have both been about Sonia's age back then. He shook his head in wonderment as bittersweet images of the pair of them spending entire weekends laughing about nothing flooded from deep within. The squeal of car tyres snapped him out of his reverie and he flicked the fag end against the white breeze block wall, the numerous cigarette butts nestling amongst the shards of peeling paint.

Boyle was round at the front passenger window before the car had stopped moving. He tapped the glass for Steel to pop the locks – he always drove with the locks on, some phobia about car jacking.

'Christ! It's ripe in here!
Open the windows for fuck's sake will you.
And no, don't bother getting out Gary. You and I are not going anywhere just now.'

'F-i-n-e...' Steel spoke slowly, as if unsure of what to do next. He obviously wasn't used to being called by his first name.

'Right! Can you show me this *alleged* puncture or can we cut the bullshit and you tell me exactly what the fuck is really going on?'

Steel banged his forehead onto the wheel and lifted his arms up and around his head.

'Sir! I am so sorry for not telling you!

I've been all over the place since the
weekend and I needed time to think
things through.'

'What's going on Steel? Another woman?
A married-'

'Aye sir. It's the wife of my best pal.
I don't know how it happened…I never
meant to hurt him…he found out last
Friday and kicked my head in…I thought
that was the end of it but she wants to
leave him for me…I don't want any more
to do with it sir…I wish it had never
happened…it was just crazy stuff sir…'

'Okay son, slow down! Deep breath,
that's it.
I wish you hadnae lied to me that's all.
Take the rest of the day off and I'll see
you sharp tomorrow right?
You've done the right thing knocking it
on the heid.
Nothing else you can do. It'll all sort
itself out in time, these things always do.
You've been a total idiot and you've
been caught out. Happens every day.
Go on, bugger off and we'll catch up in
the morning.'

Boyle lit a cigarette and watched the car
drive away fast. There was something irritating
him again. He wondered if it was early onset

dementia the fact he couldn't think of things until it was too late. Like he still loved his wife for example. And the obvious thing right now.

'Nope.' He spat angrily and stubbed the cigarette out as if everything was somehow its fault.

'Sorry son. But I don't believe a fuckin' word of it…'

Boyle turned wearily to walk back up the stairs unaware all manner of hell was about to break loose about him.

Chapter 11

It had been a couple of days since Lachie had been to the island with Archie and that obsequious prick, 'just call me Leo.' It was another dry and bright morning and it felt good to be back again on his own. He needed to get a feel for the place emotionally, to become a part of it and learn its secrets. He knew all about its history and he'd even had a drink with the only living descendant of the original owners. Fine and well but his critical task now must be to learn the geography of the place so he knew it like the back of his proverbial hand.

There still remained an incredible amount of work to do and by the very nature of the project this meant most of the work had to be done in secret, by him. He'd planned to stay for a few days to get it all done and he'd even set himself the challenge of sleeping rough for two nights. He had to see if it was feasible. He fully believed it would be possible and he couldn't allow himself to think otherwise. The whole idea would be dead in the water if he failed.

There was a boat-load of electronic equipment to be unloaded and installed, 'weather monitoring stations' and the like. He had rented a twenty foot container which sat next to the old croft and looked about as inconspicuous as a giant blue Lego block, but what could he do. His cover as a wealthy but eccentric environmentalist seemed to be working. Only shrewd Archie had seen through the act, most likely, but even then he couldn't have an inkling of what was really going on. Besides which, Lachie had dangled an extremely juicy incentive for him to help make the whole scheme work as effectively as possible. The old curmudgeon had been invaluable to Lachie and he thanked the gods that somehow he had stumbled upon Archie the first time he'd come up to recce the area.

Tomorrow there would be a delivery of live fish and using Archie's contacts, Lachie had hired the entire workforce and equipment of a wee fish farm from around the coast at Loch Ewe. The plan was they would drag a floating cage of Rainbow Trout to the north of the island with their own boat. The fish would be transferred into a couple of one-tonne plastic tubs which could then by lifted off the boat by a Hiab hydraulic crane and carried down to the Lochan using the fish farm's four wheel drive tele-lifter.

This last part was the only bit Lachie was interested in as he was going to have to do it himself seeing as none of the fish farm guys would agree to stepping on to the island. In fact they were going to spray everything down with a high pressure hose the minute it touched back down onto the deck.

Lachie got the impression that the farm manager thought he might be barking mad but after a little persuasion he'd got the guy to test a sample of the Lochan water for himself and he'd grudgingly agreed it should present few problems for the rainbows to survive for a few months until caught. With the incoming fish nearly a couple of pounds in weight, Lachie had told the farm manager he was bringing in wealthy tourists to fish the Lochan over the summer by which time they should have grown considerably, particularly as he would be installing an automatic fish feeding system for the next few weeks. After that, the fish would be on a shoogly peg.

'Put and take' fishing ponds were a common practice on estates for the *hoi polloi* willing to pay for the privilege and Lachie had caught his first ever fish like that aged only nine. The guys had been sold the lie that this could be an ongoing arrangement every spring and their wide eyes had feasted greedily on the thick wad of notes Lachie thrust into the manager's paw yesterday morning. He was dead certain this little arrangement would not be communicated back to the farm's Shetland owners and that was fine with him.

On his last trip over with the estate agent it had been like getting commonsense from a soap star to wring out of him where the original anthrax warning signs were dumped. For Tompkins, it really had been the 'A-word' and it did make Lachie laugh.

'My dear chap!' Lachie had hammed it up as much as he dared.

'All I want to do is take one of the signs and have a dozen or so replicas made. It will be so quaint to have some authentic feeling and 'retro' is so *zeitgeist* is it not?'

First things first though, he needed to investigate his two command centres a little more closely. Not wanting to appear too interested the other day, Lachie had only been shown the south bunker and even then he'd only given it a cursory glance. Today was different. He'd started with the north bunker and he was pleased that despite knowing roughly where it should be he still had difficulty working out how to find it. The thick gorse had completely obscured the entrance and it was patently obvious 'Leo' hadn't ever bothered his arse to look inside it.

The two bunkers had been constructed by government military scientists from Porton Down in the early 1940s shortly after they'd 'requisitioned' the island from its owners. Those had been dark days for all and the British were becoming increasingly paranoid that Germany was planning to introduce chemical or biological weapons. The race had been on to develop a bio-weapon of our own and to determine whether or not we could withstand any attack from a weapon of that nature. Lachie felt the bramble thorns pierce his leather gloves as he pulled apart the vindictive sprays designed to rip the ear off unsuspecting interlopers.

At least the scientists had the foresight to realise what they were planning to do was going to result in catastrophic and long lasting environmental damage over a wide area even if they were imaginatively challenged as to what form this terrible weapon was going to take. Lachie cursed the unrelenting plant growth bitterly as he imagined the white-coated boffins gathered around their little black book titled, 'Fucking Evil Death Book – only to be opened during an era of collective insanity.' So they would have carefully opened their scary book and then looked at the first page and there it was, under 'A' – Anthrax. *That will do nicely*, they must have thought.

He used a chunk of rock to break off the rusted lock, the rotten wood offering little resistance. He carefully prised open the heavy door, his fingers straining. Although not in great nick, he didn't want to destroy it totally at this stage. With a fetid gasp, the door revealed its secrets. Lachie paused for a moment conscious of the fact that this might well be the first time anyone had been in there since World War Two. Fighting the urge to cover his mouth with his trademark red checked handkerchief, he cautiously made his way down the short flight of stone steps pushing aside generations of cobwebs as he went.

The two bunkers were supposed to be identical in size but he reckoned this one was slightly larger which was very good news. Still only about half the size of his Lego block back at

the croft it would be more than adequate for his
needs and if necessary he could keep some of the
fish farming kit here too as the Lochan was only
minutes away from there. The walls were simple
block work sparsely covered with white paint
and the air felt cold and heavy with the
dampness and mould that had seeped through the
walls over many years of darkness.

Without any warning, he felt a silvery
light-headedness come over him and he thought
he was going to be sick. It happened so fast he
panicked, breaking out in a clammy sweat
instantly. Hellish images of smoky wraiths and
swarming black bacilli clouded his vision so he
turned and fell forwards, managing to stumble
up the steps on his hands and knees before
rolling out into the thick undergrowth to lie
wheezing on his back. He'd never been so glad
to see the lime green sunshine flickering through
the budding trees above.

'Come on soldier! Get a fucking grip will
you!'

He was furious with himself but worried
too. He had never been claustrophobic as far as
he could remember. Asthmatic as a young boy,
he had hardly touched his inhalers since puberty
and yet he recognised the symptoms. *This was
not part of the plan*, he despaired. And yet
another part of him rejoiced at the challenge
ahead. What was it one of his army pals used to

say when everything went pear-shaped? '*A good plan never survives contact with the enemy.*'

It would be okay. He'd be fine in a few minutes, he reassured himself. He would have to do a belt and braces job on the bunkers which he should have done in the first place. After all, there would be no point installing the latest high spec gear only to have a wee mouse nibble through a cable and short the whole bloody thing out, would there?

He'd not been to his family doctor for years and the army medical crew were out of the question but he was sure he could get some Ventolin or whatever was the latest thing in asthma prevention nowadays. If he could procure the most effective illegal knockout drugs in the world from a Glasgow barman then ordinary prescription medication should be a walk in the park. *Yeah, like the last purchase went well?* The pale-faced malcontent danced a highland jig on his shoulder.

I need to bring more stuff over anyway; he consoled himself an hour later as the rib bounced over the incoming waves. His chest still felt tight and he had decided to chance the weather by hauling open each of the bunker doors until he got back. He would only be a few hours with any luck and barring any goat squatters he should be able to get back on track pretty quick.

He reviewed the list of materials in his head, expertly turning the boat northwards to put the wind against him as he approached the beach at speed. He had to be sure he had everything this time. He saw Archie standing by the cars as arranged and the plan was he would lead Lachie over to the new doctor's house and introduce him before heading into Ullapool to pick up the additional items on a never ending list. *How many gennie's does one man need*, Archie grumbled as he'd snatched the crumpled list and strode off shaking his head.

Lachie smiled and jumped behind the wheel of his hired Range Rover giving the big engine a good loud revving just to wind up the bad tempered old goat in his tiny Fiat van in front of him. *Flash git*, Archie mouthed as he gave him the internationally recognised single digit out the side window.

Chapter 12

His phone started bleeping before he'd got half way up the stairs and he was glad to have an excuse to stop for a minute.

'Aye, I'm here Mackie! I'm just on ma way up the stairs.
Mackie, will you calm down a minute! Who's dead?'

'They're all dead sir!'

Boyle burst into the room to be confronted by every face turning expectantly towards him, as if he could somehow provide them with the antidote to the poison, as if he knew the answer to the puzzle.
He called Mackie over and signalled to another man standing by one of the white boards, marking up the role call of death in blood red marker pen.

'Johnston. Call Steel. Tell him to get his arse back here PDQ. Tell him sick leave has just been cancelled. Anyone else who's not here, get them in, now.
Mackie. Give it to me. Slowly. When did all this happen…?'

Boyle listened carefully as the young cop poured out the grisly details of this month's ever increasing body count. It was the Meekin family.

All of them, the useless boyfriend, the vacant mother and even wee Emily. It looked like there had been no struggle, they had perhaps known their assassin. Shit for brains had answered the door and he'd been popped in the back of the head as he led the killer back to the fetid living room. Mum had been shot point blank, in her no doubt uncomprehendingly vacant face, where she sat. Where she lived. Where she died. Young Emily had been in the kitchen half of the room and her body had two bullet holes in the chest and a badly scalded leg from the kettle she had dropped as she fell lifeless to the linoleum floor. At least she would have been spared that pain, Boyle surmised grimly.

He sucked the life out of a cigarette and tossed it onto his desk angrily.

'Where's Steel?
We've got 5 murders in as many days and Baxter's going to have our nuts if we don't come up with something fucking pronto!'

'Sir…' Mackie nodded, indicating for him to look behind.

'Sir! Just heard sir. Fucking terrible sir.'

Boyle did a neck twisting double take. Steel looked even worse than he had done only a half hour ago which moments before he would have thought impossible.

'Fuck me, Steel you look like shit.
Mackie get the team to follow us out to
Garthamlow as fast as you can and I want
everything – statements, pictures and as
much forensic as you can squeeze out of
the bastards tonight on my desk, five
minutes to five.
Got that?
Steel. You and I go now. Get the car.'

They sped out of town but the directions
Boyle gave him were taking them right past the
turn-off for Garthamlow. 'Where we goin' sir?'
Even his voice sounded ragged Boyle thought.

'Where *I'm* going is to find answers to all
this crap.
Where *you're* going right now is a matter
for conjecture!
I'm considering a police disciplinary and
I don't say that very fucking often, so
how about you start telling me the truth
laddie? You've got one minute to tell me
where the fuck you were this afternoon *at
the time of the murders*.
So help me, if I find out you've been
somehow involved in this today I'll rip
out your lungs and fucking feed them to
you myself!'

Steel turned to look him in the eye. His face was as white as any Boyle had seen post-mortem.

'Sir! I told you I had to go and sort myself out. I can't tell you who else is involved. The other man, sir…the husband…he's one of us sir…he's a Glasgow cop.
I swear sir! I couldn't kill anyone! Why would I even *do* that? I don't know them.
If I shot them sir, why would I come back to work sir? I'm wearing the same clothes! You yourself said I smelt like a byre!
You can have me tested if you want! Test my clothes and my hands for bullet residues!'

'Whoa! Okay, okay! Slow down will you. No point in getting us killed too.'

Boyle looked carefully at his partner as the car resumed a speed more conducive to continuing life. He didn't like it. Not one bit. But he felt the lad was telling the truth and he would have to go on trust for the time being. They had too much to do.

'Right. We're going to Edinburgh to see the army. Maybe they'll give me some useful tips on firing squads for later today.

Gonnae open the windows eh! I'm dying in here.'

An awkward silence enveloped the two men and neither of them was reluctant to climb wearily from the stuffy confines of the car less than an hour later.

'Wow sir! What a place.'

'Aye, it beats Pitt Street a wee bit, does it not?'

They had arrived at Redford Barracks and were a tad lost trying to find the entrance which a snooty man had told them to go to when they had wrongly pitched up at Dreghorn Barracks a short time before. They were standing looking at a fine old building which apparently at one time had housed up to a thousand infantrymen and was now getting ready to say goodbye to them all.

'It could be worse you know.
If we'd been doing this next year,
we'd have to have gone doon tae
Aldershot for Christ sake.'

Eventually they were hooked up with the right people and the news seemed good. Or a firm lead for a change, at least. The gun Boyle had asked about, the one used in the murder of the Garthamlow girl, or rather the *first*

100

Garthamlow girl, had been registered to the unit here in Edinburgh. It had been posted as missing during a routine officer training exercise.

This was not that uncommon, they were informed, but usually the weapons were signed back in within a few hours. The army took a dim view of their weapons circulating in the public domain, they were told. After all, the man said, they may fall into the hands of those who wouldn't know how to use them properly and someone may get hurt.

You don't say. Boyle muttered under his breath, cursing the fact he'd forgotten his vapour fags once again.

The army had interviewed the officer whose gun it had been. He said his own had been appropriated by another officer during the session and he had unwittingly been using another officers' weapon for most of the session. He had in fact signed a weapon back in afterwards and upon careful checking it appeared the serial numbers were different and so the officer's story did bear scrutiny.

So far so good, Boyle thought. He then asked what could have happened to the gun which after all has ended up killing our wee girl. The officer looked at him as if he had insulted his parentage. The army had carried out its own investigation this morning, they were told. Excluding the officer previously interviewed, there had been another four men and one woman on the course. Each serving officer had been spoken to and the army was satisfied entirely with their versions of accounts. No, they cannot divulge their names for reasons of national security. However, he allowed himself a glimmer of a smile and told them there were three officers on the list who had subsequently left the service and he handed over a sheet of paper with the three names.

'So! Let me get this straight. You're telling us one of these three men on *this piece of paper* somehow stole a 9mm automatic pistol from the army and is now running amok in ma' town?'

The soldier looked down at his feet for a second before lifted his head and glaring at some object three feet above Boyle's head.

'Well yes, that is one of several possible outcomes from this embarrassing situation, albeit a highly unlikely one.'

'Arseholes!' Boyle stormed back to the car, gasping for a cigarette, praying he'd left some in Steel's glove box at some point. 'Tae think my son is thinking about joining the army?' Then with surprising relief he wondered if they would accept the wee bampot after his recent shenanigans?

'At least we've got something to go on. You can get these names checked out today Steel, and maybe I'll have a wee morsel to throw into the Lion's den when I get the call from Baxter this afternoon. Now find me a fag-shop double quick and then let's get the hell out of this tight-arsed town.'

His phone rang. 'Speak of the devil?' Steel ventured cautiously as Boyle fished in his jacket pocket. He'd begun to recover a little of himself but Boyle was still seriously worried about him. 'No. It's my Jenny.' He then turned away unconsciously attempting to block out the other man from his thoughts.

'Hi angel! What's up?' He didn't usually get calls from his daughter during the day and he hoped everything was alright. *I don't need any more problems* he found himself thinking as she launched into her characteristic torrent of words. In the back of his mind he tried to work out who Steel had been cuckolding. There were not many copper's wives that he had ever met and not one he would have wanted to shag in the back of a squad car –apart from his own wife.

'Hi Dad! It's just to say like. It's *not my fault* like. Mum's totally gone and forgotten to tell you that I can't see you this weekend because I've got a birthday sleepover at Stephanie's and then next weekend's the prom night an' that wi' the school and so it'll have to be like next month or whatever. I just…'

'Whoa! Were we supposed to be on this weekend? I thought…'

'Aw da! You pure went an' forgot again didn't you?'

'No love!' Boyle lied unconvincingly. It had been a bad week but even so, he was sure Marie had forgotten to tell him. He would have loved to spend some time with Jenny but at the same time he knew he would have had to cancel the weekend in any case. He had to stop this nut-job from killing any more girls like his precious daughter.

'But listen Jenny, love. I'll talk to yer mum and as soon as we can manage it, we'll get something organised alright. You just be *very* careful out there. There's some loony people goin' about right now. What's this about a prom night? Is that no' a Yankee thing for when you leave the school? You're only in first year aren't you?'

'Yes…I'll be totally careful…you always say that. FYI I'm in the *second* year now, but. Next August I'll be in Year Three you know! We *all* get a prom night nowadays dad. We're going in a pure magic stretch Cadillac an' that. You're so

104

old fashioned you know. Gotta go! Love you…'

Boyle sighed and turned to Steel who had heard most of her high pitched chat. He lifted his eyebrows and tried a half grin, the effect not really working on a bruised and swollen face.

'Did you hear all of that aye?
FYI for fuck's sake.'

Chapter 13

Despite the set-back of the morning, Lachie had to laugh at the latest grumblings from his unofficial gopher at some of the more unlikely items on the revamped equipment shopping list.

> 'Excuse me.., *Hector*, but ah' dinnae really see you as the Alan Titchmark type o' bloke, no offence like.'

Increasingly, Lachie began to detect an insubordinate tone in the way Archie would sometimes put undue stress on his 'project name' as if he knew it might be bogus. Although, of course, it *was* his correct name, if one was being pedantic about it. From their very first meeting, Lachie had instinctively sensed Archie was the type of character who could only be pushed so far and he'd realised they had been getting very close to that point earlier in the morning. Nevertheless, Lachie knew he still had a firm grip of the whip hand and with the project nearing the off very soon, he had to utilise every tool at his disposal to get the job done.

Archie's main bone of contention concerned why Lachie needed not one but two wheelbarrows; one sturdy aluminium builders' barrow, which was required for the making of small batches of concrete around the island and a second flimsy looking plastic barrow for which

Archie could not see any proper use for any self respecting Highland man.

After throwing a 'back atcha' comment as regarding the likelihood of him having green fingers either, Lachie took great delight in showing Archie the true purpose of the barrow. Loading up his army backpack, he then threw another hundred kilos of kit into the lightweight wheelbarrow and trundled his way up the track from the beach whistling merrily as he went. 'This,' he had gently explained, as if to a small child, 'will mean I take half as many trips over the next few days and so save a lot of valuable time. That is, unless you want to carry some too?' The older man had stormed off shaking his head and swearing under his breath. But Lachie could tell he had been impressed.

By the time the sky had begun to turn an incredible fiery orange, he had installed solitary scaffolding poles in a dozen locations around the island, each one positioned in what he either considered would be a highly trafficked location for future activities or in some cases a calculated gamble which he hoped would pay off. There were still a few spare poles, cement and sand should he need to put up some more. Lachie knew fine well he'd have a far better idea after sleeping rough and living off the land for a couple of days but he didn't have the luxury of time on this. He couldn't wait any longer as the concrete had to go off before he could begin to install the vast array of equipment on to each pole.

He had been severely tempted to cheat and sleep in one of the bunkers but as he looked up into the clear sky he marvelled at the beauty of his location. It would be crazy to miss the chance of a rain-free night plus he wanted to give his lungs as much time to recover from their earlier ordeal. Also it was important for him to find the best place for any night-shelters so he could leave his future guests some clues. In no way did he want to make it easy for them, but to counter that he also didn't want them to use some other bizarre location he didn't have under camera surveillance. That would be pointless.

Grabbing a hand axe and a bottle of water he left the north bunker with the door wedged tightly shut and set off for a berth for the night. Heading directly south, he soon heard the healthy gurgling of the main inlet stream for the Lochan he would be magically re-populating tomorrow. The light had begun to fade alarmingly fast and he could have kicked himself for leaving it so late. He'd earlier decided in his head the best place for a sleeping area should be in the thick escarpment of trees which lay all along the western and southern edges of the spine-like ridge which ran up the left centre of the island. If he could temporarily get above the tree line then his going would be much faster.

Even at this stage of the evening, the view remained spectacular from the high point and as he traversed south he could still make out the small hamlet of Laide and the darkness of Loch Ewe in the background. He felt he had a reasonable idea of the layout of the island by this point. If you looked down from a small plane it would look very much like a speech bubble, Lachie thought, with its five hundred metre sand bar tail twisting away to the south east. The overall length, apart from the tail, was supposed to be only two miles or so, but because of the density of trees and the challenging terrain underfoot he could see it would easily take an hour to traverse that distance. Hopefully he would learn to better use the rabbit and goat trails over time and of course there would be significantly increased human traffic soon which would be bound to create more sophisticated pathways.

One of his most difficult challenges had been to anticipate where they might go at this early stage. The island was almost rectangular if you didn't count the tail and he'd been told it measured just over a mile wide which he hadn't had time to test yet by walking. Lachie guessed it would always feel counter-intuitive to cross the island widthways because it would mean climbing up through the forest and over the high rocks which formed the mile long ridge running up slightly left of centre. Standing at the highest point and looking down to the west to the left of the island's prominent spine, all Lachie could see was a long steeply sloping scree composed entirely of shale and small rocks. It looked treacherous and he'd no intentions of ever going any closer.

Dropping back down into the forest, he wasted no time in resurrecting his army skills, hacking some small branches and interleaving them firmly over the loose mulch which formed the majority of the ground on the southern sloping woods. He knew they went all the way down to his other bunker. It had become too dark to go any further down and he was relieved the wind had become almost non-existent which quelled one of his nagging worries about being far too high up and exposed for a guaranteed safe shelter.

Lachie spent the last few minutes of weak daylight in gathering as much of the substantial quantities of dry old bracken still remaining from last summer and stuffing it in and around the framework of branches. He lay back against his makeshift bed and looked up at the night sky. He knew he felt far too excited to go to sleep at this point. The blackness gradually became lit up by a sparkling array of stars which flashed their undecipherable signals enticingly at him and he felt himself sink more heavily into the ground.

Noises he had been unaware of previously began to tickle his ears; first he heard the low and rhythmic lullaby of an owl punctuated by the angry heckling of crows who must be bickering up among the rocks of the high crag above him. Once his hearing became more attuned to the silence he could detect the pitter patter of small creatures all around him. Keeping very still, he could see a whole community of rabbits emerging within a few feet of him. Smaller animals like mice and perhaps a shrew or vole would shoot out into view and then disappear almost as fast so as Lachie would wonder if he had imagined them or not.

But something else niggled away at him throughout his magical night under the canopy of stars. He'd begun to have renewed crises of confidence about the entire validity of The Project. Waves of unaccustomed emotion had coursed over him as he lay in the darkness. He'd been feeling none of his routine animosity towards the world over the last few hours and in fact if he'd been given the choice he'd have wished the night could have lasted forever. He struggled to dredge up the feelings of rejection and bitterness which had for so long been the icy cocktail he had been forced to drink.

What am I doing here? What is the point of The Project?

He scratched nervously out of habit and made himself remember some of the many incidents of gross unfairness and evil intent he had been made to suffer. Here he was, fully twenty eight years old and destined to be the stereotyped 'forty year old virgin.' The media were going to have a field day with a 'mutant' like him but he would open up their eyes to more than just his own personal depravity.

He'd planned to record the entire events of the next few weeks or even months on the island and to display to the world the fragile sham of our modern existence. He would rip off

111

our mask of civilisation and show how easily we could all revert to the base animals of our past.

He comprehended fully that the recordings would make him infamous in most quarters yet he was convinced in this era of televised celebrity jungle escapades and bizarre reality show pantomimes, his island recordings would tap into our tabloid fascination for true life absurdity laced with authentic peril and spiced with a sleazy splash of titillation. It promised to be a heady mixture of Attenborough meets Ant and Dec. He decided the standard quality natural history fare could never be enough for the chattering classes anymore and besides the format, like the old guy himself, had grown past any concept of sell-by date.

No, instead what the people clamoured for was a game show more than just a game – unless you thought of it as the only game in town. The Project would become a game of life with the twist being the distinct possibility of death. Death, blood, mud and sex. A soap opera in dire need of soap. It could be a blockbuster. A real-life *Hunger Games* but without any victors and the only prize being you might get to live a little longer for the entertainment of the masses. But this would only be if he went ahead with it. He had some serious thinking to do.

Lachie had become entranced by the nocturnal comings and goings as his eyes steadily adjusted to the darkness. Of course he was unused to keeping completely motionless and so he would often make an involuntary movement and the whole area would instantly clear. Further away, he thought he could hear larger animals snuffling in the dirt but he couldn't be sure. He'd been assured there remained a vibrant community of smallish wild goats on the island which he had factored in as an important supply of meat over the summer months. Primitive rituals of the hunt and the kill would hopefully provide a rich and gripping pageant of savage behaviour.

He quivered with what he assumed to be nervous anticipation before realising he had been shivering with cold. The temperature had dropped considerably in the couple of hours he had been lying there but as he began to think of ways to improve his nesting area for warmth, the soft hooting of the owls began to seduce him into a numbing slumber.

He awoke cold and stiff in the early dawn over an hour before the alarm of his Omega Seamaster watch had been set to go off. He sat up, groaning with the effort and rubbed his aching legs as he remembered he had elected to live rough like this for the next two long days. Unfortunately it wasn't before he'd already had indecent thoughts involving sizzling bacon and his twin ring camping stove up in the north bunker.

This might well be the start of a very long day Lachie decided, marvelling at the cloud formations across the horizon, and with every muscle of his body beginning a roll call of pain, he knew it had to be time for action. He strode

off, mentally adding a dozen chickens to
Archie's next list as he gratefully discovered a
squashed Snickers bar in his coat pocket.

Chapter 14

I didn't start all this mayhem, he reasoned with himself. He had always been a judicious man, an authority figure, someone whom people trusted to make decisions. Decisions were his strong point he could say, without any trace of immodesty. After all it had been said to him many times. He would feign embarrassment and instantly reply with one of his stock remarks he always had tucked away for such situations. 'The important thing is to make a decision. I always prefer my people to make a bad decision rather than make no decision.' *I might regret saying that one day*, he thought carefully. He seemed to have made quite a few bad decisions lately.

Or had he? He had absolved himself for the lifestyle choice he'd embarked upon many years before this latest and most serious crisis. But, he had always understood it might one day come to this. He was supposed to be one of the good guys. In his younger days, they had let him wear a uniform proclaiming his goodness, advertising the fact he was separate from them, *better* than them. Yet in the last week he had taken three lives. In his line of work, the spectre of sudden death was never too far away. Inexplicable, painful or gruesome, death was his bread and butter, always had been, always will be. Yet, like most intelligent people, he had never imagined in his wildest dreams he would one day personally be the agent of another man's demise. Of course, we've all thought about what it would be like to kill. We're bombarded with images of killing every day and night; the news bulletins, the conveyor belt Hollywood action films, endless artificial sweeteners to counter the relentless tide of real life human misery presented for our delectation.

But how many people actually knew how it would feel to look someone in the eye and then pull the trigger? Well, he had his answer but he couldn't tell anyone.

He had felt nothing.

Admittedly, it hadn't been the Prime Minister he'd killed. It wasn't anyone who had ever amounted to anything or was ever likely to. In fact, he had been doing society a great service. Garbage disposal. Thinking about it logically, his actions ought to be applauded, they should consider giving him a medal.

All the same, he'd been shocked at how easy it had been. He hadn't lost a minute of sleep over their deaths. No nightmares, no manic washing of his hands or looking over his shoulder. He had often felt more overwrought driving through Glasgow in the rush hour.

Would I do it again, though? This posed a more difficult question. It would always involve a certain element of danger, to take a life unlawfully. But the last killings had only served to secure his position. A quick decision had to be taken and he had acted accordingly. End of story. He couldn't say he had developed a taste for it. Not yet. His tastes were bizarre enough in the eyes of the great and the good. But it would certainly not throw up any psychological problems for him if he had to do it again. He could think of two or three additional killings which might benefit him greatly but then perhaps he would be straying into the realms of an addiction, a compulsion? Not the behaviour of a reasoned man, he decided. But what if they were entirely necessary?

Yes. Then I would kill again.

Chapter 15

Predictably, Baxter had been looking for him so Boyle didn't want to hang about HQ for any longer than necessary. He needed to get something concrete from all of this. It was getting late and so far Mackie hadn't given them anything of great use from over Garthamlow so he left Steel to co-ordinate a response for Baxter and chase the army retirees at the same time.

'Nimmo sir? Sorry pal, is DCI Nimmo available it's Jim Boyle here? Aye, no problem.
Sir?
Yes, sir, bloody carnage down here as usual. Thinking maybe a move to the loftier heights of Drugs Squad might be a good idea sir!
No? I suppose not, sir. I need to speak to the barman you've got from the strip club shooting sir? Can you okay that for me?'

'Bloody hell Jim! Why didn't you let me know? We let him go at lunchtime. Disgusting article! We've got his passport. His family are all here so the powers that be don't view him as a flight risk. We've got him for supply and possession with intent but Vice haven't managed to pin anything else on him so far. You interested in him for the shooting? I thought forensics cleared-'

'No sir. I don't have him down for the shooting but I can't believe he doesn't know more than he's let on. He speaks English?'

'I haven't clapped eyes on the little shit myself, Jim. Like all these chaps, his abilities with the language are dependent on who might be talking to him. I'll have one of my boys email you his address in the morning, alright?'

'Sir! Can I be a right pain and get it from you just now sir? I can nip up to the eleventh in a minute myself.'

'Well fine, if you must Jim. But see McCrindle will you? I've got to be out of here in a jiffy.'

'Thank you sir, goodnight.' Boyle placed the phone down carefully then swore loudly, the entire open plan office aware of his irritation, no-one wanting to catch his eye. He stormed over to the whiteboards scanning for the barman and any information relating to him. He hadn't been ringed which meant they still hadn't spoken with him.

'Did I not ask one of you to register our fucking interest in the barman?'

There was a unanimous shaking of heads and a general murmur which always sounded to Boyle like the lowing of cattle. Johnston gulped and spoke for all of them. 'Did you not say you and DS Steel would interview the suspect earlier this morning sir?'

'Bollocks!' He ran for the stairs and made it up two flights before the altitude sickness began to slow him down. Red faced and wheezing he burst into the room, identical to his own complete with the sprawling paperwork and stale body odours.

'Looking for McCrindle?' Boyle gasped. The closest man turned to look at the cardiac case sweating over the desk beside him. 'Sorry sir, he's already shot the craw.' The red faced man only snorted and kicked the door as he left. The rest of the men smirked and got back to work. They had all heard their boss being verbally abused many times in the past, this time they only heard the tail end of the foul entreaty but the last word rhymed with anchor, of that they were sure.

It was an hour later by the time Boyle set off for the Southside of the city. He'd wheedled the address from the uniforms downstairs, and with Steel nowhere to be seen, he requisitioned a driver to get him there and back before Baxter had his guts for garters. He had asked Steel to send her an email to say he would see her at 6pm. He hoped she would be gone by then, perhaps to see the same performance at the Opera house as their unhelpful prick of a boss, Nimmo. He texted Steel. *Whr fk are u? BB?* His answer was immediate. *Chsng sodjrs.* Then minutes later he got Baxter's email reply forwarded to him as they drove down the Kingston Bridge off ramp. *Looking forward to it, Jim.* He glared at the driver. 'Can you not go any faster?'

The address was a tenement flat in Govanhill and as he glanced around the area he reckoned Romanian was only one flavour spoken in an interesting recipe of nationalities. The flat looked to be part of yet another delicately positioned cultural trapeze act, one floor above a traditional Halal butchers and an off-licence. As the two men stepped out of the unmarked police car they nevertheless felt many pairs of eyes burrow into them as they crossed the litter strewn pavement.

A communal security entry door lay slackly open, the lock broken and useless. Exotic aromas of spiced meats assaulted his senses and his empty stomach growled as they started up the stairs. Boyle decided he would get his driver to stop for a carry-out before they left the Southside. Baxter would definitely have to wait.

The black painted door looked wet with grease and mould and as he waited for someone to come he shivered for a moment despite the warm clammy air. There were tiny Asian kids drawing with brightly coloured chalks on the next flight and in the dark corner he could see a toddler squatting over a lengthening stream of urine.

121

He knocked a second time, wishing he'd taken a quick cigarette to calm his impatient hunger. One of the little boys tugged annoyingly at his trouser leg. Boyle looked around helplessly, hoping a mum or older sibling would rescue him but the other kids were all very young. He bent down to gently detach the tiny brown hand from his trouser and couldn't help smiling back at the little boy's twinkling black eyes and the cheekiest smile, helped by the fact he had no front teeth whatsoever.

Just then the boy looked straight at him and made a gun shape with his hand while making little popping sounds. His driver laughed nervously. 'Jeezo! He's startin' early sir.'

But something in the wee face chilled Boyle's blood and he felt his gut kicking in hard again.

'Oh fuck! He's seen something, I'm sure of it. Let's get this door opened pronto eh!' Boyle yelled in frustration.

The younger man placed his shoulder against the door in preparation for a more robust movement when it swung open lazily.

'Not locked properly sir! Go in?'
'Aye!
What are you waiting for?
Get in quick will you!'

Boyle pushed roughly past, the veins in his neck pounding as he instinctively knew what he would find. 'Shit!' There he was sitting bolt upright on the sofa, former barman, Anton Stefoniou deceased. One neat little hole in the middle of his forehead being the only clue to his recent departure. *A clinical job*, Boyle thought. He pulled a small square of polythene from his jacket, slipped on a Scene Safe glove and felt the man's hand – still warm.

'Right! Call it in, the full works!
Get some uniforms out there PDQ!
And we'll need an interpreter too.
I'd better check the rest of the flat.
Gaunae no touch a thing eh?'

Chapter 16

They were both waiting in Baxter's office. It was past eight o'clock and if Boyle had been hungry earlier, then now his audibly complaining stomach had begun playing glockenspiel with his backbone. The sultry promise of a Chicken Tikka had turned rancid over the last few hours however and it would be a while before he could face another take-away from his local Indian. What he really needed was a cigarette.

Baxter had been apoplectic on the phone, Boyle guessing it was more because she knew he'd been trying to avoid her earlier, than the fact they'd uncovered yet another corpse. Some of the choice words she had spat down the phone to describe his handling of the case had included such gems as 'piss-up in a brewery,' 'dog's breakfast' and 'circus.' He knew only too well when she stormed in the door any second now she'd be expecting answers, lots of good answers. As the two detectives sat forlornly, side by side like two errant schoolboys awaiting the headmaster, Boyle sighed and tapped his foot with annoyance.

The truth of the matter was they still had very little to go on. Steel had interviewed one of the army names and cleared him of any involvement. Another was on private security work in Iraq and had been away for several months so he was also in the clear. They were left with only one guy from Perthshire who'd seemingly done a bunk over to Europe before everything kicked off. There was one wee problem being his extremely well-to-do mother had no firm idea of exactly where he had gone and when he had left, only it had been at least a fortnight clear of the first killing.

Steel had said she had one of those really annoying posh accents, so much so he swore he could hear the marbles in her mouth. 'Probably the ice in her glass of Pims,' Boyle had retorted angrily. Steel had tried to lift Boyle's mood with an admirable Jeeves and Wooster rendition of the conversation.

> 'He'd mooted something about chartering a yacht in Monte Carlo but I simply have no idea of where he is. We're *very* close you know but he's a wealthy young single chap after all and a Mother doesn't want to pry too much now does she?'

Steel had seemingly written him off too but not before broaching the likelihood of them being allowed to jet over to the South of France to check him out further. Boyle's exasperated face had told him all he needed to know. However they had so little to go on so far he didn't want to let anything go unresolved. Baxter would be screeching at him any minute now and he had to be seen to be on top of this.

He growled at Steel. 'What makes you so sure this toff isn't our gunman?'

'Sir? Well firstly he was out of the country, and then…'

'Do we know for sure? Have you checked with Border Control? Have they got a note of his passport number leaving the UK?'

'No sir. Nothing as mundane for this guy. He apparently flew out on a friend's plane and landed privately, no passport control or anything as common for him. I've checked the manifests and he was definitely listed on a flight from Inverness to Nice via Liverpool and Paris.'

'Lah-de-fucking-dah! Great life, eh? Still doesn't constitute proof though. But what would be his motive? A wee schoolgirl from a sink estate and a banker. What's the connection? It doesn't make any sense.'

'No sir. Definitely not sir. Much more likely scenario is he kept the gun as an army memento; you know how these guys love their guns, especially the hunting and shooting brigade. He either sold it on, again unlikely in my opinion sir, the guy seems to be totally minted, or he's had it nicked and was too embarrassed to tell the police as he shouldn't have had it in the first place.'

'So we're back to some kind of turf war then?'

'No doubt in my mind sir.'

'But we're the only ones who think so, right?
Us and the Daily Recorder maybe, but there's a camp I *don't* want to be in.
If it's a turf war over drugs then who the fuck is waging this so-called war? Rocky doesn't seem to be interested and the DS haven't come up with any cogent reasoning have they?
Did you get to speak to Nimmo? If the arsehole had given me the address of the barman a bit more fucking sharpish, we might have caught the guy red-handed!'

'Agreed sir. We wouldn't be sitting here, I wouldn't think.
DCI Nimmo was particularly unforthcoming on the phone.
He told me to leave the drugs angle to his department, sir. He said our killing had to be drugs related, and his boys would catch the perpetrators soon enough.'

'Aye right! Can we have that in writing then?'

Steel nodded back at his boss, exhaled deeply then abruptly pulled himself back up straight. He had felt a brief moment of relaxation. A small victory. A battle won in a war which would continue for a long time, perhaps the remainder of his life. Waiting for an inevitable bollocking from DCI Baxter was never a particularly pleasant prospect admittedly. But taken in perspective, it had to be a walk in the park compared to the other problems he faced. He would happily have swapped any one of them with his harassed boss.

He had his own reasons for publicly writing the playboy Captain Maclean off as an unlikely serial killer. None of them made him feel particularly warm and cosy inside. He had wanted so desperately to find proof the killer of the first wee girl and the man at the strip club were *not* the same person.

He couldn't sleep for worrying about who or what this person might be. If it were to have been the case then he would have had fewer nightmares. The shooting he had been embroiled in could then have been shrugged off as an unfortunate accident. Wrong place, wrong time. But this seemed impossible, now they knew beyond any doubt the same gun had been used. Add this fact to the privileged information only he possessed and you had the stuff of nightmares. During the tussle at the strip-club, the assassin's sunglasses had fallen off and Steel would never forget those hideous eyes. Savage

128

and alien, like piss-holes in the snow, only red. Like Emily Meekin had said, *pure mental red eyes*. There were only two men who knew for certain the same man committed both of these murders and that was the way it would have to stay.

It had been a different murder weapon with the second Garthamlow murders which had thrown the police off the scent as regards one solitary assassin. He had initially been pleased by this in a cold and dispassionate way. There would be virtually no chance of the Force ever connecting the Meekin case with the club killing and so he'd felt for a wonderful fleeting moment he might be off the hook from a go-to-jail-throw-away-the-fucking-key point of view.

The fact he'd been responsible for their deaths wouldn't really help him sleep much better at nights, but every little thing going his way had to be a bonus right now. What was that wankerish management course expression again? Oh yeah. *Only shoot the crocodiles nearest to the canoes...*

He realised he needed every bit of help he could get. If the red-eyed killer *had* identified him from the club, then it could be only a matter of time before the man came after him. Steel being a serving policeman had only counted against him so far. He'd tried to keep out of the limelight as regards the media but the mercenary bastards had managed to not only get his face on the 6 o'clock news standing behind Boyle, but they'd also mentioned him by name as being one of the leading detectives on the case.

He was in two minds about the toff soldier. If it had been him who killed his movie partner then this was *bad*, very fucking bad, because not only did it mean he must be a professionally trained killer, but he also possessed apparently unlimited funds. The fact he'd carried out the killings personally, rather than employing a hired thug, indicated to Steel the guy may have had a predilection for violence.

He still had bruises which bore testament to this theory. But, if he'd now gone away abroad as it appeared, then that would be very *good*. Perhaps he had achieved whatever fucked up mission he'd set out to do and meant the end of it. Job done. He might be a rich twat yes, but maybe he did work as a professional gunman, even for kicks. He would move on to the next assignment and Steel would be forgotten about.

Or he could be a clinical type of consummate professional who insisted on tying up all loose ends. An OCD killer going for his next merit badge. It didn't bear thinking about; he could be sitting in a car out there in Gordon Street right now, waiting impatiently. So he would have to be so careful. Throwing Boyle off the scent was fine but then he'd have to look like he was still working effectively as a policeman while watching his back and trying to get this guy before he got to him.

Kill or be killed.

This is what it had distilled down to. The Meekin murders had proven how high the stakes had become. For this deadly gamble to pay off, lives had to be cashed in, predominantly worthless lives, admittedly. But now with the death of the barman he was suddenly aware the gambling had perhaps got out of control and in the next run of the dice he'd be the one out of luck and cashing in his chips. He was up to his neck, he had no-one to turn to and any admission of involvement meant certain jail. Steel swallowed painfully, his dry throat telling him what he already knew – the House always wins. He'd rather be dead. *Careful what you wish for*, he thought morosely.

They both heard doors being slammed long before they saw her. Steel gulped and Boyle gritted his teeth as her stiletto heels rapped out an increasingly angry vibrato on the tiled floor as she approached.

'Here I am at last! Right Jim, tell me what I want to hear, *please.*'

The two men stood up clumsily, each one speechless. Boyle felt his jaw dropping as he stared at Barbara Baxter. Dressed head to toe in jet black, she wore a tight-fitting mid-thigh length dress which in no way hid her curves and her naked shoulders were exquisitely shrouded in a lace shawl. Her piercing eyes were directed fully at Boyle and he wondered why he'd never

noticed their beautiful aquamarine intensity
before.

Chapter 17

This was it.

At long last, it was officially Day One of The Project.

He'd done all the preparation. He'd spent days on the island, erecting weatherproof digital cameras, sound recording equipment and speakers. There were 'Keep Out – Anthrax' signs all around the coastal fringes. Sleeping rough on the island had been proven entirely possible after he'd spent two nights outside and lived. He'd caught one of the newly installed fish with a spear he had whittled himself. He lit a fire several times with ease, smashing a discarded bottle of supermarket whisky and utilising only the heavy glass bottom and the power of the sun.

His two bunkers were now clinically clean and brightly painted. He had sleeping bags, fridges, power, plasma screen monitors, wi-fi and recording equipment. To keep him from getting bored there were magazines, porn films and every ultra-violent X-box game he could think of.

But *Castaway Island Limo Hire* had to be the piece of work he remained most proud of. He'd set up the website by copying chunks off other sites, mostly based far away in Florida and California. He had admittedly spent a lot of money making them all-singing but he had to agree, the effect was fucking stupendous, even *he* wanted to hire one. The next step had been to advertise on all the forums. He set up a false business page on Facebook and purchased a few thousand 'Likes'. Copying comments from other sites was easy and he'd posted hundreds of fake photos of previous happy customers onto Pinterest and all the social media platforms. He paid for automatic opt-in forms and email auto-responders to handle all the communications to and from his website.

The final master stroke was to make the price as cheap as chips. How any sane person could possibly think a bona fide business could make money charging as little as he did made Lachie's head spin but nevertheless it was how it had to be.

Within a couple of weeks he'd built up a huge genuine fan base in Scotland with a queue of moronic wedding parties, business functions, kid's parties and prom nights all dying to experience his great service. It had been a simple enough matter to set the system to automatically email an apology to all customers, barring school prom night enquiries, saying they were fully booked and so he only had to deal with the pre-filtered list.

The first genuine hire went off without a hitch despite Lachie getting funny looks from a mother who insisted on accompanying her darling daughter for the entire trip, much to the eternal shame of the girl in question. 'Who or what are you supposed to be?' she had asked haughtily as if she'd been talking to a retarded teenager. He'd responded by informing her, as

134

CEO of the limo company, and with this being the first outing of a brand new, one hundred and fifty thousand pound investment, he had wanted to drive it himself before purchasing a further six for his fleet.

The gaggle of previously screaming girls stared at him in silent admiration. Apparently an excessive display of wealth is seen as being attractive even to twelve-year olds. The mum slumped into the leather seating as if the stuffing had been pulled out of her. Lachie smiled as he could see them all doing the maths and he was sure he heard the word 'millionaire' whispered amongst them before he left them for the relative sanctity of his cockpit.

He had collected the car earlier, impressing the same receptionist with crazy tales of Hollywood and then the decals had been applied in a matter of minutes. The hire concluded with Lachie giving each of the girls a free baseball cap and he had delivered the limo back, cleaned and stripped of its exclusive badges all within the specified time. Exhausted after this initial sortie he'd climbed into his anonymous white van and slept for three hours straight.

Today was going to be different.
This was going to be the First Take.
He'd picked the area carefully based on his research and the experience of the previous hires. He had successfully enticed previous customers into the limo for a free short ride

either later the same day or the next day after each of his paid limo hires. It was always going to be a gamble up until then. If it hadn't worked then he would be back to the same old problem he'd had before – how to get them into his car of their own volition. The whole limo hire business had been to avoid being seen as some monster child molester. By driving around in a monster car instead, Lachie was simply applying one of the most popular internet marketing techniques ever known.

Firstly, you establish your credibility and then you offer the customer a free or next to free product which will blow them away. Once you have established this 'relationship' then you are free to sell them whatever product you wish to scam them with.

In the case of Castaway Island Limo Hires, the customer will be winning a VIP ticket for the ultimate rollercoaster ride back through centuries of time. Transported to an alternative universe, she will have to use every fibre of her being to survive a heartless environment where she'll be unable to update her Facebook status or check her twitter feed. For the first time she will be without the support network of YouTube, her iPhone or her family and there will be no television programmes to tell her what she should be liking or what to do next. Ironically, she may herself become a global media personality of the fame and stature she could never have aspired to. It would be down to her and her alone to determine whether she would be alive to witness this.

Chapter 18

So here we are, he thought warily. It's a few minutes before school breaks for the weekend and everything is as planned. He'd had a hire the previous evening for a First Year Disco and all the ten girls had loved it. They were around twelve years old some a little younger some a little older but all at the perfect age where a brave new world they would shortly inhabit would have the best impact on them, where they would hopefully still have retained their innate innocence and ability to connect with the natural world.

He figured, from his experience, he would be likely to get only two or three girls today from last nights hire. He had two hires next week and two the week after. If all went well then he should be able to put around ten or so onto the island within the next fortnight giving him a sufficient stock of subjects for his experiment to work.

He could easily get more, he was confident of that even now but he had to accept every *Take* would be a potential risk and the risk would increase each time as the possibility of his modus operandi being identified became more likely.

He heard the school bell. It was time. *Alea iacta est.*

It was important to be relaxed and casual about it but even so, when he wound down the window and smiled at the three girls he

138

recognised from last night, he had been taken aback when they so readily piled into the limo. It all happened so fast he couldn't really have stopped them even if he had wanted to. As they approached the limo, he had slowed to a halt but he had totally underestimated the attention he would draw from the floods of school children once he stopped. Pouring like black rats over everything, turning the grass black, the pavements and the roadways black, they swarmed all around his gleaming white stretch limousine. The three girls called to a small group of friends to come in too and so he suddenly had six girls.

Then just as he was going to shut the door and head off, one of the girls popped her head out of the open sunroof and squealed excitedly to a further couple approaching the limo down the grass banking from the other side. They looked a little older, Lachie thought but didn't think twice as they disappeared from his view. Then the screaming reached fever pitch as he realised they had opened the small door at the bottom of the other end. Panicking slightly, Lachie slammed the main door and ran around to the other side to stop them but of course they had jumped in by the time he got half way.

Seriously worried at this divergence from the project he decided it was time to get the hell out of there. He dived into the safety of his cockpit and put the car into drive. Feeling more confident, he looked into the rear-view mirror and encouraged the girls to help themselves to

139

the ice cold drinks telling them they were all getting replaced later so they could take as much as they wanted. It had been an unusually warm afternoon and he saw them descend on the mini-bar like as if had been a spring in the desert. The snacks were taking a hammering too as Lachie cranked up the music and pushed the strobe light show up to max. The girls were screaming and laughing and when Lachie suggested one quick circumference of the area to give them a chance to finish all their freebies and to show off to their pals who was having the coolest start to their weekend there were no complainers.

Lachie drove with one eye on the road and the other on the passengers. He hadn't anticipated so many on the first try and he worried there wouldn't be enough of the sedative in the car. He held the speed steady at thirty five and he could see the girls were dancing and cavorting with abandon to the music and the videos. Once they were safely out of the town centre, he took the bypass and headed over towards the limo hire centre and to where he had his van in the courtyard of a half built farm conversion which had obviously run out of funds. With the car travelling at exactly fifty miles an hour he turned the music up even louder and released the gas.

It all happened amazingly fast. Within a couple of minutes the cabin was strewn with bodies, on the floor, half on the seats and across each other. He initially panicked that one of them might suffocate another but he reckoned he could have them out of there within a couple of minutes. The last thing he wanted right now was another dead child. So soon. It would be a bad omen and also extremely awkward to deal with. The limo slew into the courtyard without the usual style and Lachie jumped out checking first if the road was clear and he hadn't alerted anyone.

He hauled the van doors open and began to carry the girls out, one by one. He was tempted to leave the two older girls, they were perhaps as old as sixteen or so, and dump them somewhere close by, counting on them having little memory of what had happened. *Don't be stupid*, his little shoulder-squatter said. They would be bound to remember just about enough to hang him. He decided to take them and it might make the whole experiment more interesting. One girl was almost as tall as he was. He noticed one of the younger girls was also very tall but rapier thin. Lachie hoped she wouldn't fade in the first weeks before they'd learnt the requisite hunting and fishing skills.

The next TID, *time in danger*, problem would be the period when he had to leave the girls in the van temporarily unattended while he dropped off the limo at the hire centre.

He would have to do a complicated procedure which involved him moving the van as close as would be safe to the hire centre then jogging back to the limo, stripping off the decals, wiping it down and driving it back in before running back to the van.

He calculated that the girls would be out for the count safely until after they landed on the island but he didn't want to take any chances. The girls were all gaffer taped around the ankles with their hands taped behind them. Their mouths were taped with masking tape but he made sure they had plenty space around the nose. He had them all propped up against each other which he found had been made easier by virtue of there being so many of them. He remembered being violently sick when he awoke and he hoped no-one would choke on their own vomit enroute. To further disorientate the girls he had placed a black sack over each head.

He promised the girl from the hire company that he would be getting a certain Mr Depp on the next hire and she was so pleased she offered to help him for the day. He felt sad for her as he waved goodbye for the last time. Castaway Island Limo Hire had now cast off and would never return.

Chapter 19

He stopped the van in a deserted commercial area just outside Inverness to check on his cargo. It had been two hours exactly since the First Take. He pinched a couple of them and they never flinched so he took that as a good indication the others would be equally sedated. Now they were relatively safe it was time to take care of some security and experiment related essentials. There were a couple of empty oil drums he had noticed earlier and he had a good use for them.

Firstly he took their school bags and tossed them in. Next he made sure he had eight mobile phones for the eight girls. It would have flummoxed his theories about modern day life if one of them hadn't possessed a phone but none of them let him down. He carefully removed the Sim cards and batteries before systematically crushing every part of each one with a heavy pair of pliers brought for the purpose.

Lastly he had to remove the final vestiges of their contact with the old world. He was not deviant or heartless enough at this point to take all their clothes away. He was also conscious that if by any slim chance he was spotted at the next TID which was the boat loading, it would be simple enough to rip the mouth tape off making it easier to explain a girl who was merely sleeping with a blanket wrapped around her, 'my tired cousin from down south,' than some totally naked unconscious and tied up girl.

Each of them wore their own subtle variation of the school uniform which had surprised and impressed Lachie being from a strict public school himself. He took everything barring their underwear, which for most of the girls meant leaving them in their bras and pants although out of the eight girls, three of them didn't yet wear a bra and only three really needed to.

He burned all their clothing, the thick smoke casting an alarming pall across the industrial estate for a mercifully brief few minutes. There would be a black bin bag stuffed with an assortment of second hand clothing from a charity shop waiting for them over on the island. *Not exactly fashion items,* he thought as he got ready to close up the van for the last leg of the journey. He didn't imagine that they would be worried about that kind of thing for too long given the circumstances.

Lachie threw a couple of blankets over the sleeping girls, not before glancing a moment or two longer than he should have at the two older girls. The prettier of the two was not a child by any means and he contemplated all manner of sexual fantasy with her as she lay unaware. He gazed at the smooth curve of her belly, the faint fuzz of downy hair running in a line up from her navel. Her skin was of a sun-kissed brown smoothness he'd never encountered before. He fought the urge to reach down and caress her. But no, that was *not* what this was about.

144

He was exhilarated but also disturbed by
the realisation that he had the faint stirrings of
what was definitely physical arousal. His head
was still spinning as the van was slammed into
gear and they lurched off. He was a horrible
person, that much was a given but he would
gladly have driven off the nearby Kessock
Bridge if he'd thought he was turning into the
kind of monster he had come across deep in a
fetid dungeon a few weeks ago.

His mind raced faster than ever as they
approached Little Loch Broom and he could see
the mighty An Teallach on his left. Faster even
than he could drive now as the road became
rougher at this point and he prayed that the
jarring and bouncing wouldn't waken the girls.
There were still a few hours of light left at this
time of year but it should be sufficiently murky
to allow him an unseen transfer of his precious
cargo. The expensive rib was a decent size but
he hadn't planned on moving so many people at
one go and didn't want to risk leaving any of
them behind to make two trips. He just needed to
be careful when loading them, he decided.

The boat turned out to be fine as he
layered the girls rather like sardines. He used the
blankets to keep them separated as apart from
the clichéd 'dead weight' issues, his biggest
problem had been their limbs tended to flop
about and get tangled with the limbs of the
others. It had been far more complicated than
he'd expected but he'd found a workable
solution with the blankets acting like sheets of

plastic separating layers of processed meats or cheeses.

Images of gruesome overseas atrocities played across his mind as he looked down on the girls. The fact they were trussed up so tightly on top of each other and with their heads covered made them look like the bodies you would see on gritty news bulletins. The latest abominations from yet more desperate migrants fleeing from the conflicts in Syria, Iraq or from any number of religious differences in some shit-hole patch of land.

He shivered. He didn't believe in religion. Not those types at least. The life he had endured so far had cauterised any belief he may once have had in a good God. He had his own experiences of ethnic cleansing. There weren't too many television documentaries chronicling the catalogue of abuse and discrimination of albinos across the globe as far as he could remember. If he absolutely had to admit to any belief in a one supreme being then it would have to be the other bloke, El Diablo. The Devil.

The trusty plastic wheelbarrow, fulfilling its true purpose at last, turned out to be almost too small for some of the girls and by the time he'd managed to get them all up the track and past the south bunker he was worn out.

Up until then, the bunker had been as far as he had ever had to go on one trip, using it as a staging post before transporting equipment up to the northern post. The sleeping area he had identified through his own experience was much higher up than he'd realised and his legs cramped painfully as he eventually squatted down to carefully cut each girl free of her bonds. A couple of the girls were beginning to stir and so he knew he'd have to get out of there fast. So much for Rohypnol being ten times more potent than diazepam, he snorted. He decided to leave their black head sacks on to keep them quieter for longer and in case one of them opened her eyes before he was done. He knew they might get sight of him at some point in the experiment but he didn't want to prejudice their opinions of how and why they were there so soon.

Lachie walked as fast as he could in the fading light, his heart beating a primitive rhythm of survival and conquest as he anticipated the very first recordings back in the bunker. He hoped the automatic triggering systems had worked and this would be the first indication that The Project would all operate as planned.

Chapter 20

'Look angel…It's not that I'm angry wi'
you, like.
Ye ken that don't ye?
But I just cannae let this one go, know
what I mean. It would be exactly the
same wi' you, so it would.
So come on, tell me the now!
Before ma patience really does run the
fuck out an- wait!
Now hold on! Just you stay there a wee
minute, that's ma moby.
I'm not finished wi' you yet.'

Simone was terrified. Her dad was a
scary enough dude at the best of times although
she couldn't really remember there ever *being* a
best of times. Maybe, years ago, *before our Mum
ran off,* she thought. She still had very mixed
emotions about all that, seeing as the two adults
had been scrapping like two cage fighters in the
weeks before her mum went away. In public he
appeared extremely protective over his daughters
but Simone was now old enough at eleven to
appreciate most of his posturing was image
related. He was always the 'Big Man' around
here and naebody was allowed to mess with
anything of his. *That's all we are*, she knew deep
down, *we're his possessions*.
    She genuinely had no idea where her
sister had gone. Dad was going mental over
nothing. It had only been a couple of days and

Simone couldn't really see what the big deal was. The school holidays had just started and she was nearly eighteen after all and would be away from here soon enough. But it had to be something to do with Dokie, that much she was sure of, but there would be no way she would normally ever have considered grassing him up to her dad. The greasy wee shite was as vicious as a cornered pit-bull and she'd seem him slavering over her big sister for months now but he'd always been clever enough not to attract too much attention.

Oh, Oh. She gulped. He's off the phone now. The coupon looks grim an' all. What to do? If it's going to be ma' dad against Dokie then the plooky wee wank is going down, no fucking contest. Simone realised she'd all but decided this while he'd been on the phone. I just need a wee bit longer to work up the courage to shop the bastard, that's all, she thought, but then panicked suddenly as her dad stormed over to the window and threw it open aggressively. *Oh no! Not Ziggy…!*

Simone screamed in terror as her father grabbed her old cat by his scrawny neck and held him out of the third floor window. His face had turned pure white and she knew the look in his eyes. When he looked like that he could be capable of anything. His voice growled menacingly and through the window she heard the unmistakable sound of a can of ginger being crushed by a bin lorry.

'Right! That's it. Stop a' this pissing
aboot!
You know something an' yer no' tellin'
me. I'm no' stupid like.
One to ten, that's all I'm sayin.'
If your no' gaunae tell me where she's
gone, the cat's going oot' the fuckin'
windae.'

'Dad! Dad! Please dinnae hurt him…I'm
sorry! Please! I'll tell ye. I'll tell ye, the
now! Just dinnae drop him.'

'Where the fuck is your sister? *Now*,
Simone!

'She'll be wi' Dokie!'

'Dokie…?'

Simone gasped as her father's face
hardened into implacable granite and his eyes
became even smaller and blacker than a
Rottweiler's. Throwing the cat back onto the
sofa, he stormed out, muttering to himself, 'Ah
should huv' known… Ah should huv' known.'
Despite her fear, Simone couldn't help feeling a
ripple of deep satisfaction tingling across her
skin as she pulled the surprised cat up to her face
and hugged him tight.

Chapter 21

Sometimes, even in a murder investigation, the gods will do you a favour, they had both decided, but for entirely different reasons.

Baxter had been surprisingly lenient on them and had even gone so far as to gift her grateful second-in command a couple of additional officers for a week or two, to 'break the back' of this case. She had sided with Steel and had bought the drugs turf war angle, and Boyle had agreed to go along with it despite still having his private doubts and so it hadn't helped departmental morale when ballistics subsequently confirmed it had been the same gun which had killed the Meekin family and the strip club barman.

Steel was particularly devastated by this revelation as it made no sense at all given the inside knowledge he had on the case. He knew perfectly well who had killed Emily Meekin and it had nothing to do with drugs. But apart from him, the only person who could have possibly connected these two killings is the man who killed the barman. If Steel was thinking straight, he could now have two psychopathic killers who had a valid reason to terminate him. Whose side should he be on now? How many people do you have to kill these days to get through the week?

Meanwhile Boyle had been vindicated in his theory that the drugs war had been a red herring and so the whole thrust of the case had been re-directed back towards the illegal sex industry. Boyle reckoned Steel hadn't slept much in days and again he'd become seriously concerned about his partner. Obviously Steel was living on his nerves. But why? Could it be solely over a failed love affair? Boyle wouldn't ever have considered himself to be the most romantic man on earth but even so, he didn't get it. He had also been annoyed at his partner's persistent moaning that they were heading down a blind alley.

Adding fuel to the fire had been the sad fact they were making very few inroads into the case from this angle and there were mutterings from some of the lads in the department that maybe Steel had been right. Maybe, just maybe it *was* still a drugs issue. They had established firm leads from the club which indicated the dead barman had been involved in selling illegal Viagra and the like but to Boyle's mind it was hardly a surprise considering he worked in a strip club and not the kind of thing you'd get murdered for. Steel appeared to be doing his level best to slow down or derail these lines of investigation and Boyle had resumed his harassed chewing of plastic cigarettes.

All of this meant today's development had been like Christmas come early. It appeared that the mythical drugs war was back on again. One of Rocky's main men had been found at dawn by a couple of pissed up teenagers one of whom had left a tidy heap of half digested kebab a metre away from the body. The official cause of death had still to be confirmed from the lab boys but they weren't holding the front page on that particular point as he had been discovered sitting over on the M8 motorway flyover with a partially air-conditioned head.

No-one was too worked up about the death of another scum-bag like Dokie Greig, not even his foul tempered boss, whom Boyle and Steel had just left. Why Dokie would have wanted to give a handgun the ultimate blow job was anyone's guess but neither of the officers' could picture him doing it without a little 'assistance,' at least in the imagination stakes. Dokie had been, by all accounts, not exactly the sharpest tack in the box.

Rocky had been more un-cooperative than usual and appeared to have more pressing matters on his mind, refusing to give them more than five minutes of his time. Every time DC Steel asked him a question he would launch himself to within an inch of the bemused policeman and spit a further volley of invective. Between the colourful adjectives and the dubious slang they gathered he was a tad unhappy about the performance of the local *gendarmerie.*

'When are you gaunae get yer heids out yer arse's and stop yer daft notion there's some kinda drugs battle gaun oan. It's Garthamlow fer fuck's sake, no the Bronx!'

153

Apparently his eldest daughter had flown the coop a few days past and Rocky was naturally concerned about her safety. 'She's a fuckin' good kid, so she is' he reflected more to himself than to the two police officers. The implication here that she would have been without doubt in a minority of one within the cess pit she'd recently vacated hadn't been lost on Boyle. Wherever the poor lassie had gone he decided, it had to be a healthier environment than around there.

Steel went through the motions as expeditiously as the rules allowed and the two men left with the firm impression that whoever killed young Dokie had been known to Rocky but this still hadn't come across as a situation he'd been overly pleased with. They breathed in the fresh air after the stifling heat of Rocky's apartment. Boyle reached for a cigarette and the two men looked at each other for a moment, each reading the other's thoughts.

'Any chance there's *no* a drugs war going on then?
Yup, that'll be shining bright.'

Gary Steel smiled as the unmarked car sped off back through the deserted streets of Garthamlow. Any windows not yet boarded up and graffiti strewn still had the curtains drawn. Eleven o'clock on a Saturday morning was officially the crack of dawn around here. They were expecting a call from both the boffins and the ballistics guys anytime now as Baxter had promoted them to Priority One on all matters until this unusual backlog of unsolved murders started to go down. Steel knew the gun used in this apparent 'suicide' would be different to the earlier killings and so he and the rest of Glasgow could deduce his 'vigilante' had moved on to bigger and better things and so he would be effectively in the clear.

He'd started to become increasingly worried the logical solution to the recent murder equation might simply be he himself should be removed from it – with extreme prejudice, as their US counterparts liked to say. It seemed obvious the killer knew who he was. Would it not come to the point that the killer would decide to take him out and so reduce any possibility of him cracking under the not insurmountable strain? So this confirmation of it being an obvious drug war killing kept the focus of attention away from him and any other elements likely to be detrimental to him.

It therefore came as some surprise to Steel when Boyle took his flashing mobile to receive the news that forensically, this murder wasn't as clean as it first looked.

'Away! You're kiddin' me.'

Boyle spluttered, dropping his precious vapour cigarette onto the grimy floor.

'The same gun…okay…but not the cause of death?'

Boyle shut the phone off, shaking his head. He turned to his driver and told him their instincts about the 'suicide' being assisted were spot on. But never in a hundred years would he have thought it might be the same killer or rather the same gun which had robbed the lives of the barman and the Meekin family. Steel instinctively slammed on the brakes and the car stopped unceremoniously onto the hard shoulder.

'What the fuck! What's got into you man?'

'Sorry sir. Thought you'd want to pick up your fag off the floor sir. Bit heavy on the brake there! Sorry 'bout that sir.'

He's rabbiting again, thought Boyle. What is going on here? Steel had turned chalk white and his hands were visibly shaking.

'Come on! I need a proper fag! Let's go for a wee walk and I'll tell you the juicy bits and then you can tell me what's got you looking so peaky.'

Chapter 22

She opened her eyes with a start. Her head hurt a lot and it was strangely dark. Her head must be covered by the duvet but she couldn't seem to get her head from under it. *There's something over my heid*, she thought confusedly. Reaching up with a sore stiff arm she pulled the cloth off her face, only to be rewarded by a blindingly painful flash of bright sunlight. Screwing her face up with the effort to try to sit, her head went all woozy and then she knew what was coming next. Her stomach spasmed and she was sick all over her bare legs and those of another lassie lying beside her.

Chantal looked around her in horror! *I must be still dreaming*, she decided. She could see she was lying in the middle of a wood or something and there were lots of other bodies all over the place with black canvas bags on their heads. Trying to move, her body stiffened as a current of pain travelled up her body and terminated behind her eyes, painful enough to make her cry out with the intensity of it. At the same moment, she was kicked by the legs of another person next to her, the one she had just splattered with hot vomit. The girl pulled off her black bag and recoiled in terror at the scene around her. It was Stephanie or Stevie as she preferred to be called.

'Hey! What's gaun on here? Chantal? Where are we?

Who are they?
Oh, shit, ma heid. I'm gonna be...'

Her pal hunched into a ball before puking noisily into the dry grass which Chantal had realised had been put there as some sort of makeshift bedding. She sat up slowly and tried with difficulty to swallow. Her dry throat hurt like mad and she shivered violently as her body began to come to life. *Where were they and what had happened? Why were they in their undies?* Despite the sunshine it felt freezing and Chantal coughed up some phlegm which gave her throat the brief ability to speak.

'Hey! Wake up will you! Can anybody mind how we got here or what?
Stevie! You okay?
What's happened here? I can't remember nothing, so I can't.'

'Jeezo! Me neither. I feel like crap. We been poisoned and that?'

'Dunno girl. I've been awfy sick a lot lately, but no like this.
Hey! You alright there? I know, I know! We're all the same!'

The rest of the girls were coming to now and all going through various stages of the same nightmarish awakening. The air remained cold but less so with every passing minute and as

Chantal looked around her she could see they were in a flat area of a clearing of sorts. If she strained her complaining eyes she could just make out the view through one side of slightly thinner trees and it confused her even more. It couldn't be, she thought. It looked like all there was beyond them was a shimmering blue ocean.

Several of the girls were crying now and Stevie and Chantal exchanged glances as if to say, 'What the…? How do we do this?' They knew the two of them were the oldest of the girls with all the rest looking like first years. In fact, Chantal realised with a small degree of comfort she'd recognised a couple of them and they were all lassies from her school. The wee gobshite Jenny was there who'd totally idolised her over the past year.

Something twigged in the back of her mind about Jenny. She looked at Stevie and it sparked another jagged thought. The pair of them had got in the stretch Cadillac or whatever it was hadn't they? Hadn't it been Jenny who had called her over?

'Stevie? Can you mind? Were we no' in a stretch limo? Has somebody drugged us all or what?

'Aye! We were on a free go wi' yon cool limo Jenny, Simone an' Katy hud' for their Prom night. I cannae mind anything after gettin' in like. I think we've been spiked an' that!'

159

Jenny crawled over, her hair matted with sick and the two older girls grimaced at the sight of her face filthy with a mixture of smeared dirt and tears.

'We *wis* in the limo! All of us. I called yous in masel' an that, but I cannae mind what happened after. We wis huvin' a wee party like, no?
Is it a joke like? Where ur we anyway?'

Stevie looked around at all the shivering girls, some of whom were sobbing still, two or three hugging tightly together as if they thought they could magic themselves back to their own comfy warm beds. She tried to bring the voice of reason to stop the wee girls from panicking.

'Don't think this is a joke, like.
If it is, then it's no' awfy funny now is it, eh?
Me and Chantal are Sixth Years so we'd ken if this wiz some kind of end of year thing and I'm tellin' yous we've never seen anything like this before, like.
Ma new phone's gone an' everything.
This is serious, guys.'

The wailing only increased with the apparent confirmation of their own worst fears. Just then, a chill wind picked up the putrid scent

160

of the girls and swirled menacingly around them, searching out the smallest, the most vulnerable.

'Listen up! Don't panic! We'll sort a' this out okay. Stephanie…sorry Stevie is going to stay here and watch you all an' I'll go and find some adults or teachers an' that so we can all get hame as soon as poss.
Okay? I'll be back in no time, like.'

Chantal felt the weight of responsibility lie heavily across her cold bare shoulders as she looked down at the anxious wee faces. They reminded her of one of those TV documentaries with the tiny birds stretching up as their mother returned to the nest with food. She wished for her own mother just then, more than at any time since she had run off. As she brushed off the dead bracken and made to leave, an awful thought lanced through her brain. Could her evil bastard father be somehow responsible for this gig? *Was this what happened to mum*, she thought miserably. Have we all been 'disappeared'? Or, even worse, is this all my fault 'cos of Dokie an' that. She shook herself of those thoughts and nodded to Stevie as she headed downwards towards the light.

Chapter 23

Pushing through the branches and thick undergrowth, Chantal felt the fierce scratching against her bare thighs and suddenly felt extremely self conscious about her near nakedness. Least I've got ma fancy *Pour Moi* knicker set on the day, she thought absentmindedly, no like poor Stevie wi' her passion killer period pants! Her feet were signalling their unhappiness too and she slowed her pace down picking her steps more cautiously.

Despite her tough upbringing, Chantal knew out here, in the wilds of fuck knows where, she was a delicate creature really. She'd never been outside in her bare feet in her entire life. She'd never had a garden, never been abroad, never even been to a real beach before, not one with proper sand and waves and stuff.

As she emerged from the edge of the forest, she could see better what the lie of the land looked like. Down below her she saw one of those beaches she'd only ever seen in movies. Right now, it looked like one of the most perfect things she had ever seen. The sun glinted off the deep blue ocean with little snowy flurries sticking their heads up for a few seconds in a futile race against the wind.

Closer to the sparkling shell beach the sea seemed to speed up and raise its skirts to reveal bright aquamarine breakers which crashed onto the shore with a fearful thundering she could hear even up this high. Her lips were dry and her face encrusted with her own sick and she stood for a second imagining how nice it would be to feel that fresh clean water crashing over her head and gurgling around her ears. It would be salt water though? So she couldn't drink it? Makes you sick, she knew that of course, but even so, she considered it would be worth it for a wee minute. Everything made her sick right now.

Looking back up towards where she had come from Chantal could see the slope increased dramatically and there seemed to be a mountain coming out of the top of the trees. Back down on the coast the beach only stretched for a few hundred metres but she could see another beach at the far end of the island, in fact it seemed to be a longer strip of beach which disappeared into the distance. If she squinted her eyes, she could see the mainland in the distance and also straight out from where she stood. Which meant the island was in a kind of bay, she thought. No idea how far away, but there must be some people around here somewhere.

Invigorated by this idea, she struck off directly along in the opposite direction from the long beach, what she would call North. Maybe there would be a wee harbour or a fishing village. All these places have a wee harbour don't they? It would be like that lame Hamish Macbeth series her mum used to watch when she was wee.

Unknowingly, Chantal had stood only a few feet from Lachie in his south bunker and if she had turned south rather than north then she would have walked right past him. Not that she would ever have noticed his emplacement. The fact the ground had been far more heavily trampled would have been lost on the city girl and Lachie had not forgotten his army training when he built the intricately designed gorse and rhododendron screens which lay across the entrance to the bunker. As she emerged from the woods and looked down upon his landing beach she also would have been directly above his precious rib which had been similarly concealed, effectively invisible to her inexperienced eyes.

Subconsciously walking towards the glittering sea instead of directly north, Chantal found herself closer to the edge of the island and without any warning she fell into knee high marsh. She panicked and floundered ever deeper and by the time she could fight her way back onto more substantial ground she was covered in wet mud up to her chest. *So much for the posh pants*, she gasped, taking a minute's rest in the sunshine. The mud dried within seconds and Chantal felt her skin tighten and pull as she stood back up, feeling the breeze chilling her at the back of her thighs and in her groin.

Keeping west of the marshland she trudged on waiting for the first signs of civilisation. Instinctively knowing she was approaching the top of the island she felt convinced safety couldn't be far away. Straight in front of her she saw a small loch and still nervous about further marshes she considered it safer to skirt the water around the left hand side. Not realising until she stumbled upon it, she discovered there was a healthy river feeding the loch which tumbled down from the high rocks of the mountain.

Drinking the clear fresh water and washing the disgusting crud off had to be one of the most amazing moments of her young life. She stood up to her knees in a sun warmed pool and laughed as the current washed the last remnants of the dirt from her hair and body. She giggled like a primary school girl as she nervously squatted down in the welcoming water and let go a stream of darker warmer liquid, quivering with a primitive pleasure at the thrill of watching it speed away and vanish forever, dancing over the sparkling rocks.

As Chantal looked around her, reluctant to leave her watery sanctuary she thought she spied what looked like wee strawberries. Driven by a sudden and intense hunger, she forced herself to stand back up and then she gingerly made her way over the rocks to the profusion of tiny green and red fruits which seemed to be sausage shaped versions of the fresh strawberries she'd once had at her pal's house. She sniffed one suspiciously and took the smallest little bite…it was a strawberry! Stuffing them into her mouth, stalks included, she froze after a full minute of frenzied feasting. What about the others? There did seem to be plenty but maybe she should take some back. What could she carry them in? It would be crazy awkward. Anyway, she'll find help soon so they won't need any strawberries; it'll be pie an' chips more likely.

Yet as she made her way she looked back and made a mental picture of the location, just in case.

Two or three hours later a severely depressed and exhausted Chantal staggered back up the sloping woods to find the others. She told them she'd been all over the island and found no signs of life anywhere. Terrified about what the implications of this meant for the group she had sacrificed her posh bra to utilise it as a make-shift strawberry carrier. Strangely, she'd felt less conspicuous walking back topless than she had earlier in the day when she first left the cover of these trees.

The others were overjoyed to see her back and the initial disappointment of there being no others on the island was balanced by the knowledge they were all safe and barring Chantal, they all had some clothes.

'It was only a wee while after you left, I found the bin bag!' Stevie proclaimed jubilantly.

'Their no' exactly *Top Shop* an' that but better than being in the buff like! No that it seems tae bother you like! A wis thinking it must be yon Bo Derek coming up through they trees there! They wis a' Primark an' that but no too bad for a wee while as long as naebody sees us.'

'Aye! I see *you* managed to get the only decent trackies, then!'

'Come oan Chantal! They're only Kappa for fucks sake. They'd be too wee for you anyway no? I left you the matching top, see?'

'Bitch!' Chantal spat playfully as she squeezed into an old fashioned tweedy skirt and the hallowed tracksuit top. The others were all similarly attired in a hotchpotch of non-matching clothing with no footwear being evident nor any other trousers left for anyone bigger than a size 6. She unloaded the fruits of her bra and found the others had also found some edible fruits which so far hadn't given anyone any tummy problems. 'They're no as nice as these mind,' Stevie mumbled as she stuffed a small handful of the wild strawberries into her mouth. 'Some kind of berry, one of the wee ones says they're red currants 'cos she just did them at school. Good enough for me!'

'We can't live on berries for long, Stevie,' Chantal whispered as most of the girls played about the edge of the clearing. 'And we need to make something a bit more weatherproof too. What happens if we're here for a while?'

'We'll no be here for long. Wise up for fuck's sake. Who put us here? Who left the clothes? It widnae surprise me if some twat frae the school didnae turn up

167

with cameras an' that, wi' a box o' KFC for us all!'

Chapter 24

Lachie had to laugh at the Kentucky Fried Chicken comment. He liked Stevie. She was a real toughie, what they used to call a tomboy when he was younger. She reminded him at this stage of some of the girls who'd been with him in the army, most of whom he'd been secretly frightened of in case they proved themselves more able than him. The old boy network had ensured there were very few female officers for him to worry about but he could see the way it would be going. The women paid attention better and generally learned faster than the men and he was glad there had been no girls in his school. He had insulated himself from them here though. They couldn't hurt him now, could they?

But, then the awful realisation hit him instantly.

In many ways it might have been this isolation from females for most of his life that had bent him out of shape so badly. True, they probably would have called him a 'mutant' too, but maybe if he had been schooled normally with ordinary girls and boys whose daddies were not all advocates or generals then his life might have been different. Not for the last time did he hear himself curse his deceased father.

He slapped his face hard. This is not the time or place to slip back into pathetic hand-wringing about what might have been. He remained responsible for his own mistakes and nobody else. During his preparations for The Project, he had begun to notice a slight change in his outlook on life. He still hated the world but there were times when he could see the positives and not only the bleak downside to everything.

He'd picked up some shitty 'positive thinking' and business guru type books when he'd been searching for any help he could get for the planning of the mission. He'd read *The Art Of War* but it never struck a chord with him. He surprised himself by preferring stuff like Jack Canfield and even the fat old goose Trump before he went all presidential on us. He would almost start to believe he could one day be happy on this miserable rock. But then as he felt himself being suckered in, he would stop and remember who he was, and then all he wanted to do was reverse an army tank over their bollocks.

But inevitably some of it must have sunk in. If it hadn't then he wouldn't have had the courage and foresight to carry out this mission. He had visualised his success and now he was going to make it happen.

He had to admit to being cautiously happy with the way things were panning out at this early stage. The girls had found food surprisingly swiftly and one of them had scoped out the island so most of them were now under few illusions this must all be some big joke and they'd be Facebook surfing by teatime.

He liked Chantal the explorer, too. But in a different way. This disconcerted Lachie because in real life, he'd never really felt any natural 'romantic' affection towards a female before. He had lusted over the odd stereotypically attractive woman or two in the media of course, but they'd always seemed other-worldly, alien almost. He'd pondered over his sexuality as a youth as most kids inevitably did and he felt pretty sure he wasn't gay. As far as he could remember, he had *never* felt any sexual pangs for another boy. A flashback to that awful scene at the lap-dancing club tore through his reverie and he brought himself back to his task again.

The girls had all settled down together with the two older ones talking quietly. Too quietly. He fiddled with the controls in the bunker but no amount of adjusting could make their whispered conversations intelligible. He would look at sourcing more powerful directional microphones online later. It would always be a trade-off between the size and the performance. *Ooh err missus*...he laughed again.

He had his face right up to the screen, wishing he could lip-read. He had known a boy at his school, a deaf-mute, who could understand Lachie perfectly solely by watching his face. The two of them had been friends of a sort, both different from the others. In fact if the boy hadn't moved to a special deaf school in Edinburgh, Lachie would have taken lessons in sign language. He watched Stevie chatting away nineteen to the dozen and he swore at her under his breath. He felt strangely jealous of the

171

friendship, the intimacy she had with the other girl.

In the main, his technology seemed to be working well enough though. He'd accurately planted the observation poles along all the tracks Chantal had followed. For a city girl, she'd skilfully picked up on the rabbit and goat tracks he himself had used and with the increased traffic over the next months then the main routes would only become more established. During her exploration of the island there were only a few infuriatingly long minutes here and there where Lachie lost sight of Chantal and there were moments, like at the stream, where he had been transfixed.

He remained in two minds about the older girls. That they were going to be a distraction seemed evident. As he watched them around the sleeping area, he could see the younger girls were being directed and controlled by the other two. Just a moment ago he'd seen Stevie rebuke a smaller girl for apparently relieving herself behind a bush right next to where they had slept the night. She had pointed over towards some rocks which Lachie had previously hoped they would perhaps use for the purpose. To start with at least.

Therein lay the problem. His hypothesis had been that within a short time the societal norms would break down and they would revert to a more base animal behaviour. His firm belief was women were ghastly creatures, at least as vicious and black-hearted as men, if not more.

172

He'd read *Lord Of The Flies*, as a prescribed text at school of course and this had partly inspired The Project. Nowadays, he would argue we are all much less connected with our physical world or practical past lives and consequently we would be even less able to look after ourselves in an environment such as this island. The obvious implication of this is the breakdown to a primal condition should occur all the more swiftly. He had specifically chosen subjects of what he thought would be pre-adolescent ages so they would behave more naturally, instinctively even and there would be fewer complications from a laboratory control point of view.

He had heard the conversation about Stevie and Chantal being sixth year pupils with abject horror. The presence of these two, who were both effectively adults, and therefore authority figures, would almost certainly slow down the group's decline into savagery which meant the experiment could run out of time. The project timescale had only ever been intended to last for the duration of the warmer weather which meant five or six months at the very most although he secretly hoped he would get enough footage before then.

He remembered there had also been older boys in the Golding book but they were nowhere near being adults. To further complicate matters there was also the fact that children were growing up considerably faster nowadays and a twelve year old in the post war years was an entirely different proposition in comparison to one from today's fast paced technological 'village.'

There was nothing he could do about this now however, short of eliminating or removing the two girls. He had the means to carry out either course of action but he was reluctant to do so. The fact that two young adults were part of the experiment may add greater weight to the drama and make the inevitable slide into anarchy all the more powerful as an indictment of our modern culture.

He carried on watching intently, amazed at how instantly he had become tuned in to their lives. He would have been one of the first to criticise the celebrity jungle shows in the past but here he had become hooked. But this was an entirely different situation, he argued with his internal taste monitor. He had created this world and he'd been responsible for populating it with real honest people whom he would get to know and understand over the weeks. His subjects were not vain publicity seekers down on their luck at the back end of an inglorious career and therefore their behaviour would have a hallmark of authenticity which those facsimile products could never match.

Of course, he told himself; this is only because what you are doing is completely illegal and if caught you will yourself be the subject of reduced liberty and close supervision for many a long year. Hmmph.

He had surprised himself that so far he had not had the slightest inclination to even glance at his extensive porn collection. Neither had he switched on his X-box or PS3. Real life was proving to be exciting enough. Or maybe he had been too worn out by the events of the last few days. I'd better get used to it, he muttered. With the prospect of long hours in front of his plasma screens, he decided a wee exercise regime might be a good idea. Seventy five full push ups later, he rejoiced that he'd decided to invest in a halogen heated hot shower for each bunker.

It had been shortly after dusk when things first started to go pear shaped.

Chapter 25

What had annoyed Lachie the most at first had been the fact that his precious camera system was as *state-of* as money could buy which meant it wasn't exactly cheap. He had back-up equipment obviously, but he hadn't ever thought to stock up on alternative systems, different cameras or a beefed up physical protection for the system. When he tested everything he had done it in daylight which even then had been a tricky and time consuming task involving a great deal of running back and forth making his fine-tune adjustments. He knew the system worked great in the dark because he had tested it all, *from the bunkers*. This had been his first mistake.

The infra-red lenses gave him as good a picture at night as he got during the day. Beat the quality on those crappy transport cop programmes into a cocked hat for sure. What he hadn't thought about was each of the high zoom auto-tracking cameras had a little red eye which blinked like a demented cobra when it was recording. To be honest, the light was infinitesimally small and no-one would have considered it to be a problem in normal operating conditions. But he could see later on himself if somebody is immersed in the total blackness of a night sky, with zero light pollution, the little red light might as well be from a 747 with its back brakes on. And of course, *no plan ever survives contact with the enemy.*

Which had been precisely how that sharp eyed little brat Stevie had managed to clock cameras' 7 and 9 so easily on their very first unsedated night on the island? The intensity of her aggression surprised him as did her agility. He had it all on disc as it wasn't until early next morning before he discovered the group's first act of vandalism. Stevie had been fielding a stream of complaints from the younger girls, most notably Jenny and Joolz who were the most vocal elements of the group. It had been getting dark and everyone had become hungry, tired, cold and scared. Their hoped for fast food hadn't materialised and they were coming to terms with spending the night sleeping on the trodden down and damp ground.

Stevie, he was beginning to appreciate, could never be described as a people person and he'd heard her confess earlier to Chantal she might have to strangle Jenny before the day was through. Apparently she didn't do too well on a lack of food although her classification of food contrasted widely with Lachie's. To be fair to Stevie, Lachie was also thinking at this point in the recording that Jenny was a bit full on. She had the kind of incessant verbal diarrhoea he'd once heard described in basic training, about a lad similarly afflicted, as 'having a mouth like a verbal Gatling gun.'

The group had all settled down with only one or two crying quietly to themselves. Next he heard a garbled roar of anger and Stevie's white face, contorted with sheer animal rage had appeared in the picture of camera 9. Camera 7 had still been operational and so he had been able to see how easily she'd leapt up into the adjacent tree and obliterated the camera body with repeated savage blows with a handheld rock. Camera 7 was then forced to film impotently as its attacker leapt up and dealt the picture a similar hammering. The sound recording equipment had been unaffected and so he had the full unexpurgated stream of invective.

Stevie had woken up the entire group by this stage and they all sounded extremely frightened and confused. It was Chantal whom he heard calming them all down and who suggested they stay put until morning before doing anything drastic. It would be some time before Stevie's fury abated however and her language was choice as she told the rest of the group what she would do to the perverts who were trying to film them at night. The illogic nature of her argument was totally lost on the whole lot of them, as they were all wearing every scrap of spare clothing in a vain effort to keep warm.

By early morning Lachie was ready for them. He'd put his standard full camouflage gear on and painted his face up too so he would be as hard to spot as possible. He hadn't intended to be walking about on the island this early on in the experiment and so he was both angry and a little nervous about doing so.

He took his rifle and headed straight for them, knowing at this point they were all still congregated around the same sleeping area. If he could get a shot in while they were still asleep then it would be quicker and far less messy. He slowed as he approached the clearing, his movements economical, each step measured. His first sighting was the comic vision of a bare white skinny little arse as one of the younger girls squatted in the bushes. He had an excellent target to aim for and he didn't miss. With the muzzle of his gun supported by a substantial tree branch he was able to see most of the girls. He fired off round after round and within half a minute all but the two older girls were flat out cold. Stevie was set away from the others and he wasted no time in putting a round into the back of her neck.

Suddenly he was faced with Chantal walking directly towards him, panic and confusion on her tired face as she took in the mayhem around her. He swithered for a brief second as to whether he could talk her round instead but his training had taught him not to take any further chances. It was the hardest thing he had ever done in his life. He shot Chantal in the middle of her forehead and she crumpled into a heap.

The wheelbarrow had been carefully parked a few feet away and he hastily replaced the two broken cameras. Next he fired up one of his portable generators and began to construct a strong cage around the first one allowing enough

179

room for the lens to function unhindered and the view to be clear.

Next, he attached a crude spiked necklace around the scaffolding poles, the little welder being just enough to bond it strongly. He cut the adjacent tree down to prevent any further vandalism. The camera and pole were now obvious but he decided that Stevie would have told them all chapter and verse before the morning was out so there was little point in trying to hold on to a myth. There is no such thing as Santa Claus – deal with it.

He then raced around the island modifying the cameras and poles which he determined were most in danger of receiving further unwarranted attentions. He was relieved to find a great number of them were fine.

It took him a few hours and he had been getting increasingly nervous that he would be discovered. He had left the girls a sweetener, literally. He hoped they would get the message. The tranquiliser darts would be wearing off very soon now and he was anxious to see what they would do next.

Chapter 26

Most of them were stirring by the time a tired Lachie had stowed his kit and secured the bunker entrance. Confused and perhaps a little bruised, they were still waking up and trying to warm themselves up. No one had noticed the black bin liner.

It was little Katy, or Katster as she seemed to be called, who saw it first and proceeded to scream the place down. Lachie hadn't appreciated how much of a psychological knife edge they must have been on at the time. Like him. Of all of them so far, Katster had been the only one who had never once left the safety and security of the group. They could have been camped in Glasgow's Bellahouston Park and she wouldn't have been any the wiser. Quieter than the rest and very dark eyed, Lachie had the feeling she wasn't in the best of health and he had earlier resolved to try and listen more attentively when she was part of the conversations to see if he could work out what it was. He hadn't found any inhalers when he disposed of their belongings back in Inverness but still he suspected asthma and felt guilty that he was only a few minutes walk away with a stock of his own medication.

The rest of them would have wasted no time in ripping the contents to pieces if Chantal hadn't had the foresight to snatch it up briskly. The girls were now all screaming in delight, their rude awakening seemingly forgotten. It had become more like a children's birthday party, as Chantal held the sweets just high enough to be out of range and the rest of the girls danced and jumped around her, giggling and shouting for their favourites.

'Oh look… Parma Violets! Have no ate them for yonks!'

'Give's it… The Haribos are mine…Aye, you kin take the fizzy colas…'

As one of the smaller girls brandished her Curly Wurly like a chocolate Samurai sword, Lachie relaxed for the first time. The tension seemed to lift with the early morning mists and as the sunshine filtered through the trees he could see they were looking reasonably content for a moment.

To be honest, this is far too soon for treats, he scolded himself. He should be encouraging them to forage more and to think about trying to catch themselves some real food, maybe building some fires and all the other tasks he had imagined they would pick up fairly easily. Perhaps, with the camera situation now more in the open, literally and metaphorically, the girls would start to realise they were not going to be going home anytime soon. This is still only Day One, he kept reminded himself. On his travels earlier he had decided to drop his fishing spear in an obvious place to see if they got the hint. There were also three glass bottles distributed around the island; one close to the stream where Chantal had been bathing, one down at the southern end of the island by the sand bar and the other high up on the ridge. He had anticipated these would all be likely spots for traffic but as yet only one of them had been near one of those sites.

He felt comfortable for them to build fires, within reason. He had built several before jetting around the island in the rib and from the mainland at Laide or over the other side at Mungasdale it was almost impossible to see any smoke. Lachie had been open about spending lots of time on the island and he'd told Archie there was a strong possibility he'd be inviting other like-minded 'greens' to spend weekends with him.

It would be nigh on impossible for the girls to let any fires get out of control as the weather had not been that great in the run up to the mission and, with the topography being as it was, the island-long marshland which ran up the east side of the island would prevent any wild fires getting out of hand.

His attention was drawn to another screen where he saw Stevie and Chantal arguing about the cameras. He struggled to hear the whole conversations and had to turn down the volume from the main group screens.

'No being fuckin' bribed like...no wi Dolly Mixtures for fucks sake!

183

What's gaun tae happen next? Get us tae a' dress up in pink dresses an' pig tails and that?'

Stevie was livid as per usual.

'Ah know what ye mean, like, Stevie…' Chantal sighed. 'But we cannae really fight these people, can we? Mean to say, look at what happened wi' the darts…next time it could be real bullets, what would we do then? Nothing that's what. An' okay, the sweets were pretty wanky an' that, but does it not show us, whoever these people are, they dinnae mean tae hurt us?'

'So what 'ur they up tae then?
Let's dae 'nowt and see what happens next.
The cameras is whit it's aboot is it no? If we sit an' stay schtum, maybe we'll get some answers, that's all I'm trying to say.'

'Okay then. But I think it would be better tae try and explore more or even tae make a wee shelter an' that. Katster hud some good ideas for building a wee roof an' stuff. It would keep us warmer an' make it mair private too.'

'Aye maybe but let's make the shites suffer for a wee bit, eh?'

True to their word the two older girls managed to get the others to sit still and keep quiet. It didn't last too long. There had to be a delicious inevitability about it all. Even Lachie with his limited experience of little girls, knew they were on to a loser. Bereft of their digital gadgets most of them had never been made to suffer sensory deprivation on this scale before. Rather than admit defeat, Stevie jumped up and left the others. Tracking her on other screens, he saw her climb all the way up to the cliffs along the eastern edge of the ridge and as far as he was aware she spent the rest of the day there.

She had a certain degree of sympathy from Lachie despite her troublesome behaviour. He loved it up there, the view across to the Summer Isles and the Caledonian MacBrayne ferry with its red funnels breezing past twice a day. It would take an eagle-eyed passenger with a powerful set of binoculars to be able to see her standing on the top of the cliff and in his experience, most of the passengers would be more likely to be pie-eyed.

The others were restless and gradually they were drifting away singly or with others. Chantal had walked away on her own looking dejected and he had watched her until she sat down overlooking the landing beach staring out to sea. Lachie felt her deep unhappiness too and he began to wonder if The Project might be a short-lived run-of-the-mill disaster movie instead of a one off ground breaking alternative to the sugar-coated sleeping pill the planet's population

185

consumed each and every night through their screens.

No, he would be a little more pro-active and see if that would spur them into action. After all, he was expecting them to suddenly reverse the habits of generations and start to think for themselves. He wondered how many of them had even seen a real fire apart from at a council fire-work display and even then the 'experts' often made a mess of that. He remembered a Guy Fawkes fireworks display that had put the Highlands on the 'both poor and stupid' map once and for all. The footage had gone viral on the net and the beleaguered council were faced with explaining in the face of worldwide media attention how a planned half hour extravaganza had inadvertently gone off all at the same time in an expensive but admittedly spectacular 30 second ejaculation of light and colour.

He guessed the girls all came from central heated houses at best or more likely cheap electric meter heating and they would almost certainly have lived in areas where coal or wood burning fires would be outlawed due to city anti-pollution laws. As a child, during school holidays, Lachie had the regular job of cleaning out and preparing the fire every morning and he had spent many an evening staring into the red glowing coals wishing he were somewhere or somebody else.

He would leave them little option but to start a fire. The lochan needed a visit so he could top up the automatic feeding system for the last time before leaving the fish to the mercies of the girls over the summer. He figured if they fished every day there would still be plenty for at least six months but today he would give them a starter for ten. He would leave them a present of a dozen or so hand-gutted fish and so all they needed to do then was cook the wee buggers.

If they were hungry enough...

Still camouflaged, he elected to skirt up the western side of the mountain ridge which he'd not done yet. Assuming he could make quicker ground along the coast it should take him less than an hour even though it made it a more circuitous route. There would be no chance of him bumping into any of the girls. They haven't been exactly adventurous so far, he thought dispiritedly as he jogged directly south before making a sharp right and over to the fresh breeze of the coast. It was pleasant along this side he decided although colder at this time of day. He looked up at the imposing bulk of the mountain and shivered slightly as he walked into shade. The sun wouldn't hit here until late afternoon, he worked out. Maybe I could put up a wee hide or something, to keep cool when the weather gets too hot in a few weeks time, he decided.

He thought he saw a movement high on the ridge. Grabbing his army binoculars, he scanned the rocks, searching for any signs of life. He could have sworn he saw a small dark shape moving behind a rock. Was he being watched? He kept walking on but every now and then he would stop suddenly on the precept of tying a bootlace or looking out across the sea towards Harris and Benbecula.

There! He saw her.

At least it could have been her, at that distance it was impossible to tell but intuitively he knew he had seen Stevie. The lime green fleecy top contrasting vividly with the silver grey rocks around her. So, she had seen him! Well, there was nothing he could do about it now. In a way he respected her more for having the practical sense to gain the high ground in order to better see what might be going on around the island. He felt comfortable with being tracked to the Lochan. But he would have to lose her in between times as he certainly couldn't have her locate the northern bunker where he would be visiting on the way.

He hoped she would see him take the fish from the water, in a way. It would be blindingly obvious where they could fish from rather than waste precious days trying to fish from the rocks. They would soon learn if they scattered anything resembling pellets of fish food across the surface of the water, then the fish would shoal right up and the water would appear to boil for a second or two. It would be their moment.

Perhaps there could be hope for them after all.

Chapter 27

Chantal sat on a smooth rock and looked
out across the water, searching for anything to
give her a clue about what was happening in her
life. She examined her aching feet, one by one.
Normally she would have spent a considerable
part of every day caring for both her hands and
her feet. She looked down now at the muddy,
scratched foot she held. She saw a deep cut in
the heel which was black with dirt and she
winced as she pressed in gently with a grubby
finger. Her toenails which she had once been so
proud of were broken and flaking. It had taken
her ages to get them nice for her big end of
school party and now…well, now all of that
didn't really matter, she realised.

I wonder if the Prom will still go ahead.
Do they think we're both deid?

As the warm afternoon sun danced across
the water Chantal closed her tired eyes and
played a news bulletin of her disappearance.
They would be lucky to get more than a few
seconds she realised. They would be quickly
forgotten about as the latest double-chinned
councillor was caught fiddling his expenses or
yet another shaven headed gangster gave us the
bird as he was led away shackled to further
vindicate the instant judgement of the
sleepwalking audience. She knew only too well
that her entire seventeen and a half years would
be summed up with a couple of dozen poxy
cards from the local Spar shop, ostentatiously

displayed with some vile pink roses against the rusting school railings.

The last place young Chantal was seen alive.

Despite the sunshine, she shivered and her stomach cramped with hunger. At least she didn't feel sick any more. 'Must've been some well dodgy grub over by,' she thought, 'I've been feeling like crap for ages.' The constant thinking about food had gone now and in some ways she quite liked it here. Not having been an outdoor girl, she had never experienced the movements of the sky or the fresh tang of the sea as the winds changed direction depending on the time of day. It felt strangely peaceful away from all the competing pressures of her friends and she had a clarity of thought which she only remembered having once before but that had been when they'd all took an ecstasy pill and then she'd felt like a total brammer for days after.

I will keep some of this in my heart, she vowed. Once we return. I'll do more stuff, get out and about more. Learn to swim, for a start. *Why not the now*? With a shock she found herself walking down the banking and towards the water. 'How hard can it be?' she shouted to the sky as she felt the cold moist sand between her toes, soothing her sore foot. Was it no easier to float in salt water? Wasn't salty water supposed to be good for healing wounds? What about a' they currents an' stuff? And jellyfish!

She wrestled with all the conflicting stories she'd ever heard about the sea and in the end she just stood there, looking out across it. Her face radiated the reflected light and the tidal breeze blew her hair back exposing her natural beauty and if Lachie had seen her at this moment he would have known there remained a treasure of goodness in the world and a cause worth living for.

He'd been having fun himself but with fresh water not the salty stuff. Satisfied he'd thrown off his little observer, he'd picked up what he needed and headed for the lochan. It had been a strange feeling, having had the tables turned on him for a brief while. Role reversal, the hunter becoming the hunted, the watcher watched.

But at the water he'd adopted a comic over-acting role where he hoped his audience of one would see his step by step guide to 'catching a fish.' He'd sharpened up a couple of long sticks which from practicing before, he knew would be light but rigid enough to work as spears. *Talk about giving it to them on a plate*, he laughed. For their imaginary plate he lifted ten rainbows each of them weighing well over four pounds and he made a point of gutting them openly and clearly before decapitating them and popping them into his khaki shoulder bag.

He had been in his brightest mood for ages when he dropped back over to the north bunker to leave the fishing kit before secreting his harvest somewhere close to the clearing. It should have been a sign, he'd thought later. I am too happy – does not compute.

He glanced up at the screens as he worked and he was pleased but surprised to see no-one at all around the sleeping area. At last, he thought. They've gone exploring and now maybe they'll start doing things and learn a few things. He flicked a few switches as he cleaned up his gear and tried to get the stench of fish guts off his hands. Most of the girls seemed to be together coming back up from the landing beach. There was no sign of the two older girls. Perhaps Stevie would be showing Chantal what she'd learnt from watching him earlier?

He had just turned to leave when he saw Stevie out the corner of his eye. Shit! She looked really angry again and he stood stock still as he realised she was trying to shimmy up another tree to get closer to the lens of Camera 9 again. She's not going to smash up my gear again is she? Those thoughts were instantly quashed as he started to make sense of the torrent of words pouring from her tearful face.

'Fuckin' come on ya bastards! *It's our Chantal*!
If yer there, if there's *anybody* there, like, we need you tae help us!
She cannae swim like! No proper an' that an' I think she's drowning!
Please! *Do something* the now…she's oot tae sea an' none of us kin swim. Please, please help us!'

192

Lachie dropped his bag and grabbed the microphone. He would have to break another rule. Stevie fell onto her back in fright as a loud voiced boomed from the forest around them.

'STAY THERE!
WHERE IS SHE?'

A shocked Stevie held on to a couple of the smaller girls and babbled her version of where the landing beach was. Lachie only heard the first few words and by the time she had exhausted her description of the area he had run a hundred metres northwards in the opposite direction.

'Fuck, fuck, fuck...!' His mind raced even faster than his pounding legs. His lungs were on fire as the air rasped in and out in an unaccustomed flurry. He had planned for this eventuality, he told himself. This can be done. He knew it would take him the best part of twenty five minutes at full pelt for him to reach the landing beach. He doubted if he could even run that far at his present level of fitness. No. Scratch that. He would do this even if it killed him. The thought of such a sweet girl strangled in seaweed urged him onwards.

He had headed for the north coast instead. It would take less than five more minutes and there he had a hidden boat, used by the fish farmers during the transfer but also his back up escape plan if things went sideways and he had to get out fast. The smaller rib was fuelled and ready to go and although marginally slower than his 'Precious' as Archie had dubbed her, it still had a forty horsepower outboard which would outrun any other small boat for fifty miles in any direction.

He hauled the boat from under the camouflage netting, his whole body pulsating with every beat of his labouring heart. She started first time and he set off. He could tell the tide was coming in as he was being badly buffeted as the rib challenged every incoming wave to a 'square go' but he also knew this would mean the girl would be less likely to be taken out to sea. Come on girl! He gunned her engine and the rib bounced ever higher as they finally got far enough out from the treacherous northern reef. Lachie swung her around so she could lower her bow and shoulder charge their way through the deeper green-black water making better time down to the landing beach area.

He could see a few of the girls on the water's edge but no sign of Chantal. He cursed the very day he was born. This had been entirely his fault. He had brought them here. It was supposed to be an natural paradise. The dangers were to come from deep inside them, not from this sleepy island. And why? Why did it have to happen when he was so far away when for most of his time was spent at the south bunker only five minutes away?

Then he saw her!

She wasn't so far away but her black sweat-top had made her practically invisible. Lachie felt a panic rise in his throat as he realised she was floating face-down, her long hair looking like seaweed all around her. Worst of all, she didn't seem to be moving at all. He swung the rib around her coming up slower now, against the tide. Without a second's hesitation, he slammed the engine into neutral and dived in head first, surfacing up underneath the girl and grasping her expertly under the chin and onto his shoulder.

He got her over to the rib and without letting go he flipped his legs over the rubber siding and then hoisted the unconscious girl up and into the boat. He laid her down on the wooden deck and checked her vital signs. She still had a faint pulse but no responses to sound or pain. Far more ominously, Lachie could tell she had stopped breathing.

Shit. Time to do this for real.

He was a trained first aider and had been ever since he'd been in Cadet Corps at public school. He'd enjoyed it and it had got him away from most of the other pupils and it gave him a small but much needed sense of worth at the time. He'd also done a life-saving course at school pretty much for the same reasons. He'd been bullied around the pool several times and mocked for his outlandish looks or puny muscles but overall it had kept him out of the main school activities for a short while every week. In time he became a good swimmer and from there he eventually became reasonably fit with his asthma all but disappearing.

I can do this, he told himself, out loud. He remembered that day during his last summer at school. He'd been sitting alone as usual, outside in the sunshine, revising under an oak tree near the old library building. It had been one of those gorgeous summer days you only seemed to get as a child. A junior school lad had approached him crying and he had been holding his hands out in front of him as if imploring Lachie to receive a gift from him. He said he'd cut himself with a new Swiss Army knife and Lachie had jumped up immediately, steering him over to the nearest building.

The boy appeared to have cut himself on a wrist and up until then he'd done a fairly good job of stemming the blood flow simply by holding his other hand over it. 'Don't panic' Lachie had said, 'we'll get you bandage in a minute, you'll be absolutely fine then.' He'd blithely thought he'd sounded reassuring, but the boy seemed to infer from this inner calm that he wasn't being taken seriously enough.

'But, it's really, really sore,' he said defiantly. 'I know it is but don't worry sonny, you'll be fine I promise you,' had been Lachie's fateful words.

The boy hadn't been convinced. They were only ten feet or so from the library doors when he lifted off his protective hand to give Lachie a better idea of how life threatening the

196

injury was. 'Don't take the pressure off! Keep your-' Lachie had shouted, too late to stop him. The resulting jet of bright red blood shot right across the steps and coloured the ornately decorated old stained-glass windows in a way that symbolised Christ's suffering far better than could ever have been intended.

The drastic loss of blood then put the lad into shock and a bashful Lachie was later credited with saving his life. The boy's father was a professional footballer with Aberdeen FC and together with a commendation from the headmaster, Lachie received two tickets to the VIP enclosure for an upcoming international game with some top Spanish team. But Lachie never got to see the game. His father had said football was for the chattering classes and it would be over his dead body before a son of his would be seen at a match.

He unzipped her tracksuit top and placed one hand with the second on top with his fingers interleaved just like he'd been taught. Keeping his arms locked he pushed down and hard, counting to fifteen. Next, he cleared away the hair from her face. With one hand expertly tilting her head back, he pinched her nose with the other before breathing hard, but not too hard, into her mouth. Once, then again.

Nothing.

Back to chest compressions. He began to panic. He wanted this to work more than anything in the world. He breathed again, twice.

Still nothing. *Shit*! Then he heard an unnatural gurgling sound and with joy he rolled her away from him into the recovery position pulling her head back again as she threw up a pint or two of sea water then coughed hard. She was alive!

Lachie helped her sit up and gave her his army jacket as she shook violently despite the warm sunshine. He turned away from her as she struggled to put it over her own shoulders. He felt embarrassed at the sight of her exposed breasts.

'I'll take you back now,' he said gruffly.

'No…please gaunae wait a bit. Not just yet. I haven't had time to thank you.'

Lachie glanced down at her upturned face then looked away towards the beach. They had drifted further away than he had imagined. The tide must be turning, he realised. Something inside of him was telling him the sudden tidal change could possibly be due to a never seen before alignment of the planets which must have been necessary for true love to blossom in his dark heart. He wouldn't listen. He couldn't allow himself to.

'Could we no stay here? Just for a wee minute, 'til I get ma breath back?'

'Not here,' he replied and the outboard roared into life.

Chapter 28

It would be Baxter time again shortly and this time Boyle was convinced that unlike ten days ago, there would be no reprieve for him, no little black dress. He'd arranged to meet Steel away from the nick so they could try and bottom out their very own summer collection of unsolved murders. He'd been getting increasingly more pissed off with his deputy and so he also wanted to use the occasion to rip a piece off him. The lad hadn't been with the program half the time and right now, more than ever, he needed a man who could step up to the plate. He needed a leader, not a follower.

Of course one of the main reasons for this had to do with the fact he himself couldn't keep his mind on the job. He too was letting his personal life get in the way. He'd just come from home, his *old* home, where the rest of his family still lived after he had been cast out. He hadn't been allowed to oversee the case, he had told a sobbing Marie, but rest assured, he would leave no grimy, festering stone unturned and if he had to break every rule in the book to bring Jenny back home safely, whatever it took, he'd do it.

It depressed him to realise since Jenny's disappearance, he'd seen and spoken more with his wife than in the two or three months beforehand. He'd be sure to mention this as a helpful tip at his next meeting of Estranged Dads' Anonymous. *Yeah, right.* But there had been something else which burned like a furnace inside him. He knew, and he was sure she knew it too, there remained something between them. It was still salvageable.

So all of this meant he'd better things to do with his time than nursemaid his useless detective sergeant whilst they all fannied around letting every single murder case run them ragged. Case in point – he was late.

Boyle ground the cigarette butt into the grass and swore colourfully, startling an elderly man who stood patiently waiting for a little dog to finish sniffing the back of his wooden bench. He had chosen Pollok Estate seeing as it had been such a beautiful day but mainly because it was one of Jenny's favourite places. She used to spend so much time at the Burrell Collection, the stately stone building he had sat down in front of. Resplendent in luxurious sunshine and surrounded by the verdant splendour of the vast parklands, he could see why.

No Mean City here, he thought, and immediately wondered if that had been part of its attraction for her. Marie had told him she was spending an inordinate amount of time at the museum and so being a suspicious cop, he followed her one day, thinking she might be up to mischief with some toe-rag from that zoo they called a school. But no, there he'd found her, sitting on a plush leather stool sketching a bronze Rodin in the main foyer.

He had wanted to rush over and plonk himself down next to her but something held him back. She would be suspicious that he happened to be there at the same time as her. She could be as sharp as a tack, just like her mother. So he'd stood watching her for a long time, treasuring the moment. He admired her long confident strokes and the way she held her head stationary, like a beautiful statue herself. He'd gaze in wonder as she transferred the images from her eyes to the large artist's pad. He'd never noticed it lying around the house, but then he couldn't remember the last time he had been in his daughter's room. He had wondered if she could somehow escape the grind of mere existence and make a career from her art, as he now wished he had done. If he had been holding a sketch pad, he would have caught her silhouette, those defined cheekbones and the little upturned button of a nose, the spit of her mother.

Sitting here now he had so wished he'd drawn that picture there and then. It would have been everything to him, like his treasured memory of the day. Not long after, he had 'accidentally' discovered her sketch pad at home and the two of them had gone on to establish a far closer bond through their discussions on the arts.

He remained eternally grateful for those memories now. So this had become a special place for him. And if he was being honest, a small part of him also fervently hoped if it was also as significant a place to his daughter then she may magically appear in front of him today, walking carefree down the path; unlike yesterday or the day before or the many days before that.

He sighed and reached for his fag packet. He had a different picture to try and draw right now. It looked more and more like becoming a complicated and bloody piece and something told him it would still only ever be a work-in progress.

Steel appeared from behind him, silently through the grass. He sat down heavily and let out an anguished sigh. His face was the colour of Ribena, he wheezed like a man twice his age and by the smell of him it hadn't been the blackcurrant fruit drink he'd been tanning last night either.

'Morning…, sir,' he gasped. 'Sorry I'm late. Couldn't find a space…had tae walk blinkin' miles!'

'It's a *country park*! Jeezo! Yer *supposed* tae walk in the park, that's the whole point.
By Christ, looking at the nick o' yon clothes I'd say you've been sleeping in it as well.'

'Aye sir. Still no sleeping too well, but. Any news on-'

'Naw.
Bugger all.
Just like every other investigation we've got on the books right now and between

202

you and me I'm getting pretty hacked off wi' it all.'

'Sorry sir, I'm really …'

'Sorry? Sorry disnae cut it anymore Steel. We need to see results here an' bloody pronto with it.
I've got far better things to do with my time than chase around after drugged up wee scrotes hell bent on killing each other. If it was up tae me, I'd let them all just get on with it.
Now. Let's see where we are and try and get some scalps quick. I don't really care which case, I just need a result.'

'Sir, I-'

'And here's a quick heads-up pal. *You* need a result too, by the way.
Just to be up-front with you, I am under increasing pressure to have you suspended. If you can't bring anything constructive to the table in the next few days then the ball's burst. You know what Baxter's like, she's no' called U.X.B. for nothing.'

DS Steel nodded mutely and brought out his notepad. It may have looked professional but with his brain jangling like a wind chime on a stormy night, it was the only way he could buy some time to try and string two coherent thoughts together. He'd anticipated this latest bollocking and he knew he deserved it. In fact he had half thought the reason for their meeting being *alfresco* was he was going to finally get his jotters. He inwardly thanked the man sitting next to him for obviously doing a great job saving his arse and he desperately thought how he could repay him without putting himself onto a mortuary slab in the process.

'The way I see it, sir, is this.
We've got a drugs war breaking out for control of North Glasgow and the distribution rights to the North West including Inverness and beyond. There are two professional hitters out there, at the very least, who seem to be able to walk all over our patch with complete impunity.
I would say the situation is still extremely unstable, sir, and could very well escalate to all out war. We have to assume the killers had special access to some of the victims which lends weight to the gangs hiring outside contractors and furnishing them wi' specific information on their location and schedules.'

Boyle snorted in frustration and pulled out a fresh cigarette.

'Aye, nice speech Gary but can you save that stuff for yer memoirs eh?
I meant something a wee bit more specific, if you know what I mean.
Like what is the obvious connection between the first wee girl and the lap-dancing bar? There is surely a clear link there is there not? Otherwise why did the Meekin family all have to die shortly before the barman received his third eye? Is the answer not that our good friend Rocky must somehow be responsible given he is yer primo drugs player for that part of Dodge City and one of his most senior scumbags made a pumpkin out of his own heid a wee bit fuckin' early for Halloween?

'But-'

'I'm not finished yet, Gary. There is some- *Aww shit*!
Let me get that call will you, I was expecting it about now.
You better start thinking up some answers pal!
Boyle. Yes, he is… Yes. We are.
What's the Hampden roar? It's his? For sure? Fuck me sideways.
They're where? That wis a bit quick was it no? Aye, I can hear them already for fuck's sake.

I told her before, there's no need for a'
that. I'll do it…'

Boyle shut the phone and looked down
briefly at his tired old Hush Puppies. Then he
lifted his eyes and up and beyond his partner he
could see a ruck of black uniforms barrelling
along the path. Steel gulped and closed his eyes.
He knew what was coming and he exhaled
loudly. It was over. In many ways he felt
relieved.

'Gary. Sorry about this, son. That call
confirmed we have now identified your
DNA as being present at the murder
scene at the Bottom Line club. We've all
had our DNA cross checked; it was DCI
Nimmo's idea. He came up with the idea
that only a copper could have co-
ordinated all of this and requested we all
get tested. He got Baxter so wound up
that she went along with it.
I didn't know beforehand, I promise, but
I do have serious worries about your
recent behaviour which I had shared with
the boss before any of this shite.
They're coming for you. I've got no
choice.
*Gary Steel, I am hereby detaining you in
connection with the murders of Mr David
Hall and Mr Anton Stefaniou.* You know
the rest…
Steady lads! Take him out of my sight!'

It was a good while before Jim Boyle could raise his world-weary body off the bench. A part of him wanted to sit and think things even longer. He'd still to cover a couple of things with Steel but they'd wait until tomorrow at the station. Give him a chance to stew for a while. Boyle felt like a total wanker for his part in this afternoon's dramatic act. He knew in his gut Steel could never be a cold hearted killer. *Not a chance.* But as he replayed the events of the last few weeks he couldn't stop returning to the same conclusion. There's something going on for sure and you don't have to pull the trigger to be a murderer. He never would have wanted to do it like this though and right up until the call came through, he had hoped to hear the clipboard carrying prick from upstairs had been sniffing at the wrong lamppost.

Another part of him had been content to find any excuse to sit here in case his Jenny happened to saunter past. He knew he'd be on to plums on that one. He understood implicitly that for his daughter to have been gone for so long there had to be foul play involved. And he also knew if there had been any innocent reason for her departure, she would have contacted them before now.

The only consolation with her apparent abduction was it hadn't been an isolated case. There were a further seven girls missing and not all the same age either. They had all attended the same school as Jenny and some had been pals with her, but other than this, the school seemed to be the only common factor. Somebody connected with the school had to be involved and the boys were grilling all past and present staff very thoroughly.

They'd all rallied round Jim and if there was one thing the police were good at, it was protecting their own. Those found responsible for this act of barbarism would be hunted down and hell mend them if they were found by any old school colleagues with daughters of their own. He knew all of this but his experience as a policeman had also taught him that after only two or three days in a case like this they automatically assume they're looking for a body.

He had also decided deep down that if and when her body was found, he would bail out. He'd be on the last train from Central; this time he'd reached the end of the line.

Chapter 29

It had been an interesting few days for Lachie with nothing remotely going to plan. He had started to expect the unexpected almost as a matter of course now and despite his rule book now having more red ink than a politician's memoirs, he couldn't shake off the feeling of, well, *happiness* really. He suspected it all had to do with a certain bonnie lass to whom he had recently availed himself in respect of services both valiant and chivalrous.

After plucking Chantal from the sea, Lachie had taken the rib way down the eastern edge of the island directly south of the landing beach and moored her in a small sheltered bay where the sand bar begins to trail out from the island like the jagged bottom of a speech bubble. He had always intended the residents to use this as a bathing pool as with its shallow fetch, soft golden sand and protection from the wind, it made a perfect location befitting a South Sea Island as much as this miserable cast-off from the Outer Hebrides. By taking her there, he did have another worry about 'interfering with the course of the future,' but he feared *that* boat had long since sailed.

For a long time they had just sat at opposite ends of the rib, looking at each other in silence, hardly aware of anything around them bar the pop, pop of the rib rocking ever so slightly against the gentle swell of the tide. Between them, in the chasm of unexplored conversations there had been a tangle of questions, each one wrestling with the others to be the first to be asked. Chantal had proved the bravest in the end. After all, she had just cheated death, what could compare to that?

'How did we all get here? Are you something to dae with it, like? What's gaunae happen tae us?'

Lachie smiled, the remnants of his camouflage paint only partially concealing his blushes. He pulled his baseball cap further down over his face. 'I can't tell you anything about how or why you're on the island. I'm sorry. All I can say is you won't be here for ever but you will still need to try and make the best of things while you are.'

'How did you save me?'

'I'm sorry? You mean why did I save you just now?'

'Yeah, that's what I meant to say. Why?'

'I couldn't let you drown. Your friend Stevie alerted me. I was nearby with the rib. It was the only thing to do.'

Chantal gasped and put a hand up to her mouth, tasting the salt on her lips.

'You ken Stevie? And me too? Have you
been watching us wi' they cameras?
You're no wan o' them weirdo guys who
bothers wee kids are ye?'

Lachie laughed loudly trying to defuse an
awkward situation, while inwardly feeling as if
he had swallowed an exploding grenade.

'No, I promise you! I'm not a paedophile!
I happen to be living nearby myself this
summer and I was only trying to help you.
I do know a bit about what's going on
and I've done a bit of work on the island
so I have a good understanding of the lie
of the land.
I wouldn't hurt you for the world.
On the contrary, I think you are the most
beautiful thing I have ever seen.
But I ask for nothing from you
whatsoever, I promise.'

'That's the nicest thing anybody's said to
me for like…, ever!'

'Well, I am humbled.'

'Me too, I think.'

Lachie coughed and looked out across
the water, conscious they might be seen. A part
of him wanted this moment to last forever.

'Well then. This is *most* enjoyable but I think I should drop you off now before your friends' get too worried. They'll be thinking I've kidnapped you!'

'I don't mind like. It's the first time I've no felt totally Hank Marvin since I came here.'

'Hank-?'

'Starvin' like hungry! Get it?'

'Well I hope by the time you've got back the others will have cooked up a jolly nice banquet of trout for you!'

'You talk well funny, know what I mean! We cannae cook, we've got nae cookin' stuff.'

Lachie started up the engine and gently eased the rib out of the smooth water back into the tidal currents. Letting rip with the throttle for a moment, the front of the boat lifted up dramatically giving Chantal a scare. 'Come sit by me,' he suggested casually, allowing the rib to settle back to a steady tack against the waves. As the girl stumbled unsteadily and crashed down beside him, he casually removed his prescription sunglasses with his left hand, squinting against the bright sun. Surreptitiously looking around to her, he held the shades over her hands as they clutched her knees.

'Ouch! Ye burned me!' she yelped suddenly as Lachie innocently moved the lens out of the line of the sun and back over his eyes.

'Oh I am sorry!
It must have been the sun going through the glass lens. If the angle is exactly right you can start a fire just as easily. Starts a lot of forest fires, you know, people leaving empty juice bottles scattered around. Even up here litter is a terrible problem, I know there are even a few lying about the island...'

Chantal rubbed her hand, surprised to find no actual burn mark and thinking there must be a lot more to this weird looking army guy than meets the eye. Awkward silences swallowed up most of the quick return as they both attempted to make sense of what had just happened. Realising she had been taught a game-changing lesson, Chantal hadn't been slow in coaxing from Lachie the location of one of the glass bottles. She felt a thrill of excitement course through her as she looked forward to getting back and showing the others how to make a fire. The thought of a warm campfire as the chilly darkness encroached that night seemed too big a dream right then but another thought percolated through from her previous life before the island. She hated fish!

He'd been camouflaged up for so long now it proved an effort to scrub it all off and by the time he had been ready to leave he had a face like a 'well-skelped arse' as his drill sergeant used to say after a forced run with full pack. He'd told Chantal where the fish had been dropped earlier and as he quietly guided his 'Precious' away from the island he imagined he could detect the unmistakably wonderful aroma of charred fish. It was almost twilight and he had other fish to fry himself before the conclusion of this short summer night.

The heavy metal lock clanged across the water as he tried to slip into his metal container as quietly as possible. He would call Archie in the morning from the croft but right now he didn't want any interference.

Throughout his time on the island, he'd been keeping tabs on the rest of the world online of course, although he had been astonished at how little use he had made of all his entertainment toys. He had new toys now.

The container had a false division welded in at Lachie's request and so he had now ensconced himself in the secret rear third, faced with a sophisticated array of electronic equipment. Unknown to anyone else there he also had a complicated arrangement of satellite dishes and other communication devices in the spare room of the croft next door. Not all of his generators had been purchased solely for the island as old Archie had thought.

He pressed a few buttons and the wall became alive with lights and the quiet hum of the most expensive technology money could buy. Lachie had watched the developments of the case with a vain curiosity at first which had been promptly supplanted by surprised outrage then a sick dread. Events seemed to have taken on a life of their own and he didn't like the way it was going, not one bit.

It only took him a few minutes to break into the Police Scotland server accounts and he downloaded the case files for the two killings he had been responsible for plus the others which were being worryingly connected to him. To cover all the bases, he hacked into other investigation files past and present which had any connection to anything at all to do with the cases he'd got hold of. This brought up data on past foul deeds committed by numerous vicious wee bastards over the last few years. He then accessed the personal files of each of the officers who had been named as being involved with the investigations.

Next he collated all the newspaper stories about each of the murders and saved them onto the dedicated hard drive. The next hour or two had been spent splashing this information around his eight plasma screens like a massive virtual pin board looking for associations, patterns or good old fashioned gut instinct. Not having total faith in his own abilities he also had a warehouse of servers in Arizona munching through the data byte by byte.

After four hours he'd had enough suffocating in his little box of tricks. As he tiptoed out into the night back into his cottage, all he needed for the last few dark hours was peace and quiet and lots of strong coffee.

By the time the first strands of orange and red light were flickering across the bay, Lachie was feeling marginally better about things. He scratched his stubbled chin as he waited for the bacon to grill and wondered how he had got himself into this mess. *It's maybe brighter out of the window*, but he knew his situation was unmistakably darker than he could have imagined a few short weeks ago. He flipped his eggs and cursed as a yolk burst open.

It should have been so simple. The operational complications were likely to have begun with the capturing of the girls and then perhaps have increased during the island part of the plan, as he had begun to find out, not forgetting the eventual release process if any of them survived. But not surely before the mission had even begun?

After studying the purloined data through the night, Lachie had come to the firm belief that there were some desperate men involved here; cold-hearted men who either held life in even less regard than he did or panicked men who were so out of control they were liable to bring down anyone or anything remotely connected to them. He didn't like either of these scenarios.

So he'd developed a plan. Maybe a strategy would be a more fitting description, seeing as his plans hadn't exactly gone smoothly so far. It would take a certain degree of nerve, he reckoned, but in a way it would only be an extension of current operations and in the grand scheme of things it could be considered as a logical progression towards the inevitable media circus he was going to ultimately create before he was done with his Project.

In the interim however, what he was about to initiate, in the twisted minds of the attention grabbing politicians, would no doubt be construed as something grand and noble - a 'Strategy for Life' or some other bollocks like that. He certainly didn't want anyone else to die because of him. 'Maybe I'm getting soft, or maybe it's down to the other developments in my life,' he thought, wiping egg and bacon from his chin. 'I never went into this thing with the view of deliberately taking lives.' Maybe a few months ago, he considered soberly, he wouldn't have cared one way or the other. But back then he'd been a damaged and brooding blob of dark malevolence whereas now he was metamorphosing into a wholly different and possibly quite beautiful creature. One which might soon take wings and leave all of this behind.

So, the obvious consequence of this development meant not only did he wish to save the lives of others, he desired for the very first time in his own miserable existence to stay alive himself. To really *live*.

The first step in this process had to be the severing of any connection between the two accidental deaths and the subsequent carnage. The best course of action, so they always say, is honesty, so what he planned to do next was contact the plods and confess to his crimes. Risky or what? Not really, he fervently hoped. He wasn't about to let them clap any handcuffs on his wrists yet. But when they realised they were barking up the wrong tree then perhaps it would become obvious who the real 'perps' were.

He looked at his watch, *still a wee bit early*. According to the data, it would be another hour before the person he wanted would roll in to the office. This, however, had given him a great idea. During the night, he'd decided his situation had become too serious to handle on his own. There were times when no amount of technology could make up for a lack of bodies, when the urgent requirement was, to use a phrase to strike fear in every Defence Minister, more 'boots on the ground.' And in his estimation, there could be only one body suitable for the job. His fingers started tap dancing on the keyboard and by the time he had finished his coffee had gone stone cold and it was time to make the call.

Chapter 30

The heavy iron door slammed shut with an earth-shattering finality. *I'm in jail, for God's sake*! Steel stood and stared at the rusted blue door as if by pure force of thought he could slide the metal observation hatch open to see the face of the custody officer crease into a smile and tell him it had all been a cruel joke.

But no-one had been smiling earlier and although he knew each of the officers' down at the charge bar by name, he'd had to undergo the same de-humanising treatment as he'd dished out himself many hundreds of times in the past. He'd been so ashamed he couldn't lift his head from staring at his feet, never mind look any of them in the eye to see if they thought he might be guilty. He stood helplessly as his watch, house keys and other personal possessions were placed in a bag and he was expertly relieved of his belt. He had almost fallen over while bending to remove his filthy and worn shoes, wishing he'd taken better care of them and wondering why he'd never noticed before how scruffy they'd become.

He'd realised he must've looked like the stereotypical criminal and as they processed him through the custody system he felt like a dumb animal waiting to be led into the slaughterhouse towards the finality of the metal rod tapping into his skull.

The young officer who led him through the ignominy of being fingerprinted and photographed was obviously embarrassed by the knowledge his customer had performed those routines before he'd even been out of primary school. Steel had attempted a half-hearted protest at being DNA tested again as they'd obviously already obtained the data from elsewhere. He felt the life-force drain out of him as the man stared back at him. Without even making a pretence of focusing on his face, the pasty-faced Constable reeled off the standard phrases about *the rules* and *the system*, and how it 'wouldn't take a minute' before grabbing his jaw and roughly stabbing at the inside of his cheek with a cotton bud.

But nothing had prepared him for the horror of the cell. In all his years on the Force, he'd never spent more than seconds in one of these 'rooms.' He tried to think back to the days when it would have been him chucking people into places like this.

More recently he'd been working in far more rarefied locations and he'd guessed that the only reason he'd been taken here underneath this local nick had been down to the boss trying to save him the embarrassment of being banged up in the city cop shop where he would have known everyone. At least here it was quieter and slightly less personal.

But the place could sure do with a refurb, he thought, as he tore his gaze away from the door. Decades of bitter resentment were crudely etched into the once shiny mustard walls.

Steel glanced up at the pitiful excuse for a window, no larger than two house bricks end to end and cruelly designed to allow the minimum amount of anaemic light to seep through. Not that he wanted to see too clearly. He'd still not taken more than two steps and he had to force himself to turn away from the door before he lurched across the stone floor and sat heavily onto the blue plastic which could loosely have been described as a 'bed'. The crumpled sheet of torn tarpaulin enclosed a miserly rectangle of foam which he soon realised offered no support as his bruised arse began to make its presence known.

Closer to the floor now, the smell began to assault his nose and peering at the meeting of wall and floor he could see layer upon layer of rancid food, splatters of vomit arcing up the walls and streaks of human waste making up the biological collage.

Steel clutched at his collar, greasy claustrophobia wrapping ever more tightly around his neck. He allowed himself to fall steadily sideways onto the excuse for a bed and stared at the wall. There were generations of wasted lives scratched into the sickly walls, the usual bigotry and hatred he'd seen a hundred times before.

fuck the pope
UP THE 'RA

But Steel found himself increasingly fascinated with the other categories of scribbling; declarations of love, protestations of innocence, and accusations of infidelity and even indications of likely violence adding the final touch to the rich tableau of the delinquent existence.

He lost all sense of time and place and had it not been for the routine custody checks and the unenthusiastic proffering of what might have been called food in some other dark hell-hole of existence then Steel would have lost his mind. He'd asked for a particular solicitor who'd a reputation for being as sharp and venal as the villains he usually represented. But lying here on the cold stone floor he'd become obsessed with a new terror. He was safer here in this cell than anywhere else in the world. *But how could he be sure?* Preservation of life was one of the reasons he'd turned down all food, not that he would have been able to hold down any of it, the mere smell was enough to have him retching.

He knew why he was in this jail cell. Unlike the vast majority of previous occupants, most of whom would tell their own mothers' they were innocent of all charges, Steel knew he was as guilty as sin. But that was not why he was there. He was there because of what he knew. And this meant he had to be extra vigilant. He looked around the sparse cell in a panic before

222

slapping himself. No-one should be able to get to me down here!

But at the same time he was never going to be able to sort any of this out while he remained stuck in this hellish limbo. He'd been given the luxury of time to think everything through and he soon reached the obvious conclusion. A cold sweat broke out over his skin as he understood the enormity of his task. And hazardous as it would be out there, it was clear the first thing he had to do was escape from this stone box.

Chapter 31

'Boyle. *Who's this*?'

'This is a *very* important personal call for DS Gary Steel.'

Boyle clicked his tongue in irritation. He wondered if it had to do with his alleged shagging exploits. The voice sounded strange, almost like one of those automated PPI lines.

'I am sorry but DS Steel is suspended from duty pending further investigations. You might get him at home. However, I'm not authorised to give you-'

'That's fine, Jim. You'll do even better.'

Boyle dropped his pen at the same time as the penny dropped and he immediately started waving his arms in the air doing a credible impersonation of Basil Fawlty. He mouthed across the office.

'Get this call traced!'

At the other end Lachie could scarcely contain his laughter. Just like that, he had obtained one of the final pieces of the puzzle. The current status of Steel had not been updated as yet on the police computers so he guessed the hapless detective had only recently been released. Small tiny steps only but still in the right direction for a change.

'I am calling about the murders of Brooklyn McTear in Garthamlow and David Hall in the city centre. You are I believe, in overall day to day charge of these two investigations are you not?'

Boyle swallowed unsuccessfully, his mouth having become as dry as his estranged wife's sense of humour. He didn't like the tone of this conversation. Still it could just be a wee grasser who's watched too much television. He coughed angrily.

'Who the hell is this?'

'This is someone who can help you, but you *must* do as I say?'

'I'm not doin' fuck all until you give me a name pal. If you have any information pertaining to these cases and you don't want to gie me yer name then I suggest you call Crimestoppers and stop wasting my time!'

The voice whispered a single name. The room began to spin around Boyle as out of the blue, he could have sworn his office had been loudly buzzed by a squadron of supersonic fighter jets. He felt the floor jerk sideways under his feet and then looked around in astonishment to see his colleagues staring at him like he'd forgotten to wear his trousers this morning.

> 'Now hang up the phone, pick up your cell phone and find somewhere quiet. I will call you back very shortly. I don't need to remind you any monkey business would be counter productive. Do you understand?'

> 'Yes. I... Okay.'

Boyle dropped the phone into its cradle and fell heavily into his seat. The others looked at him with concern. 'You okay boss?' one called over to him. 'Trace in progress sir. We'll have the location of the call in a few minutes,' another shouted over earnestly.

> 'Aye…fine.
> I'll be back in a wee minute.'

Three minutes later and Boyle sat stunned on a wooden bench in Blythswood Square, a quiet area stuffed with lawyers' and accountants offices and the grand looking RAC Club. Of course to men of Jim Boyle's generation and occupation, it would always be far better known for its past notoriety as the locus for much of the city's streetwalking business. He sat staring at his mobile, willing it to ring and yet terrified at what the ramifications were going to be. He wished he had more than one phone as he wanted to call Marie too, but then what the hell would he say?

A stranger had called and whispered their missing daughter's name?

Jenny.

Why would he say it? What did he know? Still fearful the call might only be some malicious crank caller he continued to stare at his own scratchy reflection on the screen of his inert Blackberry. He felt the vibration before he heard the ring tone and almost dropped the device onto the pavement. Funny, he hadn't given out his mobile number to very many people?

'Boyle. What do you know about my Jenny?'

'Firstly, I want to assure you she is alive, well and has not been harmed and-'

Boyle felt the phone slip from his grasp and he made a mad two-handed grab for it, miraculously preventing it from smashing on the stone pavement. Tears were obscuring his sight and he found he was having difficulty breathing. Any office worker looking out a window at him for more than a brief second or two would have thought he'd initially suffered a heart attack or seconds later, been told he'd won the lottery. He jumped up and punched the air with his free hand and began marching up and down over a few metres staring again at the cracked plastic screen. It lit up again and this time Boyle answered it before it even rang.

'DI Boyle, are you there now?'

'Yes! Yes. I dropped the phone. Kinda emotional tae be honest!'

'Well, very good but can we try and focus on the immediate problems we both presently face?
You have a missing daughter you obviously want returned to her mother and we have a stramash of ever growing proportions which we need to solve.'

'Go on.'

'I can tell you who is responsible for the deaths I have mentioned to you which may help you work out who carried out the other killings which your department seem to have linked to these.'

'Go on, I'm all ears.'

Lachie paused for a moment. This was it, *Alea iacta est*. He was crossing the Rubicon. He felt a tremor course up his body as he heard himself speak.

'Well, to be blunt, it was me. I killed them…'

'But you're not going to tell me who you are, apart from that you're a Yank right?'

'I killed them by accident Boyle. I am not justifying what I have done. I *am* a bad man. But I am a bad man who, for various reasons, is now trying to do some good.'

Boyle was unable to contain his anger.

'I know what you're doing!
You're trying to save your skin. I want my daughter back. If you touch a hair on her head, whether it's an *accident* or not, I'll find you, you can count on that. I'll never-'

'I doubt it Jim, but let's not get into a cock fight here.
I have to go now.
Just tell me if you want to solve the murders of The Meekin family, Anton Stefaniou, Derek 'Dokie' Greig and wrap up my two into the bargain. I'll give you the killers but you can't have me. Your choice. I'll call you again.'

229

Boyle didn't remember walking back round the corner to the nick. He ran up the stairs without noticing the effort. He didn't like this spooky bastard one wee bit but for now he'd have to go along with it. He needed time to work out if there could be any grain of truth in what he'd said. He couldn't give a flying fuck who'd killed Dokie Greig or any of them anymore, but he would do whatever it took to get his Jenny back.

As he bounded into the office he heard Mackie give an uncharacteristic whoop and saw the whole lot of them patting him on the back. A result?

'Tell me Mackie? What've you got for me?'

'Sir! We've only gone an' traced the call for you sir!
We know exactly where the call came from! It's Port Stanley sir!
He's in the Falkland Islands…'

Chapter 32

The next few weeks passed pleasantly fast for Lachie. Freed from any other distractions, he had been content to immerse himself in the life of the island girls. Still keeping his distance, he nevertheless managed to get to know them better than he'd ever known anyone else on Earth.

Things had got off to a flying start after his bold move with Police Scotland. He had set enough balls in motion to satisfy himself that he would be safe to focus on The Project. The girls had luckily taken to the fishing, with one particular lassie, Debbie, whom the rest called Sticky, becoming very adept. She was the tallest of all the girls but incredibly skinny, hence the nickname. It had been an appropriate moniker in another way too as she would rarely be parted from one of her precious spears. She'd taken Lachie's ideas and bettered them. He'd watch her standing over the southern edge of the lochan, slightly in shadow, like a Heron, her long thin body stationary for extended periods of time. Just when you would think she'd been petrified into stone, her body would flex slightly and her long arms would send a spear darting forward, jerking back a split second later with a twitching fish impaled on the end.

It was only after a few weeks that he realised most of the girls had been malnourished when they arrived. Despite the limited culinary options available on the island, most of the girls had fleshed out considerably since arriving. In most cases they were stronger, fitter, more energetic and had a healthier complexion than before. He guessed from listening to them that the combination of poor quality food, no exercise, cigarettes, booze and drugs had added to the already impossible pressures put upon them to live up to the air-brushed ideals of their pop princess idols.

He'd been totally flabbergasted to find out girls of their age would have been popping pills and smoking dope. Whilst never claiming to be a man of the world, he found most of the girls had a far better understanding of drugs than he did.

Understanding had become a concept often foremost in his mind these days. He had anticipated after a short period of time, he'd see the girls become feral in their behaviour. They would lose all the structures and norms with which they had been brought up with. In the very early days, his elitist public school attitudes had only strengthened his initial opinion. He'd thought they would turn savage in the blink of an eye because in his mind they had had very little education in the ways of correct society before then. But by now their stay on the island, away from the civilising constraints of normal life, had been longer than their Lord of The Flies predecessors and yet their behaviour had not sunk to the animalistic.

As he listened to their uninhibited chatter, they seemed to have all but forgotten about the cameras, he learned so much more about his own life as well as theirs. He'd begun to have wild thoughts about these recordings of his becoming prescribed listening at boys' schools like his own, much as the Golding book had been on his required reading list. He now felt if he could have learned some of his recently gleaned nuggets about the fairer sex back in his younger days then he might have made a far better crack at his own life, elitist upbringing notwithstanding.

Despite his apparent privilege he hadn't experienced an iota of the life events of some of these girls. He had never realised how much of normal life he'd missed out on. He'd never exchanged Valentine cards with anyone for example. He'd not sent or received flowers, nicked from the council cemetery as often seemed to be the case, or otherwise. When he listened in rapture at their exchange of stories about the simple things like holding hands, kissing under a bridge, being walked home by a boy, parental interrogations or playing doctors and nurses he would often find tears rolling down his face. He could lose four hours listening to them and not even notice the time go by. He'd become one of them, the invisible elephant in the room no-one ever talked about.

He became an expert in anticipating how they would react to situations as he began to understand their characters. There was little Charlie and Fee who were literally inseparable and who'd turned into wee chimps, always climbing and tumbling over each other and they were the first to climb the delicate branches and knock down gifts from the ever increasing bounty of nature they were gradually discovering. If ever the mood of the group became too sombre their antics would be sure to spark them all into laughter again.

Least liked by Lachie was Joolz, perhaps because she was the misfit of the group, a haunting reminder of the outsider in him. Short and dumpy, she remained the least capable of all the girls and only had the lowest of energy levels, relying instead on her acid tongue. With a vicious temper, she behaved like a wounded animal and the others tended to leave her to her own devices. It struck Lachie after several weeks that perhaps she had been the only girl who'd been truly happy in her former life back in civilisation and this was what constantly rankled under her skin.

They had constructed a sloping terrace of shelters in the lea of the hill above the original sleeping area and most of the thinking behind the work had come from Katy or Katster. She had become the nest builder of the group and she never strayed far from their settlement, disinterested in swimming or exploring the rocky cliff. Although not the oldest by far, she took on a matronly role with the others and it would be Katster they would come to with a cut or a bang to the head.

Again Lachie could see a stronger element of her previous life conditioning continuing to mould her even in this alien environment and he imagined her own mother to be a very similar character. Katster was without a doubt the least healthy of the group and had a small appetite and again like a mother, she would often fuss around the others while they were content to eat the lion's share of the food leaving her to pick at a few paltry scraps left behind as they set off for more swimming fun.

Stevie had become more aloof from the group since the near drowning of Chantal although she could still be actively involved when she was around. She, along with Sticky had been most adept at finding 'proper food' as she called it and she'd a series of rabbit snares around the island. Stevie was the only one who had learned to skin a rabbit without rendering the pelt useless and she had proved to be particularly dextrous in her ability to then convert the skins into passable items of rough clothing which the girls were beginning to prefer over their too warm and now fairly shoddy charity shop clothing.

Lachie had overheard her complaining about missing her cigarettes but it had been a few weeks later when he remembered whilst doing some shopping. He'd been dropping in treats for the girls every so often and also the odd essential items which he'd never have thought of until the Project started such as tampons and an inhaler for Katster. Stevie had been working well with the others so on a whim he bought a few packets of B & H cigarettes which he'd heard her talk about a lot in the evenings when they would sometimes sit together and fantasise about the things they missed most of all.

There was an old silver birch close to the original sleeping area which had a small oval shaped natural alcove due to the peculiar growth of the tree and Lachie had left gifts in there every so often. They would be little trinkets considered to be insignificant items back in the big world but a couple of small packets of Haribos sweets for example would be kept until the evening then solemnly shared out amongst them, each girl competing to see who could make theirs last the longest.

So one day he placed a packet of cigarettes there, feeling slightly like a drug pusher but hoping they would be taken as a reward earned for good behaviour. Lachie would always be cognisant of the ability Stevie had to cause serious disruption to his whole operation. He'd been fairly sure she had been watching him as he returned from the mainland one evening and he'd been forced to circle the rib a few times in the bay before giving up and sailing up the coast to berth on the northern edge beside the smaller boat and then getting up early and moving it again in the morning.

He remained grateful she had taken it upon herself to go with the flow for the time being. He didn't see so much of her as the summer progressed as she was skilful at avoiding the constant gaze of the cameras and had discovered her own tracks and pathways which he couldn't possibly cover with the existing equipment.

So he had been extremely surprised when after a day, then another, the cigarettes were still there. He left a small packet of sticking plasters on top of the gold box and by the next evening they were gone but the cigarettes remained.

Later the same night they were all discussing how they'd changed for the better since the start of the summer and Stevie had been the first to speak up. She confessed to stealing cigarettes off her mum for years but now she was so glad she'd kicked the filthy habit of smoking. She told the girls how she was looking forward to 'winching' with a boy who didn't smoke as she'd never had the luxury and she had always hated the taste.

Without a shadow of a doubt however, Lachie had to give his vote for the most entertaining member of the group to wee Jenny. She may have been one of the smallest but she had a voice which could pierce Kevlar. By virtue of the volume and rapidity of her banter, she had become the unwitting conduit of most of Lachie's intel on the psychology of the group. Hers would be the first voice he'd hear as he switched on in the morning and she'd still be going like a train until somebody told her to shut up at night.

Her jokes were unrelenting and for a twelve year old they were outrageous, often as bad as he'd ever heard in the army. He imagined

Jenny using her future publicity from this summer as a springboard to international success as a stand-up comedian. She'd give that loathsome oik, Frankie Boyle a run for his money he thought. He had narrowed down his favourites to a short-list of three, all apparently about the school in the next estate on the other side of the motorway. Their hatred for Warlaw was comparable to the love and affection held by the inhabitants of Gaza for the state of Israel.

The whole group had been feeling ill for a week or so. The summer weather had turned cold, wet and windy and Lachie reckoned they all had a bout of flu, including himself. He'd noticed his press-ups getting harder instead of easier and he had a constant dull headache. So to cheer everyone up, a few evenings ago Jenny had put on a wee show for the girls, ably assisted by 'Seamus the sheep' who was an old sheep skull one of the younger girls had dragged back to the shelters and the others had subsequently stuck it up in a position of authority watching over them as they slept.

It had been funny to note the coincidences and contrasts with the depiction of the pig skull in Lord Of The Flies, Lachie thought. There had been no doom and gloom here. On the contrary the girls had stuffed the skull with wild flowers and recently it had assumed the personae of an old hippy grandfather with a wig of bright white Sea Campion, tufts of Bog Cotton for ear hair and a double ribbon of wild daises around his neck.

The girls would often bring old Seamus into a conversation and so it had been for this reason Jenny had incorporated him into her act as her straight man.

> 'Seamus! How do you stop a Warlaw girl frae getting' pregnant?
>
> *Cut her brother's baw's off.*
>
> What does a Warlaw lassie use fer protection during sex?
>
> *The bus shelter on Stirling Road.*
>
> Why did the Warlaw first-year go tae school wi' square boobs?
>
> *She forgot tae take the Kleenex out o' the box.'*

So it had been Jenny who above all had kept the girls going through the tough times and Lachie heard himself promise he would return this little ray of sunshine safely one day to her grumpy wolf of a father. Ironically, it was shortly after thinking this when young Jenny unknowingly squirmed her way into a small piece of his heart where she would remain for the rest of his life.

Of course, while it might be wee Jenny who could make him smile broadly in his little control bunkers, there was only one girl who could stop the breath in his chest. Chantal had blossomed along with the other wild flowers and she had now become the unassuming leader of the group. Now taller and much heavier than the others, her abundant hair flowed out behind her in the breeze as she stood proudly on the huge flat rock overlooking the bathing pool which Lachie had taken her to.

She had long since dispensed with her Kappa top and with her muscular shoulders and arms burnished a deep golden brown by the constant affections of both sun and wind she reminded Lachie of an old film his mother had made him turn off one hazy summer afternoon many years before. Even clothed in her makeshift rabbit fur waistcoat she had become to him the living incarnation of the goddess Venus. With Stevie preferring to spend long hours high on the cliff watching the faraway ships passing oblivious to the island and its new inhabitants, it would be Chantal who the girls looked to for guidance and authority.

They hadn't met or spoken again together since the day of her rescue but she often spoke to him indirectly, her head lifting above those of the smaller girls as she swept back her mane of hair and directed those radiant eyes at his cameras. Always talking in a coded fashion, she would let him know how she was faring or what she thought of a particular situation and he would stand up out of his chair and stare, his tired red eyes unblinking until she flicked her hair and turned away.

He knew she hadn't been unhappy on the island. He had known this for a long time. He heard her say many times she had never felt so strong or so well in her entire life and he'd stood hiding nearby, watching nervously as she firstly became a proficient swimmer then in turn taught each of the others the rudiments of the doggy paddle. By the middle of the summer some of the girls were spending as much time in the water as out of it and they had feasted on crab, mussels, periwinkles and Fee and Charlie had become like little water nymphs.

Lachie had changed alongside them. He had long given up on his notion about The Beast, which dwelt in all our hearts, emerging savage and unyielding during this summer experiment. He had deposited these innocent girls onto an island paradise, an unlikely Garden of Eden, expecting them to exhibit the worst facets of the human condition and to poison the unspoilt beauty around them.

Instead of a vicious dark battle for survival, scrapping amongst each other like packs of wild dogs, the girls had worked together, forming a tight unit in exactly the way a family should do, in a way few, if any of them, had ever experienced. Somehow they instinctively knew how things were meant to be. Lachie rationalised this by deducing that the girls were still, in the main, young enough to have kept the inherited decency and goodness which their genetic predecessors had gifted them, before their deprived 21st century lives could have the chance to destroy it.

He wondered if it would have been different with boys instead of girls. Could it be all down to our culture that boys became savage animals but girls turned into peaceful team-builders? This seemed far too simple he decided. He'd met too many hard hearted bitches in his bitter life to believe it was all down to gender. Plus he had recently had dealings with one representative of the female species who most certainly gave the lie to the notion that girls were only made from sugar and spice. Lachie had thought he was one of the coldest people around until he'd met her.

But then, this summer had melted his heart in a way he could never have anticipated. His scientific indifference towards his subjects had evaporated like the early morning island mists off the sea. He felt like a subterranean Quasimodo watching over his treasured little friends, subconsciously glad they'd turned the island into their sanctuary. He'd sit at his monitors and watch their unadulterated pleasure from simply playing around in the gentle surf and then later when they'd gone, he'd go down himself and stand there, trousers rolled up to his knees, his toes sinking into the sand. The rhythmic crashing of the waves and subsequent undertow from the tiny grains pulling underneath his feet felt intoxicating to him and he wondered why he'd never noticed the beautiful sensation of it before. These girls were teaching him how to live.

He would find himself sitting at the water's edge up in the relative safety of the North of the island. There was a beautiful black rock which had been smoothed and shaped by the constant affections of the waves and small shells into a curvaceous and curiously sensual object. The waves would curl around it, creating a little vortex here and there almost like slender fingers tenderly twirling the chest hair of a lover. It made him feel quite strange, unlike anything he'd ever experienced before.

He had initially construed that he maybe he had become attached to the girls in the same way as one could be fond of a pet. After all he would have done anything for his black Labrador gundog as a lad. But he knew it wasn't the same thing at all. He'd long ago lost all interest in masturbation and his pile of magazines had lain unread, gathering dust with his DVD's and computer games, not one of them viewed. They were now buried underneath the hours and hours worth of recorded discs.

The wonderful truth of it was he had overestimated the power of the beast within him, within us all, and he'd discovered, to his great joy, he might be more human than mutant after all.

But unfortunately, he had been wrong, so very wrong.

243

The beast had been merely lying in the shadows, biding its time and patiently waiting. And now, the clock hands had swept back around to a time of darkness and great evil.

With the fattening now complete, it readied itself to unleash a pent up fury borne of one of the blackest nights in the history of mankind.

Chapter 33

'The Radisson please.' She slumped back into the sumptuous leather of the chauffeur driven limousine. She'd accepted it might be a little ostentatious for a wee jaunt along the M8 but she had been tired and she always liked to make a good impression on her way to meet a new client. *Especially here*, she groaned and closed her eyes.

Most people would expect a traveller with her moneyed good looks to head straight for the Hilton or the Marriot or perhaps even the grand style of the boutique hotel 1 Somerset Gardens. But no. She detested the bland sameness of the two American hotel chains and to her mind they were only good for fat businessmen and wine-bar hookers. The other place scored even worse in her estimation, trying too hard to be something it would never be. It always came down to attitude as far as she was concerned. What would be the point in her staying in a thousand pound a night hotel if the staff were ignorant fools who thought it acceptable to wear the same uniform for several days in a row? She had worked very hard to be a professional and she expected no less from the rest of the world. This helped account for the fact she'd just got off a flight from Geneva where her two daughters were attending the last finishing school left in Switzerland.

It wasn't only her who'd come a long way in the last few years she realised as the powerful engine sped her smoothly through the new motorway system right into the heart of the modern city. Glasgow had changed. Must have, she supposed, *if it can afford people like me.* Her last contract had been in the goldfish bowl of Hong Kong. Whilst lucrative enough, she had felt nervous operating there. With her Aryan looks she'd found it harder to blend into the shadows. For the job before that, she'd been in Moscow. She'd found it so much easier.

Ice blond killers were ten-a-penny over there.

Not that she *always* killed people for money. She happened to be so damned good at it and then word spreads and well, *what can you do,* she thought contentedly. It had been five years since she'd left this city. She found it funny how the chapters in her life seemed to revolve around the number 5. Perhaps it's a lucky number for her, she wondered, like the fascination the Chinese had for the number 8? *Not likely.*

Helen Kerr didn't believe in luck. You make your own destiny in this world. Everything is a choice if you boiled it down to its minute constituents. Being 'unlucky' enough to get pregnant at sixteen after allowing a spotty adolescent one mercifully brief opportunity to scratch an early notch on his bedpost, had not been her best choice. Neither had been drinking a bottle of the fortified Buckfast tonic wine so beloved of Scotland's winos and underage kids prior to the clumsy encounter. But it had still been her choice to be flattered by the primitive attentions of a drunken braggadocio and to believe him when he said he would take precautions. That was one job she would do for free, if she could even remember his name.

Thankfully her mum had been only too happy to look after little Amy Louise and allowing her to run away to the army. There she learnt who she really was and what she could do. Not for nothing did her fellow recruits give her the nickname, H.K. or Hunter Killer. But within five years she had bounced her head off the glass ceiling too many times. Her accent didn't fit and she scared most of her contemporaries shitless. Except from when they were trying to wedge her shapely legs apart. But she hadn't been about to make the same stupid mistake again, or so she'd thought.

Helen felt her jaw tighten as she looked out at the legions of overweight shoppers lurching past her window, all rotated shoulders and lordotic postures. No doubt about it, she should've opened an outlet in Glasgow for sure. But she'd always known it.

Post-army, her next 'not so great idea' had been to open a gym in the leafy English suburbs which became a roaring success as it tapped into the profitable fitness zeitgeist at the perfect time. Her personal trainer persona had been formidable and she quickly realised how much money people would pay to satisfy their most primitive needs. Back then she had been in the business of extending lives.

Her 'GI Jane' army-style classes took off to the extent she very speedily recruited a dozen staff including one suave ex-army PT instructor who swept her off her feet and made her his wife. It was while taking time off to tend to her second baby Claire, that she discovered he liked keeping a lot of the young female customers off their feet too. Unfortunately it would be their feet being mostly behind their ears which seemed to be their default position. If it had not been for her post natal delicacy then he would have met a foot coming from a different place entirely as Helen was a second Dan Black Belt by this time and so sadly she had to forgo the karate and settle for dismissal and divorce.

The car slowed to a stop on the busy street and her door instantly opened. Thankfully, check-in proved to be quick and efficient and her shoulders relaxed a little further as she allowed herself to be shown to her room by a stylish yet smart young girl. The hotel was bright and modern and as they walked across a frosted glass floor she glanced down to the cocktail bar where her meeting would be in a few hours. Plenty time for a massage and a long bath she figured. But first a call to Lake Geneva to let the girls know she'd arrived safely in the town of her birth.

After her five years as a gym owner she sold at a good time and invested half her money in various properties including a villa in Switzerland where she had based herself ever since. H.K. Investigations had been set up shortly after and a few months of divorce and missing person's cases stood her in good stead with a reputable business front but it had almost driven her mad. So, it had really only been in the last five years she'd truly started to work for herself. Ostensibly still just a private investigator, but now she rarely did any missing persons work. Rather, her line of business now involved the creation of missing persons. And it was *way* more profitable.

Her little reverie, prompted by this homecoming, had of course set off several alarm bells in her head. It would not take a brain surgeon to work out the probability of something significant going to happen around now. Still only 31 and at the pinnacle of her profession, but how long did she want to keep taking the sorts of crazy chances inherent in the international assassin business?

This partly explained why she had taken this contract, subject to a satisfactory meeting this evening. It was unusual for her to be working in the UK and very rare she would agree to meet a client face to face.

However the circumstances of this contract were very different. For one the client had been willing to pay exceedingly well for what appeared to be an easy assignment and secondly she and the client were known to each other. In fact, if she remembered correctly, he had mentioned during their telephone negotiations, something about her kicking him in the balls. She of course flatly denied this could have been her, citing mistaken identity and so forth. But when he had followed this 'negotiating hurdle' by saying he would only pay her a quarter of a million pounds per kill plus outgoings and a guaranteed contract fee on the sole condition she *was* in fact the same person who'd so injured his adolescent pride all those years ago, then she had been savvy enough to say one word.

Yes.

Chapter 34

Truth be told, even as he awoke back in his damp and cramped bunker, Lachie felt so glad to be back on the island after his 12 hour reminder of all that was wrong with cosmopolitan Britain.

He'd arrived at the modern hotel still dressed in his 'Hector mode' and due to time constraints and, admittedly, a certain comfort-blanket reluctance to change, he foolishly decided to remain in the same gear for his meeting downstairs. He'd no sooner stepped out of the elevator when he was hit by a garish cascade of glitzy colours and bright reflected angles of light from which ever direction he looked. Feeling like a refugee from Last of The Summer Wine he hurriedly found a seat and tried to blend in. Vainly hoping the plush leather sofa would somehow assimilate him, he instead felt like a complete ass.

He'd been thirty minutes early as planned and he carefully swept the large room looking for obvious undercover police or even less welcome observers. But no one even slowed down long enough to catch breath never mind give him more than a pitying cursory once-over as they pranced past his table. It reminded Lachie of visits to bustling European cities such as Paris where he used to sit in pavement cafes to be amazed people could talk so rapidly, so loudly or have so much to say. He would calculate that in the space of his coffee and crème brûlée, they had possibly spoken a greater volume of words than he had in his entire life. He couldn't remember ever having had a conversation like these people, not ever.

Sitting now in this noisy Glasgow bar, he likened the cacophony to the sound of the gulls jostling for position as the summer thermals flowed over the tall ridged backbone of the island and he realised how far he himself had come over the last weeks. No longer comfortable in this artificial jungle he longed to be back in the wilds with his ready-made family.

It had been at least seven or eight years since he'd had his last 'full contact' with Helen Kerr or whatever she called herself these days. As a former member of his battalion she must have pulled a few strings to land herself the contract for the 'street fighting arts' self-defence course which Lachie had attended as a stripling youth. There had been no doubting her seriousness nor professional abilities however and he'd not been the only soldier to have hobbled into the bar after the first night nursing a 'pink bowtie' courtesy of GI Jane.

Any doubts as to whether he would recognise her were swept away as she literally blew into the room as if being propelled by invisible winds. Lachie could have sworn the music became instantly louder and more throbbing as if a hidden DJ had taken this cue to ramp up the atmosphere from cocktail to cocktease. The expression 'dressed to kill' flashed in red neon across his cortex as he took in the sheer stockings and the smart but sexy black suit. His jaw dropped as he saw her halt her stride for a brief moment and she scanned the room dispassionately as a killer shark might survey a shoal of intended prey before the intensity of her piercing blue eyes became focused directly upon him. He felt his cheeks burning as she grinned and set a collision course straight for him, her jet black bob bouncing provocatively revealing an immaculate set of cheekbones and an array of gleaming teeth.

Lachie stumbled awkwardly to his feet just in time to receive a double air kiss before she had planted her tight posterior on the seat opposite him. He attempted a nervous smile and looked around for some waiterly back up, noticing several male customers crossing and uncrossing their legs as he did so.

'Hope you don't mind me being a little early, honey?' her elegant accent betrayed only a hint of her humble origins. Lachie coughed.

'On the contrary, I much prefer it. Nothing personal but the sooner I get out of here the better. Here is a stick with all the relevant files. How soon do you think you can start?'

'Already on it, honey. Subject to your agreement on the advance payment, I can have your first report ready for this time tomorrow. Take it from me sugar, from

253

what you've told me, we don't have a great deal of slippage on this one.'

Ms Kerr had been as clinically professional and straight down to business as he had been led to expect but even so, he had felt infused with a new strength as he'd powered the Range Rover out of the festering miasma he'd once thought of as home. For whatever the problems and uncertainties he might have to face over the next days and weeks, he remained certain he wanted her working for him and not agin him.

Dead certain.

Back on the island, it was still early morning and he spent a few minutes limbering up before commencing his irregular exercise routine. He'd been suffering from the same summer cold as the girls and he had noticed his limbs were even stiffer than normal these days and the good old dependable press ups were getting harder than ever. After a half hearted attempt he switched on the bank of screens whilst sorting out his camouflage gear and a spot of breakfast.

It had been late when he had returned to the island and he had taken *Precious* up to the northern bay so as not to be discovered traipsing too close to the girls, his unpainted face glowing like a car dashboard in the twilight.

Not surprisingly it had been Jenny's voice already in full flow before his picture had even fully formed on the screen. What she said however stopped him dead, one leg in the air; waiting for a sock which had fallen unnoticed onto the chill concrete.

'We cannae just leave her lying there! What if she's infect-'

'She's NOT infectious Gaga. Jeezo! What could she huv caught all the way oot here?

Chantal stood up in the middle, towering over them all, her hands out placating but authoritative. She looked at every girl in turn as they all turned their faces up to her for guidance. She spoke quietly and measuredly.

'Stevie's right. Let's keep the heid here. We've all knew she's no' been well for ages. For aw' we know she could've had appendicitis or something, some wee thing they could've fixed if we'd no been stuck here. It's ma fault, so it is. I should've done somethin' sooner. We could've got her some help if we'd just screwed the nut a bit quicker.'

'But how would we get...'

Stevie punched the smaller girl hard on
the shoulder.

'Shut up Joolz. You know as well as me
our Chantal has got *special privileges*
with whoever the fuck dumped us a' here.
It's nae your fault Chantal. If it wisnae
fer you half of us wid be deid anyway so
dinnae start wi a' your shite.'

'All I'm saying is we cannae leave a deid
body lying next tae ma bed like nothin'
has happened! That's aw, okay?'

Jenny's plaintive voice rose up again
increasing in volume with every word and the
panic of their awful predicament engulfed the
huddled group.

Chantal raised her bronzed arm again and
the girls were silent, waiting for her to speak.

'No, Jenny. No-one-is-saying-that.
No way. We'll have to bury her, an that.
Give her a proper send off, like.
Anyone got any ideas for where tae put
her?'

Lachie sat and listened, surprised to feel
tears dripping hot onto his cold arm.
It was Katster. She had died, apparently
in her sleep.

256

He hadn't even cried when his own father died. Not a single drop. He'd taken Chantal's comments to heart, feeling like they had been directed at him. He wondered how many other things had been said for him to hear over the last few hours. His heart sank as he tried to imagine what Chantal must be thinking of him. He set one of the screens to rewind to the point he'd left the island. Filled with a deep despair he'd begun contemplating closing down the whole thing when he heard Stevie talking live.

> 'Ma vote's fer the wee bit of marshy ground near the loch.
> She'd never made it there herself and it wid be cool tae huv her looking over the water, like. She'd be able tae see one of us every day when we came to get fish. Aye...well, true enough.
> She'd see *Sticky* every day then.'

Lachie saw the girls weren't for giving up. No-one had said they wanted to go home despite this, their worst set-back so far. He looked around the bunker and saw it, his prized stainless steel spade. He could run up there in no time and leave it standing there for them. Maybe he could adjust camera 11 too and get better coverage of the burial. Feeling like a heartless bastard for thinking such a thing, he grabbed the spade and set off at full speed, punishing his legs as they were repeatedly torn by the now rampant brambles, but not slowing his pace to make his going any easier.

He made it back just before they set off and he felt a lump in his throat as he stared at the screen. He had been totally unprepared for what he now witnessed. The girls were all gathered in front of something he couldn't quite see and they were singing gently in a lilting harmony as they were bending over and doing something with their hands. Lachie watched in awe as the girls at the back of the group were handing flowers and other bits and pieces over and through to the girls in front.

He could hear none of the usual babble of talking and apart from the haunting melodies the girls were silent, working as a team. At last, after what seemed like forever, the group parted as if subconsciously obeying his telepathic stage directions, to allow him full view of the proceedings.

Lachie caught his breath. The little girl had been wrapped in a shroud made from a small shred of yacht sail which had washed up on the beach a few weeks earlier. The girls had initially set it up at the bathing pond as a sun shade and it had been bleached as white as if by any biological washing powder.

She lay on her back on a stretcher-bed of silver birch interweaved with strong freshly pulled fern stems. Cushioning her from the unforgiving hard bed the girls had made a thick blanket of Rosebay Willowherb and white Hawthorn flowers, the two colours perfectly matching her little pink scrubbed hands folded together as if in prayer.

Lachie noticed they had even taken the time to stain each of her fingernails with the juice of the brambles which he had observed them doing occasionally when trying to replicate the nail varnishes which they missed so much. Katster's long hair had been woven into ornate tresses around her head like a crown and through this the girls had placed large wild daisy flowers. The effect was truly magical. Together with the haltingly beautiful voices and the flickering sunlight across the bowed heads of the kneeling girls it felt to Lachie as if he was intruding upon a private and ethereal other world. A world of elves and pixies which the darkness of man should never have violated.

As he watched, spellbound, he saw the girls standing now and he could see they all had made an effort to look respectful, their unkempt hair tied back with wild flowers and their ruddy faces freshly scrubbed.

Chantal sniffed nervously as she took the lead position whilst behind her the younger girls carried the delicate stretcher between them, stepping carefully over tree roots and rocks with a practiced ease. Ignoring their own individual agonies as they shared the collective sadness, most tried not to think of those from their own lives whom they missed so very dearly and whether they would ever see them again. Stevie followed the unusual looking cortege carrying in her arms an unwieldy bundle of flowers and tributes from the group and Lachie stood listening until long after they had all disappeared from view.

Chantal smiled as they all saw the shiny spade glinting like an agricultural grave stone marking the spot where they must bury their little friend. As the girls struggled to remember the right things to do with their limited personal experiences of a social setting such as a funeral, they continued to sing together as much for mutual support as for any more significant purpose. Sticky made quick work of digging through the soft ground. It was only as the girls were nervously recycling their favourite songs for the second time when Chantal raised her arms and they became silent.

'I don't know what words to say about Katster and a' this what's happened.
I hope she's away to a better place an' she's happy an' that.
We'll a' miss her, like, an' we'll never forget her. Never ever.
If any of you maybe wants to say something as well, please come up an' do it now, like. It's okay. It doesn't matter what you say, just say what you feel.
Eh..., amen.'

As Chantal looked around at the solemn girls they all bowed their heads and backed away slightly, looking at their feet. Then suddenly little Fee and Charlie stepped up, hand in hand. They glanced at each other, eyes wet with emotion and Fee coughed and put her hand up, like she was still at school. Chantal blushed with a strange embarrassment at this unasked for reminder from a previous life. 'Go on.' She waved the two girls up to the front brusquely.

> 'It's just us two wanted to say how Katster was like a ma' tae the both of us even though she was only one year up from us, like. We dinnae want tae be here wi' oot her an' we wish she wisnae deid, an' that.'

The two girls burst into tears and rushed into the arms of Chantal who bowed her head and wept quietly with them. Before she could stop them she became surrounded by howling girls, some of them who hugged the others around her and some even falling down at her feet.

As Lachie stood some way off at the edge of the woods, he gave up trying to capture the moment on film and dropped the camera to fall heavily around his neck. His viewfinder had been too blurred with his own tears. Seconds before he had looked at Chantal with the sunlight glowing from her bleached white goatskin tunic and the scrum of wild haired little girls around

her and he'd thought it was the most resonant
image of religious majesty he had ever witnessed.

Chapter 35

Boyle chewed hard on his plastic
cigarette before realising he'd finally broken it.
He threw it into the metal bin with a satisfying
clatter and turned his head.

'Stee-
Bloody hell! Mackie?
Nip out and get me some fags will ye?
No, never mind!
I'll go myself, I could do with the fresh
air.'

His nerves were getting to him and
besides, if the call he'd been waiting for all day
finally came in he'd have to be somewhere
private. If Baxter got wind of what he was up to
she'd have his arse on a silver platter, of that he
was sure. He was glad to be sure about
something. This whole situation with Jenny had
got far too leftfield for his liking. If it wasn't for
the small detail of the guy holding his daughter
captive then he'd have had every Armed
Response Unit in the country looking for him.
The other thing he knew for certain was the
smart wee bastard had been nowhere near the
Falkland Islands.
He'd worked out the guy was shit-hot
with technology which accounted for the weird
accent as well as the bounced transmission. It
had been a voice-altering software gizmo. He'd
been reading up about all that stuff during the

night seeing as he couldn't have slept a wink even if he'd wanted to.

So who was this guy and what had Jenny and the girls got to do with any turf wars? Boyle had been so tempted to take a drive out to Garthamlow and see if he could work out where Jenny might be being held. He remained positive she had to be somewhere close. Much as he wanted to do it, he knew implicitly that talking to scum like Rocky would be a bad idea. He would never be able to keep a lid on his anger. Granted the big guy had also lost his daughter in all this but Boyle was convinced he had to be implicated and after a little unofficial torturing he'd soon reveal what the hell had happened. Boyle was more than a little prepared to bend the rules right now and with his experience he knew how urgent they needed to find the girls first. Free from the hands of her loony captor or not, Jenny would be little safer if the wrong gang members got to her before he did and worrying about a little collateral damage wouldn't keep any of *them* up at night.

Typically, he had only begun fumbling in his pockets for a crumpled tenner in the mini-supermarket when he felt his phone go off. He threw the money at the startled woman, grabbed his cigarettes and ran for the door.

'Boyle. Aye, okay, I'll go for it.
But on one condition-'

'No conditions Jim. I hold all the cards.

264

Without me, you will never see your
daughter safe and well.
I am a bad man but in this case I assure
you, you're far better off with
the Devil you know. So let's-'

'Now wait a damn minute!
That's just it. How do I *know* she's safe
and well?
You've got to give me some proof.
Let me speak wi' her, is she there, now
wi' you?'

The smothering blanket of silence
seemed to go on forever and Boyle had a flash of
panic. Now he'd called the guy's bluff the awful
truth would have to come out. He would turn out
to be another dirty perverted bastard who'd
killed her and the others ages ago and they'd
discover this absurd charade had been him
stroking himself off at the whole stupid lot of
them.

'No Jim, that's not going to happen.
No phones.
What I will do and this will be my *only*
concession, as a token of good faith, is
to have each of the girls record a short
video and I'll send you the links.
This will prove they are safe and I am
genuine.'

Boyle swallowed as a wave of adrenaline coursed through his body. She was alive! And he could see her! He dreaded to imagine what the video would look like and his next dilemma would be whether to make the videos public or not. He knew he wouldn't be able to keep it from Marie and he clenched his jaw tight before attempting his most authoritative voice.

'Okay. Agreed. When will you have the videos done?'

'Let me worry about that. But it will be soon, I promise.
However in the meantime, this is what *you* need to worry about...'

Lachie stretched and yawned. It had been a long night, his eyes rarely lifted from one screen or another. He knew he would have to leave the island for a short while and he didn't want to miss another second of the drama unfolding in front of his weary eyes. He might not have a hunched back but that didn't stop him being a monster, nevertheless, he'd also become their protector. This tribe of rag-tag girls were his family now. He felt this strongly. It had been a new experience for him. He'd never felt a sense of belonging before, not even in the army and certainly not with his own biological relations.

Rag-tag had been an appropriate description he thought, as he tried to work out the provisions he needed onshore. It was high summer and most of the girls had dispensed with conventional clothing especially since the funeral but Lachie knew he couldn't allow them to appear like that on any videos. Glancing over at the dusty pile of unwatched porn videos and magazines, he shuddered at what sordid images the filthy-minded police would conjure up if they saw the girls as they were today.

He could sense something else had been going on, the girls were even more excited than usual and it was as if they were anticipating an event of some kind. They couldn't possibly know what he had planned could they? Confused and then terrified for a brief moment, Lachie had taken a frenzied head count, fearful there had been another death in the camp. The flu bug hadn't relaxed its grip on the girls yet and he felt like death himself and so he thought perhaps some real clothes might do the girls some good despite his reluctance to bring the modern world crashing back into their lives. It could be cold during the clear summer nights, even here in the bunker, so maybe a few items of warmer clothing would be all they needed.

Chapter 36

The powerful rib sliced through the choppy waves with its customary disdain and despite the bright sunshine overhead, Lachie felt the cold wind cut into him. He slowed the engine, telling himself not to panic but feeling something like what he imagined a new parent must go through the first time they have to leave their new offspring. He mused on his chances of ever becoming a parent and as he expertly brought the boat alongside the small pier and waved over to a waiting Archie, a shiver of adolescent excitement replaced the usual feelings of dark despair and isolation which would accompany any thoughts of having a conventional life.

The normally ever patient and easy-going Archie seemed to have a bee in his bonnet this morning about something.

> 'Good morning *Sir Hector*, or is it afternoon?
> Good God man, you're paler than ever. D'ye never get any fresh air over on yon island of yours? An' you're dressed for winter!
> Better no' turn out to be one of those posh druggies.
> We had a bunch of them up here a few years ago. Old Malky was right taking the piss so he was. Six idiots crammed into one of his filthy old cow sheds each

paying three thousand pounds for a week
of cold porridge and hard labour.
Cocaine it was! Can you imagine? It was
the only way they could break the habit
so he was telling me and then he-'

'No Archie! I am not on drugs and as an
albino I find your comments regarding
my complexion extremely offensive.'

Lachie pretended to look annoyed for a
moment but was secretly very pleased to have
someone to talk to. First he needed to get the
business arrangements in place.

'Now have you arranged a safe berth for
those components we discussed?'

'Aye... It's all sorted, just like you asked.
Had to pay a fortune for delivery mind
you! There's folk thinking yer making
another Braveheart or something of the
like!'

'Am I not paying you enough Archie?
Have you checked your bank balance
lately?'

'Aye I have and I cannae believe how
much money I've got from this up to now.
But that still doesn't make up for feeling
a wee bit funny about all this. I do trust
you Hector and you know I wouldn't be

here if I didnae but there's lots of
questions being asked and I cannae keep
a lid on everything folk do and say
around here can I?'

Lachie felt his guts tighten and he fought
to keep his face relaxed. There was always going
to be a shelf-life for The Project and if he was
being honest, when he'd planned this whole
thing, he'd fully expected the girls to have torn
each other to ribbons by this point and for him to
have been long one. It suddenly struck Lachie
he'd not really thought much about his future
after The Project. He'd not planned anything
because in his empty heart he'd known he
wouldn't escape from this with his life.

But things were different now. For the
first time that day he felt a warm caress from the
sun's rays and he turned to give Archie his most
winning smile.

'I hear you Archie but I'm confident a
man of your talents will be able to
control a wee bit of village tittle-tattle eh?
I need the wood, plasterboard and fabrics
to make a small studio for some new
promotional videos and the health and
safety rules mean my stocks of normal
medicines is pitifully low for the quality
of guests my business will be attracting
and-'

Lachie had been utterly unprepared for what happened next. Archie whipped around and Lachie found himself staring down the barrel of a shotgun. His face had gone an unhealthy deep purple and white spittle gathered around his snarling mouth.

'Enough! *Hector* or whatever your name is.
I know you've got wee lassies over there and I'm not moving a muscle until you tell me whit yer up to with them! I've seen the news and so if it's all the same to you ye can stick the money where the sun disnae shine for all I care aboot it!'

'Whoa steady man, take it easy will you!'

Lachie moved fast and disarmed the bewildered old man who suddenly found himself sitting in the heather facing a smiling lunatic.
He extended a helping hand and passed Archie back the gun as the man looked up at him in consternation. His beetroot complexion had paled and the edges of his mouth twitched as half formed words struggled to make themselves audible. The wind freshened off the sea and Lachie was struck for the first time how old Archie must be and a cold hand of regret twisted tightly around his throat making him feel light-headed. This man was much older than his dead father but in a strange way Lachie felt more of a

271

bond with him than with any of his own flesh
and blood. It must be time for some plain talking.

> 'But you *have* got a point Archie. There
> any malt kicking about in the back of the
> van? I'm frozen.
> Let's go into the bothy for a wee chat,
> shall we?'

Chapter 37

It turned out Archie had a considerable amount of whisky and so it was almost dark by the time the two men passed out over the ancient kitchen table. Many hours earlier, Lachie had stunned the other man by admitting to having an alias and that his whole 'environmental toff' persona had been fictitious.

Despite his complete inebriation, Lachie didn't worry the old man about the kidnappings or deaths prior to the girls arriving. He portrayed The Project as a left-field psychology experiment which had to be kept secret to keep the media away and he promised it would be over soon and the whole thing would be on the television by autumn. And an important part of the whole TV formula for these types of programmes would be the individual video-diary recordings which each girl had to record.

Lachie artfully dodged the issue of why the recordings couldn't be made out in the open by emphasising the videos always had to be made in a confined 'confessional-style' atmosphere hence the requirement for a makeshift studio which Lachie was going to have to rig up later. He added that the production company executives needed to view these videos but they could not be allowed to know the location of the island at any point until The Project was complete.

The two men had poured out their life stories along with the Macallan and Lachie learnt for the first time how much the island meant to Archie and his family. Archie spelt out the hideous way his predecessors had been treated by the treacherous Westminster mandarins in the name of national security and he promised to uphold his part of the bargain regarding ownership of the island. Once The Project had completed, Lachie would sell the island to Archie for exactly £1 and it would once again be back in the family as it once had in the time of his granny. Lachie tried to convey the spirit of the film Dr Strangelove which Archie had somehow missed entirely and then they both had a laugh at the expense of the poor estate agent.

It was only in the chilly hours of the early light when first a weary Archie and then Lachie came to same deadly conclusion about the 'summer-flu' he and the girls were suffering from.

'It's the Anthrax, I'm telling ye!'

Lachie shook his head, which turned out to be a bad idea as the canvas tool bag full of spanners inside his head clattered painfully against his tender skull. The birds joined in and so he clamped his cold damp fingers over his ears and across his fevered forehead.

'It can't be!
The whole island had been declared free of Anthrax in the late 80's. I researched

all this meticulously when I picked the location. I spent a whole day online!'

Archie slammed the heavy kettle onto the range unsympathetically.

'Aye well! That's where all yer cleverness wi' computers get's ye now isn't it?
Ah remember it well. Bunch of English poofters wi' degrees in fuck knows what, who didnae have a clue what they were up against.
Mind you, it was a bonanza time for the locals. Everyone and their auntie was working with the chemicals although how much of it actually got used is another matter, know what I mean? They spent hundreds of thousands up here; how did ye think I came tae own three holiday houses?'

Lachie accepted a mug of tea gratefully. Once again he wondered why people subject themselves to the horrors of alcohol on a regular basis. But this hangover had taken suffering to a whole new level. It couldn't be true could it?

'But I thought you were always dead against it?'

'Aye! But only after I realised they didnae have a clue!

Before, I thought maybe there could be a wee chance my family would get their island back.'

'So what about the Government Minister who came up! I've seen archive footage on the internet. It was very dramatic; he pulled a warning sign out of the ground and declared the island safe. That was what convinced me to buy the damned place!'

Archie spat back in utter contempt.

'Well ye should know better!
You being in the television business an' all!
Do you know how long he was here for? Between landing in his helicopter outside there to taking back off again, I doubt if he was on the island for more than ten minutes.
You've been living over there wi' those poor wee lassies for weeks!'

Lachie allowed his head to rest on the table. His brain continued to scream in pain and then the awful realisation that he'd killed Katster hit him like a rabbit-punch in the guts. He'd been a fool. And now he saw them as his family, it seemed inconceivable that he'd risked all their lives so callously. And Chantal!

'But it's curable Archie! With antibiotics!'

'Aye, it's possible but it depends on how you've been infected. To be doubly sure the wee prick from the Government had a doctor up wi' him. He sat in yon chair at this very table talking to me all about it while he waited the whole ten minutes. Had a briefcase stuffed wi' medicines so he did!'

'You were here?'

'Too right! I wisnae going over. I'm not daft.
You fire up that wee iPad thingy of yours and look for Dr Whatshisname, it'll come tae me in a minute.'

Lachie switched on his tablet and they found the scientist Archie had been thinking of who'd said categorically "he would not go walking on Gruinard" and also revealed news about spores uncovered near Edinburgh which had survived for hundreds of years.

'See?
And a bootfull o' the stuff could wipe out half o' Edinburgh if they didnae catch it in time! And there's mair, look!'

Archie had been right. More recently, anthrax spores had been found in Egyptian archaeological excavations which had remained alive after thousands of years. Lachie felt a panic rising up in his gut and he ran to the toilet.

As he staggered weakly back he thought of the guns he'd stashed next door and how easily he could end this nightmare. Great idea you idiot but where would that get the girls and Chantal? He instantly quashed any selfish thoughts and made a tough decision. This was no dystopian computer game and now he had a responsibility for real lives, precious young lives which he'd foolishly endangered. Now it had to be him who sorted things. He had to get them off the island and to medical assistance as soon as possible.

The Project was over.

According to what he could glean from the internet, it would be highly unlikely the girls could have inhaled any spores directly but instead there was a strong chance they might have eaten some infected plants or other food. This meant the onset of anthrax poisoning would be much slower and at this stage might hardly be noticed by girls of their age. He felt such an idiot and despite the colossal advancement in his emotional evolution since he came to the island, he realised he was still a child feeling his way through the darkness. It seemed ridiculous now when he'd thought his lack of vim had been down to being in love for the first time! He wasn't sure if a monster like him should ever be allowed to know what love felt like. But then maybe love truly was the answer. He shook his head and tried to focus on the practicalities.

They could still make the videos later today which would keep the police off his back for a while at least. Archie would need to set up a friendly medic to provide the medicine and after the videos he would have to take the girls back down south and leave them somewhere safe to be found. His relief at the thought of the girls being safe was tempered by his sense of loss at losing them. He couldn't imagine life on his own now and Archie stared back in amazement as his normally stuck up boss broke down sobbing in front of him.

Chapter 38

'Honey, it's all fine at this end.
Honestly, it happens every day, believe
me. I won't even charge anything extra
for it like a lot of them do.
But I do need an answer from you today.
Now.'

Lachie swallowed and tried to think
clearly. This day had become more and more
bizarre by the second. He'd just watched a
couple of the videos and either he was going
mad or wee Jenny was trying to send coded
messages to her dad and then there was Chantal.
Talk about dropping a bomb. How he'd never
noticed it up until now he didn't know but it
wasn't something he would have considered and
it was quite possibly the last thing in the entire
world he could ever have wanted. But there it
was right in front of him. He had the screen on
freeze and there could be no mistaking what he
had been looking at. Her swollen belly, exposed
for the camera, brown as a brazil nut. Chantal
was pregnant.

And now he'd got an assassin on the line
asking him if he would 'okay' her having to kill
a policeman on his behalf. He couldn't argue
with her cold logic. It had been Lachie who'd
provided her with the initial data, the hacked
files from Police Scotland. But now she knew

more about the Garthamlow and Bottoms Up murders than the police did. All apart from maybe one man. A bent cop in every sense of the word. Lachie had intended the police to re-arrest DI Steel after he'd informed Boyle about his involvement at the strip club. There had never been any intention to kill the pathetic swine, much as it would have served the good of humanity to do so.

No, Lachie had expected him to be banged up for many years and as far as any further killing had been concerned he'd only been prepared for the murderer to die whoever he or she turned out to be and even then only if it was necessary to protect himself. Killer versus killer, live by the sword and all that Bushido code stuff.

But now he had been told Steel had gone AWOL. According to Ms Kerr he might even be the person responsible for the Meekin family killings and the barman as she'd found out the same gun had been used in each murder. Steel was the link. He had a strong motive for killing the barman and she promised to keep digging until she found a reason for the Meekins' deaths.

'And he's coming for you, no doubt in my mind.
He's been tracing the gun you used, which I have to say was spectacularly bad judgement on your part if you want my professional opinion. You realise, honey, if you'd secured my services

earlier then you wouldn't be in this situation.
He's eliminated all the other potential gun-owners, he knows who you are and he's spoken, as I've had the pleasure of doing also, with your charming mother. This-'

'Hold on a minute!' Lachie's head was spinning. He pressed a thumb hard into his forehead and squeezed his eyes shut.

'He couldn't have got anything from my mother, she's about the last person on earth who would know where I would be, so how does-'

'Sweetie, she good as told *me* where you'd gone. You bought the island with your father's inheritance didn't you? Well, you must have triggered some property tax paperwork which landed on your mother's doorstep so she gleefully told me you'd apparently bought some country estate somewhere. Two minutes on Google and Steel would have got every substantial Highland acquisition over the last ten years!
Of course he neglected to furnish any of this information to his superiors, which makes him prime suspect in my book and therefore he must be liquidated immediately.

I've just had a ping on his car registration coming up the A9 so I need your kill authorisation right now so I can get to him before he gets to you.'

'Give me a second will you.' Lachie rose to his feet and walked out of his bunker, blinking at first as he allowed the warm afternoon sun to loosen his tense shoulders.

The die is cast.

He gazed up at the hill to his left, hoping to maybe catch a glimpse of Stevie on her usual island circuit at this time of day. He loved this place more than anywhere else in the world. And these girls had become more precious to him than he could ever have believed.

The Project was finished. And they couldn't stay on the island that much had become obvious. But the girls had to be protected at all costs and Chantal was going to have a baby. A stampede of wild thoughts raced through his mind for a few seconds before the wind freshened and a dark cloud obscured the sun. He lifted the phone back up to his ear.

'Helen, can you stop him?'

'From reaching the island? I'm still in Glasgow, so short of hiring a chopper, I can't get ahead of him. You know what those roads are like, honey. But if you mean can I prevent him arriving... then of course I can sweetie.'

Chapter 39

Rocky slammed his fist into the table. 'Fuck knows *where* it is!' He jumped to his feet and as he did so, every other man in the room backed away. They'd not seen him like this since the wee lassie first went missing. And they'd all seen the pictures of Dokie in the Recorder.

> 'Just get me the biggest bastarding four-by-four in Glasgow, fill the boot wi' guns and make sure it's one wi' a decent fuckin' Sat Nav! Okay?'

They would do well to keep me at arms length, Rocky decided. He knew he wasn't the calmest of blokes under pressure but sometimes the only way to keep from going off his head was to hit something or someone hard. Again and again. He wondered if he had begun to lose control of things. Maybe he should look at all of this as a sign it might be time to pack it in. After all, he'd outlived most of his contemporaries hadn't he?

But it didn't seem to be getting any easier. As if it wasn't tough enough running a crime empire these days without every wee scrote thinking they were 'the man' because they saw a telly programme about the Kray brothers. Next he'd have the filth breathing down his neck every five minutes, trying to justify their miserable pay packets. *Or supplement them*, he snorted.

This was the problem these days. You couldn't trust anyone. No respect. That wee cunt Dokie, interfering with his Chantal. No doubt it had most likely been his own fault that she'd got herself into this other mess, the fact he'd not been able to protect his own, right under his nose. Well he'd fixed the wee fucker but even there he'd had to accept the embarrassment of outside help.

He'd been pleased the situation had been speedily resolved, no worries there, but he'd have preferred to have had the chance to have a wee 'chat' with the lad first. His hard-man reputation may have been bolstered but if the truth were told, he might *not* have killed the boy – it would've all depended on what he'd said about his relationship with Chantal.

But with this bent cop, he'd deal with him as soon as he got back. There would no possibility of leniency there.

Rocky checked over the vast arsenal of weapons his men had displayed for his inspection. Once quietly satisfied he had enough to wage a one-man war up there, he nodded and made for the car park. No, the disrespectful prick is a dead man walking and I'll be the one who ends his miserable life that's for sure. No point in delegating jobs like this. Has to be some perks to the job.

He didn't know what to be more annoyed at but at the same time the last few hours had also made him feel happier than he could ever remember so right now one of the wee twats could shoot him in the kneecap and he wouldn't really be too bothered. One thing he knew for sure. He would never let anything hurt his family ever again. He knew now what was important to him and he'd torch the whole fucking business to the ground if it meant his girls were safe and happy.

No, what had wound him up so badly had been the way the cop had tried so blatantly to con him. At first he'd been relieved to know how she'd died. He'd realised there would be no chance of her being alive. A dozen or more people had met a grisly end themselves over the last few weeks in his quest to find her. He knew what happened to teenage lassies who were abducted and he'd not met one pervert yet who'd ever let a girl go free afterwards.

So when Gary Steel had promised to tell him where her body was and who had killed her, he'd felt truly indebted to the man. But then when he started the 'I know all about you' crap then demanded money and guaranteed safety or else he'd sell the story of his gay affair to the Daily Recorder...

Rocky growled. 'Best gie me a real fuckin' map an' all.' This was too important to trust to a piece of software.

His daughter was alive!

Minutes after he'd promised to shove his phone up the polis bastard's arse, he'd received a video message. A fucking video! He'd never watched one on his phone in his entire life but now he couldn't stop replaying it. He was even thinking of getting someone to make the trip with him so he could get them to drive so he could watch the ninety second clip over and over.

Rocky had never seen her look so beautiful. Radiant and healthy, her face was glowing. Fair enough she might be pregnant with Dokie's wee bastard baby but all of a sudden he found he didn't care anymore. The wee shit had gone for good and his daughter was alive and he would be a grandpa!

Way across town there was another relieved father. Boyle had carefully explained to Marie that they shouldn't get their hopes up too much but she should know Jenny remained most definitely alive and he would do everything in his power to make sure the mysterious character who had come good on his promises so far would deliver his final part of the bargain. Boyle had earlier put out a nationwide hunt for Gary Steel although part of him still clung to the hope his erstwhile partner might yet be able to explain this satisfactorily.

But it had been Marie who'd first noticed the bit about the T-shirt. Boyle, the Detective Inspector, would never have guessed what she had been meaning and he'd just been so deliriously happy she seemed apparently unharmed. So there she had been, wearing one of those disgusting T-shirts, far too tight in Boyle's opinion and all the time she had been talking she had been giving them this weird two-fingered pointing at the wording on her shirt like one of those demented rap singers.

'She's trying to tell us something Jim!
Look!
Why is she pointing at that word? It's one of those rock bands I think.'

'No idea love. What does it say, is it *Anthrax*?'

His wife dug him in the ribs hard.

'Shoosh! Will you be quiet and listen?'

'... an' so ah really miss Joey and that. It's true what they say like, home is where the heart is so Joey Belladonna I pure love you. Been ma second home here Mum, so it has but will ye' tell Da' I love Joey so much...'

'John! Get down here! NOW!'

'Aww mum I'm revising, what is it?'

'Who or what is Joey Belladonna?'

'What? Random!
Joey Belladonna is in a heavy-metal band I used to like ages ago. Called *Anthrax*.'

Chapter 40

Lachie had to give due respect to the old man. When he'd asked him to get something special, he'd envisaged some Happy Meals courtesy of the Inverness McD's at best. As he loaded the fragrant cartons back out of his straining oven and into an insulated crate he was thankful the old grump hadn't forgotten to get him a curry too. He hadn't realised just how bored he'd become of his sensible sandwiches and healthy cold cuts of late.

In a gesture which would have been alien to him a few months previously, Lachie had taken the time to match up each Indian or Chinese dish with the individual girl whom he thought would enjoy it the most based on listening to their incessant food fantasising. Archie had also had had a fruitful meeting with both a junior doctor and a friendly local vet and so now each meal had been adulterated with a strong dose of horse tranquilizer and the girls' first round of antibiotic to begin reversing the effects of any possible anthrax poisoning. Each meal with the exception of one. Chantal's carton had a private message imploring her not to taste the other dishes and to try and persuade the others to eat all of their allocated food.

He arranged to rendezvous with Chantal later and he'd also got Archie to procure a bottle of chloroform for emergency usage just in case.

Once safely off the island, Archie would carefully take the vanload of girls to the nearest large town and Lachie would have by then informed Boyle where the girls could be found safely.

Despite the inherent dangers to the girls and to Lachie's future beyond the confines of a prison cell, there had only been one thing preying on his mind. Chantal. Very soon now he would have to say goodbye forever. Or he could ask her to stay with him. They could go anywhere; he had the funds to support any lifestyle she desired.

But somehow he knew it would not be as simple. What about the father of the child? What was his relationship with Chantal beyond the obvious prior coupling? Would Chantal accept him as relationship material once they were out of danger? It all remained uncharted territory for Lachlan Maclean.

In the meantime he didn't have the time to indulge in romantic fantasies. H.K. had called him to say he'd soon have both DI Boyle and Ricky Bean on his doorstep but rather than a case of 'police and thieves' she reckoned it was more a case of personal vendetta with one a whole lot deadlier than the other. Lachie had asked her to keep tabs on them but it would be dark in an hour or so and the plan remained still to have the girls off the island just before dawn and away before anyone else could show up and get in the way.

As to the whereabouts of DC Steel, she had laughed and said not to worry too much about him.

This day couldn't get any worse Steel had thought as he'd hauled the car round another tight corner while being completely blinded by yet another arsehole who couldn't be bothered dipping from full beam. He held his bare arms out straight in the manner he'd been taught many times and noticed how white and puny they seemed, almost translucent in the pre-dusk gloom. Blood dripped from the gash above his right eye which had been inflicted, he believed, courtesy of the air-bag. Another great invention, along with Vehicle Licence Plate recognition software. He'd been nearly 100 miles along the A9 before he'd had the good sense to realise his schoolboy error and pull off onto the treacherous smaller roads. But not the sense to ameliorate his speed after leaving the faster road behind and consequently becoming airborne at a particularly vicious hairpin bend about forty miles back.

Thankfully the car had still been driveable and his injuries wouldn't be life-threatening. He really didn't want the hassle of changing cars, retrieving hidden guns and all that palaver. It couldn't be too far now and so he lowered his head and pressed on faster than ever. The thought of that sanctimonious prick Boyle laughing at him at crashing after having undertaken so many advanced driver courses only served to make him go harder still. The old git never did appreciate his driving.

It was too dark now to see anything but he kept imagining he could hear the sound of a helicopter above him although why that would be the case he couldn't imagine. He wished he could have had used the Police Scotland budget for this trip and he decided there and then the next course he ever took would be learning to fly his own helicopter. There couldn't be any fellow officer's after him at this point and no way would there be any local 'bullet-catchers' looking for a Glasgow detective all the way up here. He guessed the noise was the blood pumping in his ears. The sound of adrenaline.

But in hindsight he might have been better served by getting Boyle to send him on a course to learn the delicate art of negotiation after his less than successful telephone call with Ricky Bean.

Of course he should have held back on the location of the island until the appropriate remuneration had been agreed and it was now abundantly clear the foul-mouthed gangster didn't take too kindly to being called a poofter.

Truth hurts.

He hadn't written the deal off completely just yet but in the meantime he had decided he would endeavour to milk as much cash out of this 'gentleman-killer' toff before the boys in blue got their mitts on the case. He would never work again in this rain-infested shit-hole so he needed to grab as much as he could. *No more cock-ups though,* he couldn't afford to get to close with this guy in case he turned out to be a bit handy.

The plan had been to hit the island literally mob-handed with Rocky and his boys working alongside him. Now he was back to being on his own again. He didn't know what he would find up there but there could be no witnesses left alive and only he knew what would be at stake if he made any more mistakes. This time he would get it right.

Getting it right had been exactly what he was thinking about when he rounded the bend at ninety five miles an hour only to see two Armed Response Unit vehicles parked nose to nose across the road, their lights flashing impotently in the dark.

Chapter 41

Lachie had begun to seriously panic. Lugging the food up the island had worn him out and it had been only then he'd realised how much weaker he'd become since he first came to the island. He'd known he'd been slacking off with his exercise regime plus he'd been uncommonly fit when The Project began but despite that it had become patently obvious a darker agent was afoot this evening. He found himself praying to a God he'd often scoffed at for the safe passage of the girls and the unborn child, all of whom were at his mercy. One short year ago, if this had been a scenario in one of his violent X-box games, he would have happily firebombed the entire island and skipped off merrily into the night.

But here he was preparing to carry them carefully away as if they were the most precious treasures on the planet. Only this time most of them had virtually doubled in weight and he'd become as weak as a teenage boy after a fevered night of internet porn.

It had become very dark now and feeling strangely exposed without any camouflage make-up or fatigues, he was glad to stumble into the bunker, his heart thumping and his throat raw. He ransacked his drinks supply and downed two bottles of sickly sweet energy drink while he waited for the bank of monitors to fire up.

Two things struck him immediately. They'd started that haunting singing again although this time it seemed lighter somehow. And the screen for camera 5, the main sleeping quarters, had been de-activated. It had been a long time since Stevie had messed with any of the equipment and Lachie's first thoughts were there must have been another death. He scanned the monitors frantically without seeing any of them and his heart felt sore with grief. If it was Chantal then he didn't know if he'd have the strength to see this through.

It only took him seconds to realise they were all together and it was in the sleeping area where he could hear the singing coming from. He hefted the food-filled rucksack onto his back and limped as fast as he could through the now familiar woodland. Crashing into bushes and cursing under his breath he wasn't concerned about being heard.

If one of the girls had died then they'd all be around her like the last time. How he would get them off the island he couldn't imagine and as far as a funeral was concerned then it would be out of the question. It was too horrible to contemplate and he forced his aching thighs to push faster up the slope towards the girls.

He walked right into her sharpened spear and felt a stinging pain as the fire-hardened tip scratched his sweat drenched neck.

'Stevie! Whoa what's-'

'It's *Stephanie* to you pal!'

The tall girl flicked her wrist and Lachie felt himself suddenly unbalanced, his body making the instantaneous calculation that it would be safer to fall on his arse than have a spear embedded into a main artery.

'That's far enough.'

Lachie looked up in the gloom and he could see that although the girl was plainly terrified, she had him under control so with the spear hovering in front of his face, he made one of his better battle-field decisions. He held up his hands in mock surrender and started talking.

'Sorry!
Listen Stephanie, I don't know what is going on up there but I'm on your side, I really am, I promise.
I've got a whole pack of take-away food for you all but I'm here to tell you that you have to leave the island. Tonight! It's not safe anymore!'

He could see a tick develop on the girl's face and she kept looking nervously over her shoulder like she was either expecting some monster to come lumbering through the bushes or more like she was hiding something.

'No way, pal.
We cannae go anywhere the now, so just fuck off an' leave us alone!'

'Listen! This is serious. There's some really bad men coming here tomorrow and it's not safe for you to-'

'Not safe for *you*! That's what ye really mean right?
You're the bawbag who started a' this and now you're pure pissing yourself 'cos your gaunae get caught.'

'Yes! It's my island! But I am *not* the danger here.
You know who Chantal's dad is?'

He saw her pale face nodding in the moonlight.

'You know what he's capable of? Well he's mixed up with some crooked cops and they all want me dead but they don't care who else gets killed into the bargain. Now I'm not bothered about myself, truly, but I don't want any of you to get hurt. Especially-'

'Chantal. Aye, we ken...'

Lachie felt himself blush and despite the ridiculous situation, it wasn't an unpleasant sensation.

'Yes, well maybe, but I want *all* of you to be safe and she's the one who's going to have a baby, not my doing you understand and-'

'Ye got that right, pal. She's *having* the baby - the now!'

'What! But – she can't be! We've-'

'Well she is! Who the fuck do you think you are anyway? God Almighty? Ye cannae control everything, even if it is your island.'

'Is she alright? I mean who's-'

'Is she *alright*? She's havin' a baby! In the fuckin' woods – what do you think?'

Lachie clambered to his feet, sloughing off the rucksack in the process only to be met by the sharp end of Stevie's wrath once more.

'Where the fuck do you think you're going?'

'But I have to help! I'm army trained, maybe-'

'She disnae need your help. The girls have it a' under control. It's only me who cannae handle the blood an' stuff.'

With her admission Stevie lowered the spear and Lachie saw his opening. He snapped out his hand in the gloom and snatched the stick from the surprised girl before breaking it over his knee in one fluid moment. Stevie began to back away expecting him to lunge at her but instead he raised a placatory hand and spoke softly.

'I'm not going to harm you I promise.
You might find this hard to believe but you guys are the only family I've got and I will not let anyone hurt you, ever-'

'Aye, right! Didnae help Katster did it?'

'That's why you have to leave! The island is contam-'

'We ken a' aboot it. At least some do.
I found some of yon signs up on the ridge an' I told the older two but it 'wis Jenny who worked it oot. She's the brainy one.'

'So will you help me save the girls?'

'Aye alright, fair enough.
We're no' wanting tae go. But we ken we can't stay here forever an' so I'll help.
It'll a' depend on whit's going on wi' Chantal like so what's the idea?'

So Lachie had found himself an unlikely ally and he explained how the food should render most of the girls unconscious and Stevie agreed both she and Chantal would share a portion and let the others succumb. He had two wheelbarrows and so that would make transporting the sleeping girls twice as fast. He radioed back to a relieved Archie and made his way to the bunker to wait.

Chapter 42

The pilot carefully positioned the helicopter before gently easing her down between the two old barns as instructed. He'd been here once before he remembered but landing at night had been a different challenge and not something he'd done since being over in Helmand. Still, his diminutive passenger had paid him ten times the going rate plus she had been a lot easier on the eye than his usual clientele. In the last week he'd transported some ugly farmers and even uglier politicians but he somehow doubted this flight would ever be appearing on any official expenses claims.

He prided himself on being able to spot ex-military at a hundred paces and despite the girl being devastatingly attractive he knew he must be dealing with some kind of Special Ops situation and he also knew he could never tell his ten year old son about it no matter how much he was dying to. If pressed on the issue, he would say to people you could always tell a military person by the way they stood. Simple.

For fun, he again tried to help her with her baggage and just as when she boarded, she made it impossible for him to get his hands on the two bags and an aluminium briefcase. He smiled knowingly at her as she waved him off and decided if her case didn't carry a high-powered rifle then he'd retire there and then and start driving tractors instead.

Helen Kerr smiled her fake smile and turned away before mouthing *sexist pig* under her breath. Typical. They can't handle a woman, a successful woman, in a so-called man's world. She watched the chopper bank expertly away from the only trees in the area and swoop up and over the hill to be instantly forgotten as she re-checked her watch. She had efficiently computed Lachie's updated time-in-danger based on the reports received as they approached the landing zone and she remained satisfied the risk was minimal, especially as she had now arrived on location.

A flashlight twinkled as agreed and she breathed a sigh of relief. It was always the extraneous factors which let an operation down and she knew this old man had a lot on his plate so it had been reassuring to know he was still on point. She only needed a quick ferry and some local knowledge but everything hinged on the next phase of her mission.

Lachie didn't respond to the first message. He might as well have been on a different planet by then. The camera had been miraculously switched back on and his nose was barely a foot from his monitor as he watched the girls pass the baby from one to another. Warmly wrapped in soft fleece carefully washed the same morning, the little boy's still beetroot face shone in the candle light. The rustic setting gave the whole picture a powerful Nativity feel and as the singing rose and fell, Lachie was spellbound. He knew he shouldn't react so strongly but it was still all very new to him to feel any positive emotions and right now his heart felt swollen like it might burst. He felt so proud of Chantal and the girls and no new father could have been giddier than him right then.

The girls had propped Chantal up and surrounded her with candles. They'd taken a sun-bleached cow head and placed candles in the eye sockets and fringed the skull with wild flowers. Lachie watched in awe as the girls knelt and presented the skull to Chantal one by one as if worshipping their Queen.

That must be how they felt about her, Lachie now realised and the little boy would be their prince. Little Fee and Charlie were kneeling at her feet and even the acerbic Joolz seemed to have melted into a softer more malleable creature.

But always there remained the spectre of death and the skull reminded Lachie of the urgency of his evening mission. He had been pleased and a little surprised to see Stevie had taken on her new role with great enthusiasm and she'd reheated the exotic fare on a small slate fireplace they'd set up before the weather had become so warm.

'Come and eat this before it gets cold,' she urged the other girls. 'You sound just like oor ma' said little Charlie and they all laughed.

Lachie's receiver crackled and this time he was ready.

'It's me honey. I'm with Archie at the bothy and we're all good.
He's asking how long before you arrive?'

Lachie looked at his watch.

'Three hours if the girls all sleep as planned. Tell him I've recruited one of the girls to help which'll make it easier at the other end too.
What about our visitors? Do I still have enough time to get the girls away safely?'

'All good as I said, sweetie.
Your Scottish plod hasn't improved much since I went away. Gave them your boy on a plate. Asked them to do one simple thing – set up a road-block. Usually the general idea is to place vehicles in road to impede progress of target vehicle. Not park at a jaunty angle and allow fugitive to smash straight through a space larger enough for a proverbial bus and thereby rendering their own transportation unusable. Four out of ten – could do better.'

'So is he still a threat then?'

'Still a theoretical threat, honey, but it's me he'll be dealing with from now on so as I said before don't worry yourself about him. The other two are still on the road with your gangster ahead by several furlongs as we speak. Bait is set and it's a case of springing the trap and then deciding how many you want me to reintroduce back into the wild. Or cull.'

Lachie gulped. He felt way over his head with Ms Kerr and he didn't really know how to handle her. Sure he'd killed people recently but none of it had been planned and he wasn't sure he could murder someone in cold blood. Boyle posed no threat as far as he was concerned but he doubted if H.K. would have any additional qualms about killing an honest police officer as compared to a dishonest one.

He'd also become distinctly uneasy about the prospect of Chantal's father getting involved in the situation. He'd heard the guy was a psychopathic maniac and so was naturally terrified of the man's reputation but at the same time he didn't want to start a potential relationship with the only woman he'd ever cared about by wiping out her own father and rendering her an orphan. With any luck the cops and robbers scenario would work itself out and if this DC Steel ever appeared then he would have to get past his highly paid protector first and he didn't think much for his chances.

It was time to get ready.

Chapter 43

'Even if I felt up to moving, I wouldnae
be going.
Ye ken that, right?'

The girl glowered at him, her strong arms
enveloping the wee child and rocking him
backwards and forwards in an age-old rhythm.
He could not defend himself against such a
beautiful sight. But this had to be it – now or
never.

'And I don't want you to go. Did *you*
know that?'

Her eyes shone wet in the flickering light.

'Naw, but I sorta' hoped you'd say it,
like.'

'But you can't stay. None of us can. If
you trust me, I promise to help you and
the child. I will take the others to safety
and then I'll come back for you. We can
go somewhere, anywhere you like. You
can decide what to do after you're safe.
But you can't stay here or you'll die and
so will he.'

'An' you'll come with us? Honest?'

'I promise I will move heaven and earth
to keep you safe. But there is one other
problem – your dad knows where you are
and he's on the warpath. I don't think
he'll be so keen on our idea, do you?'

Chantal stood tall and again he marvelled
at the sheer animal intensity of her presence.
How he longed to be with her, to learn about life
with her, real life, and in turn to show her the
world beyond Garthamlow. Her voice sounded
flat and exhausted.

'Naw. He'll no' be too happy, but I
suppose he never was.
But things have changed, know what I
mean? The time's passed for him tae tell
me what I can and cannae dae.
I amn't his possession now. No' anymore.
I don't care why you did this. In a way
I'm glad it's nearly over but still it's the
best thing that's ever happened tae me
and it's a' down tae you, so it is.'

Lachie could see Archie was itching to
get going and the light was even now
brightening over the sea. He reached out
tentatively and touched her shoulder, a tiny
gesture but containing more pent-up emotion
than he'd ever experienced. He knew Chantal
somehow understood and as he made to move
off she turned sideways smiling through her
tears, showing him the sleeping baby.

307

'I will be back very soon, I promise,' he said with a certainty the young girl could not mistake. 'Be safe and wait for me here.'

Chapter 44

At last he could see the coast again and he could switch off the bastarding Sat Nav. A more annoying voice he couldn't imagine and it made him think of a funny video the boys were always pissing themselves laughing about where there were two Glaswegians in a posh hotel lift which used voice recognition software to take patrons to their chosen floor. Obviously their coarse accents were unrecognisable to the machine and the two men get more and more enraged with comic results. Of course his lads would have resolved the predicament with the more traditional remedy of extreme violence.

He'd finally got a successful mobile connection to check his youngest was safe although she had still been sleeping at such an early hour. There might be more men guarding her than the entire Royal Family protection squad right now but he wasn't taking any more chances.

Rocky knew there couldn't be any new turf war in the making but it wasn't just the crooks he worried about. These days the cops were streets ahead in venal duplicity, particularly concerning drugs money, partly the reason he had come up here on his own. The wee prick Steel had got him spooked and if there remained the slightest chance his Chantal was still in any danger then he would have to do this alone. Any fucker who crossed him before he'd got her safely home would be six feet under a stinking bog if he still had a breath in his body.

He chucked the phone down and scanned the scenery looking for any bearings. He'd made a mental note to torture the bastard who had talked him into changing mobile phone provider a few weeks ago. This new one wasn't worth a toss and the next unfortunate person who breathed a word about universal coverage would be breathing out of a plastic tube for the rest of his miserable life.

Despite his infamous success in the business of crime, in the last thirty two years he'd rarely strayed far from the confines of Greater Glasgow, so to say he might be out of his element had to be the understatement of the year. If it wasn't for the arsenal of weapons in the boot of the car he'd be for turning back.

He'd not passed another car in ages and looking at his petrol station map, he guessed the distant lump out to sea must be the fucking island he wanted but he'd already travelled at least two or three miles along the coast without seeing a single fucking boat he could purloin. No ferry either – too modern for these sheep-shagging bastards. As the road turned northwards again his heart sank. Any further and he'll be going past the ugly dump and falling off the end of the earth.

There! Jeezo! Two boats at least and a wee pier. He bounced the Range Rover off the road at speed, destroying the wooden markers planted to supposedly guide vehicles away from the treacherous marsh. He heard the loud rending of an expensive sounding hole somewhere under the car as he found one of the enormous granite boulders lurking in the muddy reeds. '*Fuck.*' He'd have get one of the boys to collect him if it all went well. But with a proper car, not one of these cumbersome boxes that keep wanting to bloody tip over every time you came to a corner.

The place looked as deserted as the moon apart from some old cottages with no lights on this early in the morning. Rocky decided they must be rustic holiday homes, if you liked that sort of thing. He could see a Sky dish on one stone built bothy although it was twice the size of any he'd ever seen before. *Nae wonder*, he growled.

But finding a boat which would work, that was all he could think about. He looked them over. One was only a poxy rowing boat but the other proved to be a real beauty. As the early morning light brightened his mood, Rocky clambered on board and gazed in admiration at the massive black engines on the bulbous rubber inflatable. He'd never been so close to one before and hadn't appreciated their sheer size and complexity.

A small wave slapped the boat and Rocky felt his confidence wobble along with his footing. The absurdity of his situation hit him just then. Here he stood. The tough guy who couldn't swim the length of himself. He could see where the ignition keys should go but the owner hadn't been kind enough to leave them handy. He searched the boat with increasing frustration as the daylight grew stronger.

Worried someone would soon wake in the holiday cottages, he made the panicked decision to take the wee wooden boat instead. How hard could it be? He'd always been touted as a strong man and now he'd have his chance to prove it once and for all. *Wait 'til the boys hear about this* he thought as he manhandled his two bags of weapons onto the boat.

Looking out across the water, he suddenly felt extremely exposed and vulnerable so he took out a shotgun and laid it close by him. A deadly comfort blanket. The island looked a long way away all of a sudden and so he thought the sooner he made a move the better. He grabbed the oars and pushed off.

He had no idea about the tides or currents and he'd never been in a rowing boat before but at first he felt rightly proud of his progress. Then he realised the boat seemed to be heading the wrong way and unless he could change direction he would drift South of the island and back onto the mainland albeit two or three miles away from where he started. He yanked harder on his right oar and to his shame and embarrassment he felt his skin tearing with the pressure. *Office hands*, he grunted with dismay. But it didn't seem to help and then he saw the front of the wee boat sticking pretty high out of the water which he guessed was making it harder to steer. The guns! It must be the weight of the guns at the back which was tipping the boat up.

He stood up gingerly and stepped over to the bags. It felt really awkward to balance and for a brief panicky moment he wondered if he should maybe let the boat drift back and either wait for the weather to calm or find someone who knew what they were doing. *Aye Ricky and how'd ye explain the fuckin' shotgun?*

He bent his legs and lifted one of the bags over towards him and stumbled. He stepped sideways to avoid losing his balance and dropped the bag at his feet. It happened in a second. The two bags were now on the same side and so was he and before he could even think what to do next, the boat had tipped sideways and he found himself underneath it and swallowing ice cold sea water, falling ever further from the light up above.

Chapter 45

What a beautiful morning Chantal
thought and the nicest one since they arrived on
the island, a lifetime ago. Typical they'd had to
endure the coldest weather and wildest winds
and now it would all be over just when full
summer had arrived. It felt very strange being
alone on the island, well *almost*. She gazed down
and smiled at the baby who was sleeping
soundly, his face still sticky with milk.

With the camp deserted the place looked
even more untidy than usual and so Chantal had
decided to practice moving about a little by
sorting things out and making the place look the
way it had before all the recent madness. She'd
never have considered tidying up her flat back
home. Would it *ever* feel like her home ever
again? But then she'd changed so much in the
last few weeks. It was only as she'd said it to the
guy, Lachie, *weird name*, that it had hit her what
a transformation this island had wrought on all
of the girls. We could do anything after this, she
decided. And it was true. There would be no
going back for any of them. It might be easier
for the two wee ones to drift back into their old
ways but she knew Stevie would never fit in
back in the depressing schemes and she could
see Sticky living here perfectly happily if it
wasn't for the anthrax.

Chantal wondered what would become of
the island after they left. Would anyone else
come here and what would they imagine had

314

been going on? She felt like some kind of custodian for the place and no way did she want people to think just because they came from a poor council estate in Glasgow it meant they lived like tinkers.

She had a million questions about what had happened here. Somehow she trusted the strange man who had watched over them. She implicitly understood that his story was intricately woven with hers and she felt comfortable he would soon share the reasons for why they had been kidnapped and taken here. For her, the simmering resentment had vanished many weeks before and she swore even Joolz had become happy living here. But whether or not it had been the right thing to do had to be another important question. Garthamlow had become a different life for her and she had even stopped thinking about what it must have been like for their families. She thought more about her mum than anyone although her memories had been vague and somehow intertwined with this place as if maybe her mum had also been here many years before.

Could it be so impossible? Who could have believed all of this? If she'd been told this would happen a year ago she'd have called for the wee yellow van for them. The truth of her disappearance remained another question she would determine to get to the bottom of after they left here and she felt confident Lachie was the kind of man who could help. Maybe after all this was over, he could help her find her mum?

She had been lost in pleasant thoughts, hazy memories of her mum and dad together and not fighting when something alerted her. She sensed danger, movement from below the camp. Someone was crashing about and getting closer. Too big to be an animal and none of the girls would have been making so much noise. Fear gripped her heart as she edged noiselessly towards her baby.

Then he appeared in front of her. A man. Ridiculous in torn suit trousers and a pink satin shirt to match his florid complexion.

'Da! What are you doing here? You're soaked through!'

Chapter 46

Despite the seriousness of the situation, Helen couldn't stop laughing. She'd come across to meet Archie and the girl, Stevie, who'd proven to be one very useful resource. In the space of two minutes she'd provided her with an accurate hand drawn layout of the island complete with details which seemed to have even surprised Lachie including pointing out several secret escape routes and shortcuts. Helen felt confident this intel would certainly be a huge help in evening up the odds if it came to the life or death stuff. And she knew in the end, it would always be about life or death.

So she'd managed to ensconce herself in a windswept slate and stone bothy Stevie had built with her bare hands. It clung resolutely to the contour of the landscape high up on the southernmost tip of the jagged ridge that ran down the left of the top half of the island which the girls called the Spine. From her position she could see the main camp where the girls used to sleep and where Chantal and the baby still rested.

To her right she could see all the way to the main Laide road which gave her plenty warning of any visitors before they even reached the coastal road. To her left sat the flattest landing beach but the height of the bothy meant she could see right down to the bathing pool and sandbank which she knew would normally be the first area of the island most newcomers would be likely to aim for. Even better, with her

317

military grade binoculars she could make out Archie's pier over at Mungasdale and over to the mighty An Teallach which the unknowing Stevie had poetically scribbled down as The Telly.

Hence the reason for her current hilarity. Helen had enjoyed the comedic spectacle of first seeing Rocky take a header off the boat and then his heroic usage of the upturned vessel as a flotation device to push it all the way to the sandbank using his little legs alone. She guessed that accounted for the way he had been walking afterwards as he gave a wonderful imitation of John Wayne before landing himself waist-deep in the biggest area of marsh on the island. It had been easy for her of course with a map to follow and the girls all had all known to avoid The Swamp.

But then she stopped laughing. She had taken some great shots of Ricky Bean and had them confirmed by Lachie who had still been racing back up the road and not so far away from the island. She'd also ID'd Gary Steel from miles away despite his limp. What is it about these guys and their limps? Mind you, she smirked, she was very experienced in making guys limp and she knew *all* the ways to do so.

Steel had confounded her initial appraisal and managed to not only evade the police but then also commandeer a workhorse Defender and she could see him currently sniffing around the few boats moored in a row where the road first meets the coast. If he did get a lift over there she'd see him all the way and it was a sea

318

journey three or four times as long as he would have needed to take if he'd known about Archie's pier.

There was no doubt Steel had proved himself tougher and more resourceful than she'd given him credit for but he wasn't why she'd stopped laughing. He'd got lucky, big deal. No, it was another incident relating to a man getting lucky which niggled away in the back of her mind. And Helen Kerr didn't believe in luck.

As he sat shirtless in the sunshine, cradling his wee grandson, Rocky Bean watched his daughter busy herself around him, fussing and pushing him out of her way and he decided he must be the luckiest bastard who ever lived. Never the most loquacious of men, he had now rendered mute by the overwhelming emotions cascading through him. At last, he thought, we've thrown off the family curse. The taunts from the other kids at the school after his dad had walked out on the family for the final time. *Where's yer Da, Ricky Bean? Been and gone, no tae be seen*! And then years later, the sudden departure of his wife, sickened and ground down by his violent lifestyle.

Having come to the island prepared to wreak death and destruction, he had instead, for the time being, been blown away by the beauty and serenity of his surroundings. He felt as if a grubby veil had been lifted from his tired eyes and he gazed at Chantal in admiration as she

319

turned his shirt on the makeshift line and checked on the hearty breakfast sizzling on the hot slate. Gone was the bored and sulky teenager he'd thought he'd known and instead he saw she'd blossomed into a strong and resourceful woman. He couldn't remember the last time he'd seen her without her face being caked in a mask of make-up, like all the other lassies at school. But now he saw her natural beauty as if for the first time and it made his heart soar.

She'd become strong too! He watched her tanned arms flexing like rusted steel rope as she tossed another batch of neatly cut logs into the fire. He couldn't even work out how the fire worked.

'What's that a' aboot hen? Where did ye learn tae-'

'Frae the school, in history an' that. But a lot was common sense.
Ye' get good at stuff quick when yer freezin' cold at night.
See this space here? We dug it out the hill. Then we lined it wi' slates tae make an oven. Then underneath we dug a wee tunnel a' the way through tae the other side, where the breeze comes in off the sea so it's like a flue of a chimney like at Gran's old hoose, remember?'

Rocky nodded and thought back to the old council house where he'd been brought up.

Riddled with damp, the only saving grace had
been the old fireplace and one of wee Ricky's
jobs had been to go and steal coal with his
brother. Some days they'd hang about near the
sharp corner where the coal lorry would enter the
first of the council schemes and bits of coal
would fall off onto the road. Fair game, he
thought. His amazing wee girl had been right.
You do get good when the only alternative is an
awful bone-numbing cold.

He saw Chantal glancing over at him and
he hoped she could see the proud look in his
eyes even if he couldn't yet find the words to
convey what he felt. For some reason he felt so
much older than when he'd last seen her and
when he looked down at his bloated white torso,
he felt so out of place. Here in this natural world,
nothing had accumulated as surplus or waste and
everything had a useful function. His daughter
seemed at home here, yet to him it felt as alien as
the bottom of the sea.

> 'So the wind whips in there and keeps the
> fire burning hot. We found this massive
> bit o' slate here and put it oan' the top,
> like, for tae make a griddle and that was
> it. Sorted.'

Rocky looked up at the roofed sleeping
area and the drainage ditches running down each
side of the camp. 'So there's no been any men
here? Ye've done aw' this yerselves, like?
Where'd ye get some o' this stuff, I cannae-'

Chantal stood stock still and glared at her father. He guessed she'd been waiting for this.

'No dad. No men. We did this. The lassies an' me. Ye'd be surprised at what blows in off the sea an' that. But aye, it was a man did *that*, right enough!' She pointed at the sleeping child, still nestled in Rocky's fleshy arms.

Rocky bowed his head for a moment and took a deep breath.

'Aye lass. Ah' ken aboot the man what did that. That's why I-'

'Well ye' can stop right there!' Chantal roared down at him and Rocky panicked for a second as the baby wrestled in his sleep before cuddling back into the warmth of his bare chest. He tried to pass the wee boy up to her as a peace offering but she lifted her hands in protest, her eyes glaring. 'The man who did that will never see-' But then he saw her stop dead in mid-sentence, her face registering the obvious shock at what she was witnessing. Rocky raised himself up to his full height, blocking all the light from the sun for a brief dark moment in a way he had done many times before, causing men to fear him. But no-one had ever seen him do this. Hot tears poured down his face.

'Why I came. Was just to say I am sorry...'

Chapter 47

The island would be in sight soon and Lachie forced himself to slow down as he checked in with first Archie and then H.K. She seemed to have unlimited pick-up from her position high on the ridge but he knew he'd be out of reception soon.

'Yes, honey. The godfather of Garthamlow, or should I say *father-in-law*? Sorry, sweetie. Out of line, I know-'

'Thank you for your concern Ms Kerr, duly noted. Can we please just stick to the plan?'

'*Affirmative*. So, Rocky's made contact and all seems fine and dandy from what I can tell up here. No gun-fire at least and no other arrivals thus far. *Over*.'

Lachie smiled, despite himself. He knew when she was gently mocking him but if he was honest he loved it. He'd learnt a little of the art of taking the mickey out of someone from listening to the girls and this had been the first time in his life he'd ever had a 'relationship' for anyone to rib him about. He also knew the 'sugar honey' routine would no doubt be all part of the show but all the same he did enjoy talking to the woman and he sometimes wondered what it would be like to be genuinely friends with an assassin like her. For some reason he would then always start thinking about praying-mantis females biting the heads off their mates after copulation.

And *was* there a genuine relationship between him and Chantal? He liked to think it might be possible and it had been something he'd been pondering for most of his journey back from Ullapool. The transfer of the sleeping girls had gone to plan without him having to use any of his bottle of chloroform which he had still affixed to his belt. Stevie had even given him an awkward hug when he left and he'd given her a wad of bank notes and a throw-away mobile so the girls would be able to let their families know they were safe. He knew she would be able to return to the island if she'd wanted to and she could also inform the police too but he instinctively knew this would never happen.

As he'd turned to head back up towards the island, a fleeting thought entered his head. He could just leave. Drive south and never look back. It would be far safer than his present course of action. He had enough money to make a new life anywhere in the world. New identity – restore to factory settings. No-one would ever be able to connect him with his grotesque failure.

But then it would have all been for nothing, wouldn't it? He *had* to go back. For the Project files at the very least. That was it. He would have to go back to rescue the files for posterity and if Chantal wanted to be with him afterwards then so much the better. Assuming he wasn't dead by then.

Archie looked at him with his customary steadfast gaze, while tapping his watch almost as if by accident. But Lachie knew better.

'Afternoon, *Hector*, nice of you to show up. I'll need to be charging ferry prices soon I'm thinking, with all this coming and going. Maybe paint a name on the front o' the rib. Lord of the Isles Two maybe!'

But Lachie had been prepared for him this time. He knew Archie's wee van was far more practical for zipping around these country roads and how all the locals scoffed at the unwieldy 'Chelsea tractors' the incomers persisted in buying in a last forlorn attempt to prove how wealthy or successful they'd been in their previous lives down south.

'Great idea Archie!
You'd be saving me a fortune if you were as cheap as Cal Mac to be honest, and if I remember, it's my rib is it not? And anyway, you'll rightly be The Lord Of Gruinard Island soon enough if you can keep to your part of the plan...'

'Aye right you are!' Archie spat into the sea. 'If I'm no deid or in the jail.'

Lachie knew Archie had only voiced what he himself had also been feeling and again he questioned the sanity of his return. He had to force a smile as he gently poked the older man. 'It wouldn't be the first time you'd faced that dilemma eh?'

It had been during their whisky-fuelled night of bonding when Archie had revealed the major part he'd played in the covert scheme of several locals and early eco-campaigners to get the whole anthrax fiasco on the media agenda.

'Aye but a long time ago!' Archie had replied glumly but he couldn't hide the smile which crossed his face at the thought of it.

Lachie remembered the story well as at the time it had seemed so at odds with the gruff no-nonsense man sat in front of him. 'It had been more the posh boffins from over at the yoonie mostly,' he'd told him over the kitchen table. 'They gave us some anthrax spores, they weren't even from about here and we put them into a wee bag of dirt and posted it back to the bastards who infected us all those years ago! Then we sent a few other bags, just wi' plain soil mind, to the Tories at their Blackpool conference and a few of the newspapers if I mind right. We called ourselves 'Operation Dark Harvest' which had been my idea,' he had said proudly, 'mostly 'cos of all the footerin' about we'd had to do in the dark for to dig up a wee bit of soil!'

Archie slowed the rib as they eased past the two incisor shaped rocks guarding the safe passage onto the sandy beach and with one hand nonchalantly reached down and retrieved a full sized shotgun from beside his feet.

'And I don't remember any of us havin' tae carry guns back then! Mind you, it's all about the kinda' company ye keep isn't it?'

Lachie tried to mask his surprise but failed miserably and his heart did another little drum roll on his rib cage. 'Where did you get-' but he knew the answer before the words were out his mouth.

'From the wee darlin' that came over before! Five feet nothing and bonnie with it but she had a bag o' guns and stuff for getting ready to start World War Three. She gave me this – *just in case* – she said! Then she told me there's another arsenal lying in four feet of water over there beyond the point. An' butter wouldn't melt in her mouth!'

Chapter 48

He left Archie down on the beach with the firm instruction that if he didn't get an hourly update from either himself or his new wee friend then he was on no account to approach the island but instead to contact the police, the proper police, over in Inverness and to give them the full truth of the situation.

H.K. had given him no further cause for alarm and they'd gone through their battle plans for the initial contact with Rocky Bean. Despite this preparation, Lachie felt very much on his own now as he walked up the familiar track, feeling more nervous and pumped than at any time since he'd first landed a lifetime ago. He glanced up at one of his observation cameras, now sitting idle and he kicked himself for not leaving the system on automatic. If anything it would leave an honest account of his final hours and hopefully prove he hadn't been the monster they'd inevitably make him out to be.

Rehearsing his lines like a nervous suitor, wondered too late if he should have brought a present, before immediately discounting this as idiotic fancy. This man is a powerful criminal mastermind and I'm the person responsible for drugging and kidnapping his pregnant daughter! *What was I thinking of*, he thought madly, cursing his own birth whilst predicting an imminent death.

Then he saw them.

It wasn't how he'd expected to see the infamous Rocky Bean and he felt instantly relieved. For a start the man seemed smaller than he'd been led to believe although the bare feet would have accounted for some of that. But the soft flabby skin of his bare upper body and the fact he was cradling a wee baby, his baby, *no not his baby*, so gently, made him wonder if this island had a strain of some miracle redemptive spores rather than the dark evil they knew about.

Chantal had positioned herself in a potential buffering position and she motioned him to keep his distance whilst they negotiated these vital few seconds. The man glowered at him for a second before looking back down at the sleeping child. Closer now, Lachie could see the power in the man's shoulders and reckoned he would have been a formidable fighter a few years back. *He might still be.* But he could see that providing he didn't fall into the grip of those meaty arms which were currently occupied holding the baby so tenderly, he knew he would be safe.

'Da' this is the man who saved me from the sea.'

Lachie nodded uncertainly and looked at Chantal before smiling with genuine affection. 'How is the baby?' he volunteered, deciding to keep the conversation on a safe topic.

'Baby's fine.' Rocky replied his deep bass echoing through them all and contrasting all the more vividly with Lachie's nervous squeak. 'Ma lassie here's told me the score an' that and for now I'm prepared to be reasonable. The other wee lassies huv' been returned safely so I believe and I understand...' The man slowed his voice and deepened it even further, 'you've no' harmed a hair on their heid's throughout this..., this *sit-u-ation...*'

Lachie attempted his most convincing smile and began to die inside, his heart pierced by the fatal flaw in his plan. He'd no idea what Chantal might have said to the man whether truth or not. Why he hadn't thought of this beforehand escaped him and so with there being an absence of conveniently placed sink-holes to swallow him up, he decided to go on instinct and what he already knew about the pragmatic and resourceful girl standing smiling at him. He wanted to kiss her right there. *No Lachie, wouldn't be wise.* So he started to talk fast instead.

> 'Yes, the girls are safe and should all have spoken with their parents by now and we just have to get ourselves away from here as soon as possible. I don't know if Chantal told you but this is my island which I recently bought but have now discovered it's contaminated with anthrax. But don't worry, I have

331

medicine for her to take, but we couldn't administer it before the baby was born in case it-'

'Whoa sonny! Slow it down will ye? Yer giving me sore ears and-'

'Sorry! Been a tough few days...'

Rocky laughed and the tension caused by Lachie's outpouring evaporated like the sea water from the new grandfather's satin shirt baking on a warm slate beside them. 'Nae shit Sherlock,' Rocky snorted amicably enough.

The pressure building from a new torrent of words that needed to be said had begun to make Lachie's eyes see little red lines like fine cracks. His aching brain felt too small to hold the vast ocean of everything he wanted to say to this girl. But first things first.

'Unfortunately, the anthrax is not our biggest problem. I'm a soldier, or I was rather and I know certain things about the police which has made them very angry with me. The normal rules don't apply here. They've killed people you probably know about and other people besides and I know they'll be perfectly happy to kill both you and me if it helps keep their stories safe. Especially you...' he nodded carefully towards Rocky.

332

'Doesn't surprise me much.
This wouldn't have anything to dae wi' a
wee scrote called Gary Steel by any
chance would it?'

'Yes! How do-'

'The wee cunt tried to blackmail me
about a' this shite a couple of days ago.
He said you'd kidnapped the lassies and
killed them. Told me you'd still be here
and then called me a fuckin' poof an'
asked me fer money!'

Rocky turned suddenly and gestured for
Chantal to take the baby. The sky had begun
clouding over but just then darkened ominously
and Lachie felt himself checking his footing, just
in case. 'Sorry for the coarse language in front o'
the wean, Chantal, but nae cunt calls me that an'
get's away wi' it. Nae cunt.'

'Dad! I dinnae want to hear words like
that neither I dae. I've no' heard those
words all summer an' that's the way I'd
like to keep it okay?'

'Aye, okay, sorry hen. Fair point, like.
So eh, *Lachie*, right? So Lachie what the
fu-, I mean how dae you think this is
going to play oot? I can normally take

care of my own business, know what I mean?'

'Oh absolutely! No question, I'm sure of it.' Lachie certainly didn't want to offend the guy's masculinity as it seemed to be a particularly raw nerve at the moment. But at the same time it offered a prime opportunity to emphasise his own authority and in a way which shouldn't rebound back on him. This was something they had planned to do if required. 'But I have the backup we *both* need right now.

Lachie stepped backwards out into the clearing and undid the red bandanna from around his neck with a theatrical flourish. He then tied it to a thin branch of birch over to the right of where they all stood and moved back towards the other two. One second later there was a whip crack and the branch snapped in two as the high velocity round tore through the air.

Rocky had instinctively ducked but soon regained his nonchalant composure.

'Jeezo! Watch the wee bairn! You've got a shooter up there?'

'Yes! Ex-army.' He beamed foolishly. He thought it best not to tell him it was a girl for now.

'Have you got a gun for me an' all? I dropped all ma' weapons in the sea on

334

the way over, plain stupidity, what can ah' say?'

'Lots! But we've got to move from here. Too exposed as you've just seen plus I've got two underground bunkers, the southernmost one which you've already walked past and it's only just back down towards the landing beach. I'd like to let Chantal and the baby shelter there until we can find this guy and sort things out once and for all.'

'Cool! Lead on. Chantal, can I help carry anything hen?'

Lachie could tell Rocky had been impressed by the show of marksmanship ship, *strange expression*, and he guessed that far from being afraid in a perilous situation like this, he was the kind of man who enjoyed the adrenalin buzz.

Once he'd pulled aside the camouflage screens he ushered Chantal down the stone steps but stopped her father at the top. It would be fitting for his Esmeralda to obtain sanctuary in his underground Notre Dame but there wouldn't be room for a second monster. Plus he definitely didn't really want Rocky to see what was going on with all the monitors and the like. He needed to keep him on-side.

'It's too cramped down there but totally bomb-proof and lockable from the inside so they'll be safe until we get back!'

'But ah' just-'

'Will a 9mm semi-automatic pistol do you? Good! Two minutes then!'

He hurriedly moved aside some of his junk and cleared a space on the bunk for Chantal to lie on. He hoped she wouldn't poke around too much as he was conscious of all the recordings and he'd not even considered the porn stuff which he'd totally forgotten about until then. He dug out a spare gun and a box of shells before cracking open his last box of treats and some chocolate he'd been saving for a special occasion.

'Sorry there's no milk for coffee but I didn't think I'd be back down here again so stay safe on the bunk and I'll be back very soon. There's a chemical loo through the back and the water is fresh to drink, more or less. Apart from deadly anthrax spores obviously.'

He laughed, trying to fake a bravery he didn't feel.

'Be careful up there...' Chantal looked up at him with a tenderness in her voice that twisted his guts. 'And look after my dad too eh? He's no' as tough as he kids on he is, ye know.'

Lachie smiled and then had an idea. 'I will, don't worry. But thanks! You've given me a good idea – me the bloody soldier too!' He dashed back down the steps and rummaged through his pile of clothes. 'Your dad is going to stand out like a sore thumb with all his exposed flesh!'

'Exposed belly you mean!' and they both laughed like nervous kids on an awkward first date, not sure what to do or say next. So he kissed her on the top of her head, noticing for the first time the smell of her hair, fresh like the sea and he silently vowed to make it back to hold her in his arms for the longest time. 'Back soon okay!'

'Here! Have this.' Lachie chucked a dark green army jersey up to Rocky as he tiptoed up the steps conscious all of a sudden of being in a battle zone and he'd got a hell of a lot more to lose these days.

'Cheers pal.' The way the man pulled the old jersey on so fast spoke volumes as to how awkward he must have been feeling and Lachie smiled. He knew more than most about social embarrassment and if there were medals to be won for how fast you could cover up a white complexion then your albino boy here would be on the top podium every time.

'What ye doin' now?' Rocky looked at him aghast as Lachie had pulled out some dark black paste and started smearing it across his face.

'It's camouflage! Here's a green one – put it on in thick stripes like I'm doing and I'll swap you the black for the green in a second.'

The big man snatched a tin and did as he was told, muttering under his breath.

'Sorry? Didn't quite catch that.'

Rocky looked around nervously as he wiped the paste across his forehead. Then he laughed quietly.

'Ah was just thinkin' if yon wee cunt Steel could see us the now, he'd have a fuckin' field day so he would!'

'Let's hope not.' Lachie glanced warily around him at the sound of the cop's name, before his brain had fully worked out what the man had said.

'Here. Should be enough. Let's swap now. But what did you mean?'

338

'Och, what the fuck. May as well tell ye, we could be deid by tea-time eh?

Way back when we were teenagers my brothers an' a few pals had one of oor' first bevy sessions after ma' dad fucked off like, and we all had a shot of the old dear's make up and fucking dresses and stuff. Pure blootered we were, havin' a good laugh but one of the lads had a fuckin' Kodak Instamatic intae the bargain.

So tae cut a lang story short, some o' these photos turned up years later like the one wi' me and ma' brother Neil sittin' up in fuckin' bed like a couple o' pantomime dames.

We'd have given the Ugly Sister's a fuckin' run for their money! It wisnae' a big deal at the time, like, as we'd always shared a bed, ye know, head tae toe. It was a normal thing back in those days.'

Lachie felt the air grow colder as a two piercing eyes rooted him to the spot.

'See but by then Neilly had died wi' the cancer an' that, so he couldnae defend himself and some cunts put oot' the story he was a poofter. And me an' all intae the bargain. An' that's what yer cunt Gary Steel tried tae lay on me the other day. That's why he's got tae die...'

Chapter 49

He's got to die, she had decided.

A lifetime of resentment boiled in her veins as she watched the men move cautiously through the edge of the forest straight towards her. Neither man had been being particularly adept at finding cover and Helen had trained her laser-sighted crosshairs on one forehead for long enough to have emptied an entire magazine through his skull without making more than a tiny hole. About the width of a biro, she thought. She's killed a man with less than a plastic pen before.

I'm a professional, she repeated back to herself. She knew this had always been her problem. She was better than the rest and that's what they paid her for. It had been her mantra, what had kept her going when the sexist pigs had written her off, first in the army then as an entrepreneur and now as a private contractor. But she'd proved them all wrong. Until now maybe. So if she was going to start popping people at the slightest whim then she might as well hand in her gun right now. A little voice inside her head whispered, *but isn't that what you really want to do?*

Question. Would she have taken on this contract if she'd known any of the players beforehand? Her first instinct was to say of course she wouldn't. What she would have done instead would have been to kill him herself, a lingering and pain death. But then she'd be as bad as the people she usually killed. Or sometimes, if this was the time to be brutally honest, as bad as the people who *paid* her to kill the others.

When she had first started out it had been her policy not to question the motives or the rights and wrongs of a contract. All she had to consider was the quickest and most effective method of fulfilling the terms of the contract in such a way that left the customer delighted and with no danger she could ever be implicated.

It had worked out fine for a year or two but as she became a more prominent player in the international assassin industry, she'd found her lens had become more and more blurred and it had only been the contract before this one where she'd had to politely decline for the first time in her career. It had been for the CIA, not so they'd told her in so many words, and she'd been instructed to kill a rogue intelligence agent who'd gone viral.

She'd rationalised her decision to forgo the healthy fee by telling herself she'd vowed never to work for a government agency and particularly with the Americans she'd always be looking over her shoulder for the rest of her days.

But the real reason had been was she simple didn't agree the hit should ever happen. This had left her with an unexpected space in her schedule and so this easy private matter on home soil had seemed like the perfect stop-gap. Plus, if the media reports were to be trusted, the American agent was still alive and causing huge amounts of trouble around the globe making it perfectly obvious no other contractor had taken the job either and so she'd felt vindicated. Until now.

She scanned the vista below, safe in the knowledge nothing could escape her notice from up there on the ridge. The clouds were racing across the island and the sun had now risen above and behind Stevie's bothy making her job even easier. Not that it would be difficult to spot these lumbering bears, even without binoculars or rifle sights. She saw a quick reflection and hunkered down again to get her range exactly right. She again placed a tiny red bead on a man's forehead without his permission and thought more about the emotional journey she'd just made up here in this eagle's nest.

Because she'd totally shocked herself by coming to the conclusion she didn't want this man dead after all. Not particularly because he'd impressed her with any redeeming traits although she had seen something she'd liked and it had been something she'd missed a lot over the years but had never told anyone. Compassion. Apart from that, she had become well versed in the finality of her profession.

Often she'd killed people who on reflection might have gone on to remedy their past misdeeds and overcome their associations.

If she killed this man today then there were certain things in her life that would or could never happen. People would be affected by her actions. The people she cared about more than anyone else on the planet. She decided in the end she didn't have the right to end this person's life.

Suddenly she saw movement. Multiple targets. *This is getting interesting.* All personal thoughts became secondary at that moment. She knew she couldn't allow herself to soften towards anyone down below her. It was a fluid situation and she had to be ready to take the shot no matter what. She blinked once then closed her left eye, knowing her next act would influence the rest of her life.

Chapter 50

Steel winced in agony. He'd made only the smallest of movements this time yet the pain had been almost unbearable. He guessed his right leg had probably been broken above the ankle and he couldn't put any pressure on the foot without lightning bolts arcing up through his body. How he'd get back over to the mainland without help he couldn't imagine.

Killing the young boat lad had been a tactical error but he couldn't have allowed him to cross back over and alert the authorities and there'd been zero chance he'd bought Steel's garbled story. No, there was no doubt he had dropped himself into some serious trouble this time, but he'd escaped from difficult situations before and all he had to do was eliminate the toff and Rocky Bean and anyone else who got in his way. Then he'd have time to sort this out.

There was blood everywhere, which wasn't helping. He must have hurt his head in his third crash of the day and there had been no worries about a fucking airbag in the old Land Rover, he'd have been safer crashing in a cast iron roasting dish. He hadn't had the strength to push hard enough on the brake pedal and consequently the car had tried to bury itself into the thickly-cushioned heather hillside which had undoubtedly been the only thing which had saved his life.

And now he needed to get up off the ground, to pull himself higher up this tree but his hands were slick with his own blood and every other part of him seemed to be in the way with branches digging into his aching flesh at every opportunity. Steel had never considered himself an athlete, unless you counted snooker, but he would have thought he could have hauled himself up with his upper body strength alone. He guessed he must have pulled a muscle in his side when he whacked the lad with the oar and it felt as if the devil himself was pushing a knitting needle under his shoulder blade and piercing his black heart. He'd nearly shot himself hauling the rifle up behind him and he could see it being commandeered far better as a walking stick for the trek back to the boat.

He'd made the decision to get as high as possible because of his leg. He had to keep walking to a minimum. It made sense for a number of other reasons. He didn't know the island but he knew enough to figure that he would catch sight of them at some juncture and as long as he didn't pass out with the pain, he'd get his chance. The sun would be in his eyes when he got higher up the tree which wouldn't help him for now but he knew he was a good shot and they wouldn't be expecting such a bold move. His only other worry had been if they'd passed him along some other track and he'd be found here months from now, picked clean by crows.

At last he'd fought clear of the worst of it and he tried to make sense of what he was looking at. It should be straightforward enough he decided. They had to be in the clump of trees ahead of him as the rest of the island he could see was either scrub or marsh land apart from a high cliff which he'd never be able to climb.

Wait! He saw something move. Balancing precariously on one elbow he dragged up his binoculars and peered into the trees. He could have sworn he'd seen something. It had looked like a bare back and arms, pasty white like a marshmallow fallen onto the dirt at a barbeque. Like his own flesh would be like. A city boy. Could it have been them? Must be.

Again... this time, he saw an indistinct movement but in the end it had been the deep murmur of voices which drew his eye. He'd got their range now and so next time it would be quicker for him to locate the source. He saw two men, covered with dark mud or something and he guessed they'd just emerged from some secret lair in the trees. They were walking straight towards him and he'd never get a better chance. He rubbed his face roughly across his left arm, wiping the sweat and blood from his eyes before awkwardly manoeuvring the rifle up to his right shoulder.

He found them easily. Not knowing or even caring which one was which he focused on the first head and squeezed the trigger.

Chapter 51

Boyle put the phone back in his pocket and let out a long sigh of relief. It had been Marie. She'd had a call from Jenny and she was safe and unharmed like the guy had promised. *Come home Jim*, she had said. Home. He knew she'd been talking about *their* home, the one they'd shared for all those years. He felt somehow this whole ridiculous business had brought them back together again, as a family, as a couple.

He looked out towards the island, where who knows what had occurred, and he felt sorely conflicted. Part of him wanted to jump back into the safety and warmth of his car and race back down the road to intercept the police liaison vehicles who'd be ferrying the girls on the last leg of their journey back to Garthamlow. To take his daughter into his arms and tell her how much he loved her.

But there would be time for everything later. First he would find this guy and wrap his arms around his neck in an altogether different fashion. Safe return or not, there would be no way Boyle could allow him to walk away from this.

He'd seen the abandoned Range Rover and a quick ANPR check had revealed it to belong to one of Rocky's associates. *So he was here too*. Were the pair of them in this together?

He walked up towards some converted farm buildings when he heard the unmistakable

347

sound of a gunshot echoing across the water, abruptly followed by another. Boyle dropped to his knees and looked around him before clumsily standing back up and brushing his coat as if he'd dropped a crumb as an angry looking old crofter guy came charging out of the farthest building.

'D'ye hear that?' The man shouted accusingly. 'Was it *you* they were shooting at then?'

Boyle felt stupid and shook his head mutely as he felt his phone go off. He held up his hand, glad for a moment to think. 'I'll be with you shortly' he mouthed.

'Boyle. Who's this?'

'Never mind who I am.
Find Archie the boatman and tell him to stay put. Got it?'

'But, how will-'

The line went dead. It had been a woman. A young woman he would have said, maybe Scottish but more West End than Gallowgate for sure.
He saw the old man was still staring angrily at him as if waiting for him to explain himself. Boyle couldn't think of anything else to say.

'I'm looking for Archie the boatman!
Any idea where I might find him?'

This didn't help the man's demeanour
one bit. He spun around in a circle and stamped
a boot hard on the grassy machair.

'Archie the boat...! The cheek o' it! Who
were you speaking with?'

Boyle stepped back, his frustration
spilling out despite his best efforts.

'Steady pal! I've no fuckin' idea, okay.
Are you Archie by any chance?
My name is Boyle, Detective Inspector
Jim Boyle.'

'Aye, is that a fact pal? Well good luck to
you!'

Boyle watched the man turn and storm
off back to his croft. If this was indeed the
famous Archie then he'd have to get him to
cooperate and there was no way he could get
over to the island without him. He rummaged in
his pockets for a cigarette before remembering
he'd finished the packet on the drive up *and* he'd
vowed to stop for good as long as wee Jenny
would be found safe and sound.
He cursed out loud but didn't feel any
better. 'Bastard! That's put the tin lid on it!' For
some reason he thought of Gary Steel and he

349

wondered what had happened to him and if he was lying dead in a remote bog as his colleagues had thought. They needed answers and he more than anyone had both the reason and opportunity to find out what was going on here.

He dropped his head and trudged over to the stone building and rapped hard on the blue wooden door. Barely a second had passed when the door was wrenched open and again those blazing eyes were directed at him. But this time he had on an oilskin jacket and he held an enormous twelve bore shotgun in his hands.

'Aye I'm still here! Nae need to waken the dead!
Come away in, but be quick for I'm just heading out.'

'Cheers. All I know is it was a woman's voice and she told me to find Archie and for the two of us to stay put. Does that mean anything to you?'

Boyle felt himself force a cheery smile as he scanned the tidy room looking to see if the old man had any fags around the place.

'Aye well, *Detective*, ye've no doubt guessed who I am. And I'll tell you straight, there's no chance of me staying put if my pal is in danger wi' all these loonies running around over there wi' guns!'

Boyle saw a packet of tobacco and smiled a real smile this time. 'I hoped you'd say that.'

Boyle didn't do boats, a fact he'd conveniently forgotten until he stepped on to the wooden boards and felt his stomach lurch. Grasping for anything immovable to hold on to he sank weakly to his knees as Archie fired up the two massive engines and unleashed their raw power. He'd never experienced anything like the noise and it reminded him of when he'd taken the family to an air show down at Prestwick when John had still been at primary school. It hadn't been an unmitigated success. The supposed highlight of the afternoon was supposed to be when they were buzzed by a Vulcan bomber which had only made Marie feel sick and wee John had burst into floods of tears.

He understood now exactly how they must have felt as he clung tightly to ropes looped along the sides of the boat, his body buffeted by the constant rise and fall of the floor. It seemed like the huge rib was determined to leave the water entirely as the front rose up like an angry whale desperate just once to slip its weighty burden and take to the skies.

Although conversation would be impossible with the ear-splitting racket from the engines, Boyle still carefully edged his way along the boat to get closer to the man piloting the black missile with an implacable determination. Surprise couldn't obviously be part of the plan and Boyle desperately hoped the boat would slow down enough so he could attempt to find out what was going on. As far as rolling a cigarette was concerned he might as well have chucked the tobacco pouch in the sea.

Thankfully the voyage was as brief as it was terrifying and the prow of the rib lowered sufficiently so Boyle could see the island and a small stretch of white sand where he prayed they would soon land. But Archie seemed to have other ideas. Boyle saw him looking over towards the direction they had come from, scanning with an impressive pair of binoculars and barking into a cumbersome radio telephone of the like Boyle had only ever seen in films.

'Right, get oot' here!' Archie shouted at him over the burbling of the idling engines. Boyle stared back in horror, the water being at least three feet deep still.

'But? Can't we go in a wee bit further?' he asked.

'Naw! There's no time.' Archie leant over and grabbed Boyle on the shoulder pulling him roughly towards him.

'Now listen good. See the wee track coming straight up from the beach? Right, then you'll need tae follow it up-' He saw the look of shock on the policeman's face.

'Aye that's right! I'm no' going with you the now. But listen and you'll be fine!

See yon track, well go up it until ye' see a hidden bunker, well it's no' hidden anymore, an' you're the Detective after all! At the bunker, take the left hand track and keep going 'til ye find a pal o' yours about a hundred yards along.
It's up tae you what ye want to dae after ye get there!'

Archie inched a little closer and gestured for Boyle to get out. 'And, here-' he shoved a revolver into Boyle's hand, 'you might need this too!'

Wondering what the hell he'd got himself into, Boyle squelched his way up the beach and found the track easily enough. It was obviously a well used path and he felt cautiously optimistic about not getting lost forever as he'd initially feared. Who or what he was going to find occupied all his attention and so he stumbled onto the site of the bunker far earlier than he'd imagined. Archie had been correct about the casually strewn screens of woven bushes and branches not being hard to spot although he would never have had the imagination to think they were covering an underground bunker. What would he find in there? Resisting the strong temptation to investigate further, he pressed on. He'd hopefully find out soon enough.

He could see what appeared to be three distinct paths leading off from where he stood, with the middle and right hand ones being more

354

worn down and substantial. He'd been on a steady incline ever since he'd left the beach and although it hadn't seemed very obvious mainly because his mind had been on other matters, he could feel his heart beating faster with the exertion and he realised he'd become short of breath.

The left hand track looked wilder and more uphill but it had been the one Archie had instructed him to take. *Par for the course,* he muttered. But he somehow trusted the old man and the last thing he wanted was to get lost. He crouched down nervously as he heard a low animal rumbling close by and then laughed as he realised it had been his own hungry stomach. It seemed like a lifetime ago when he'd wolfed down a plastic roll and sausage from one of those spooky burger vans in the middle of nowhere. *How do they make money?*

Decision time. He went left, ducking under a lethal spray of bramble and watching his footing as the incline increased and the width of the path decreased. Someone else must have recently cut themselves on the vicious bramble thorns as he had begun to notice blood smeared at hand height at several points. *Who's the detective now,* he thought smugly.

What he encountered next took what little breath he had out of him entirely and he felt his legs crumple beneath him as he sank to his knees. It was Gary Steel.

It looked as if Gary had been crucified except in an upside down position. And what the hell had happened to his leg? Boyle saw the white gristle of bone sticking out, and as he heard the buzzing of flies he knew what was coming next as he knelt forward and vomited the disgusting remnants of his wholly inadequate last meal.

Professional experience deemed he must reach up and ascertain if Steel might still be alive but it had been no surprise to Boyle when he couldn't locate a pulse. He forced himself to look more closely at the disfigured corpse of his former partner. Then the true cause of death became obvious. Steel's face had been so encrusted with blood, of both the dirty black vintage and a little of the fresher claret variety, it had taken him a few moments to notice he'd been shot in the middle of his forehead, a neat high velocity round which hadn't departed his skull with the same clinical precision as it had arrived.

Boyle had taken a couple of firearms courses, much against his will, but mercifully his eyesight had been sub-par for any serious weapons training. But he knew the handiwork of a full metal jacket round, the preferred ballistic weapon of choice for professional shooters; quiet, accurate and designed to kill. Despite their prickly relationship, Boyle had been genuinely fond of the lad and as he looked up at the mutilated body he could now see numerous other injuries and he wondered with a shiver if perhaps Steel had been tortured before he died. If someone had told Boyle the man had fallen out of an aircraft then he wouldn't have been too surprised notwithstanding the cranial ventilation.

Hating himself for doing it, Boyle reached into his jacket and retrieved his phone before snapping a couple of quick shots. That's when he noticed how badly his hands were shaking. No matter what madness Steel had got wrapped up in, Boyle vowed someone would pay for this depravity. He knew the physical evidence would be severely compromised by the time the white suits got up here and so he forced himself to take a few more photos while trying not to look too closely.

Swearing under his breath, he checked over his handgun to make sure he could use the damned thing and set off further up the path to confront an enemy who now seemed to be more evil and ruthless than he'd given them credit for. So he'd become a slower, quieter but angrier man who tiptoed deeper into the heart of the forest. So much quieter in fact that he walked right in on several men in army camouflage standing in a makeshift clearing.

'Jeezo! What the fuck are-' was all Boyle took in before a huge black fist came out of no-where and then the lights went out.

Chapter 53

'Bloody hell! Is he who I think he is?' As
Rocky rubbed his hand, Lachie stepped over and
looked down at the man who he'd been taunting
for so many weeks. Limp and out of condition,
the detective made even Rocky look fairly
healthy in comparison.

'Aye! Fucking DI Jim Boyle, the bastard.'
Rocky swung a vicious kick into the
unconscious body at his feet then pulled his foot
back to repeat the action when Lachie reached
over and grabbed him. It would be the first real
test of who thought who was in charge.

'Quiet!' Lachie hissed, his mouth a thin
red snarl which seemed to tear his blackened
face in half. 'There's time for that later. Now
pick him up and let's get moving!'

'Aye, fine!' the other man muttered
angrily, handing Lachie his weapon before
bending down to grab Boyle around the
shoulders 'but if you'd half a notion o' the grief
this prick has given me over-'

Crack!

The bullet missed the back of Rocky's
head by inches and ricocheted off a granite
boulder sending both men diving for cover, just
as Boyle was coming around.

'Stay still! Lachie's hand pointed
accusingly at both Rocky and Jim who froze in
fear. 'That bullet was meant for you Rocky and
if you hadn't bent over you'd be minus a head
right now. And it was no air-rifle I can tell you!'

They both knew how lucky Rocky had been. The echo of the gunshot still rang in their ears and without being asked further, the Glasgow crime boss grabbed the Detective Inspector, pulling him away from the more exposed centre of the clearing, more for a physical shield than anything else, he would maintain later.

'So it wisnae part of yer plan then? Tae shoot me?' Rocky asked.

Lachie put his right forefinger to his mouth and glared at the two men before shaking his head and gesturing towards the lower slopes of the woods.

'No it bloody wasn't and I don't understand what the hell's going on! We've got to get into cover, the bullet came from the right direction I'm positive but it sounded different to the earlier rounds. She'll have an arsenal of guns but why would she want to kill you? First we've got to get to safety and that's our main priority right now.'

'She?' Rocky growled.

'It's a long story,' Lachie glanced down at a still woozy looking Boyle.

'Can you walk?'

Boyle rubbed his face and nodded quietly before something occurred to him and his head darted around madly. He lifted a hand almost as if to ask to speak except he was waving like a drunk man and then pointing back in the direction he'd come. 'But, that was a gunshot right? I've already found a body a few yards further back there. My partner, Gary Steel.'

Lachie and Boyle both jumped at this. 'Steel's dead?' Lachie asked and Rocky just smiled. 'Cunt deserved all he got, saved me the bother.'

'It *must* have been H.K. then,' Lachie spoke his thoughts aloud as if sharing them might help put some sense into what he was saying. 'Then why did she try and kill you? Wait a damn minute! Of course it wasn't her. But then who?'

Lachie had too many pieces to fit on his board game all of a sudden and this had most definitely not been part of their strategy as far as he understood it. They needed to get to a place of safety and contact Helen Kerr. Then it hit him. Chantal and the baby! They must be in danger. He whipped round and looked at Rocky whose wide eyes told him he'd had the same thoughts.

'We have to move! Now!' Lachie jumped up into a crouch and punched Boyle hard on the shoulder. The man hardly reacted.

'You're not in a fit state to keep up with us, sorry my friend. Stay in the shadows and follow along as best you can. Rocky! We go *now*!'

The two men ran back down the track towards Lachie's south bunker, two men from different worlds, but united in a common goal. It was only minutes away, Lachie reasoned with himself. The bunker was one of the safest places on the island wasn't it? Wild thoughts went through his mind. Could this Steel have got to them? Or the people who killed him assuming it wasn't Helen Kerr? But she had to be the one! He'd given her carte blanche to take out anyone who was a threat to him, Chantal or Archie, no questions and no recriminations. But Rocky? Why would she have perceived him as a danger?

There ahead, he could see the clearing with the hidden entrance area which looked so totally obvious now, like it had been trampled by a herd of wildebeest. They were getting closer now, running as fast as the terrain would allow. He panicked when he saw the rhododendron screens had been pulled aside and quite different to the way he'd left it. Chantal would never have left of her own volition, not with the baby. Someone had found them!

Feeling sick, Lachie sprinted the last few feet and as a hail of automatic fire strafed the flattened grass only inches in front he tripped falling flat on his face with Rocky tumbling on top of him. Elbowing him off, Lachie stared down in horror at the bullet-torn earth then turned in panic. A voice boomed down at them.

> 'Nobody move!
> Hands on your heads.
> Now!'

Lachie raised his hands in mock surrender, using them to shield his eyes from the bright sunlight. He could see a tall figure on a small escarpment about twenty feet below the main ridge line and he was amazed he'd never noticed it before. Funny the things you think about just before you die was all that went through his mind as he saw the man raise a weapon.

A rustling noise from his left made Lachie turn and he saw DI Boyle stagger out into the clearing shouting rabidly, 'Stop! No!'

Lachie tried to swing round and stop the man from committing suicide just as a fresh volley ripped up the ground between the two of them and he saw Boyle fall to the ground. A wave of hopeless despair washed over him as he realised the inescapable truth. They would be next.

He looked up at the black outline of the man and the towering rock and it reminded him of a massive cathedral. So this would be his Notre Dame and he had been another monster who'd failed to protect his love. He knelt defeated as Rocky steadily edged towards the trees, both men still staring back up hopelessly at their attacker. Their executioner.

The sun still dazzled painfully but through his half shut eyes Lachie saw something happen, a shadow moving fast on the high ridge way above the man and then something large and round seemed to fall out of the sky and hit him directly on the head. The man crumpled and remained still.

Still not fully understanding what he'd witnessed, Lachie felt himself being pulled up roughly. The two men stood leaning against each other in silent awe as they squinted up at their beautiful warrior princess silhouetted against the blue sky, her strong arms waving down at them like a mighty statue come to life. Behind her came the black shape of a smaller figure cradling a baby and Lachie thought he saw the head dip in a cautious nod.

Chapter 54

Boyle woke up coughing and cold with a headache bad enough to have brought down a buffalo. He had some kind of cloth tied across his face and he clawed at in panic. Someone had tied a red bandanna across his mouth and nose and it smelt horrible. He didn't drink alcohol but there lying beside him on the grass sat the evidence for all to see. He shivered in horror. For an awful moment he thought he'd somehow been on a terrible bender and this had all been a hideous alcohol fuelled nightmare. He picked up the brown bottle – *chloroform*. His stomach convulsed and he couldn't believe that there could have been anything left to throw up.

It was a minute or two before the cramping in his guts had ceased and then he pulled himself onto his knees, hauling at some long grass to wipe his face. He looked around cautiously then stood up holding on to a nearby tree, his entire body shaking. He tried to piece together what had happened before he'd passed out. Or had he been knocked out? Boyle looked back down at the bottle, unsure of anything, even his own mind. Gripped with a sudden fear, he fumbled under his jacket for his phone. Still there! He punched the screen, instinctively calling Marie. No reception. *Bastard!* But his anger gave him renewed energy and he pushed off the tree in the direction of where the shots had come from.

There were so many questions and so much to understand he struggled to make sense of what had happened. He decided if someone had wanted him dead then he'd not be breathing and so whoever had been with Rocky couldn't be considered an immediate threat. But the other shooter mustn't have been after him either. So had all of this madness been a turf war over drugs as Steel had said in the first place? Images of the blood-splattered detective streamed through his mind and he stopped for a moment. He felt drained. He looked up at where he intended to go and saw it was going to be hard work. He turned and looked back downwards, amazed at how much height he'd made.

Then he saw the smoke. Why hadn't he noticed it down there? Thick black smoke poured out of where he guessed the bunker must have been. He scanned the rest of the island and saw more smoke, less dense, drifting over the highest point of the ridge moving faster on the high winds. Boyle growled and spat into the heather. *Burning the evidence.*

He looked up ahead, trying to decide whether there would be any point in going further without back-up. The chickens had flown the coop by now he guessed and he doubted whether he'd ever find out the identity of the mysterious kidnapper from anything on the island. Had he been the man with Rocky? But what had been the connection? He realised he'd possibly saved their lives, however clumsily. But for how long? Would he stumble across more bodies before this day was done?

Boyle thought about his blood splattered partner and felt suddenly weary. Time to head for home he decided and his spirits lifted at the promise of a family reconciliation later. He made to turn back just as something caught his eye up ahead. A glint of gold was it? He squeezed his eyes together and his blood chilled as he saw what seemed to be a watch. It looked like a gold watch attached to an outstretched black hand.

Shit! It might be someone still alive! He'd perhaps get some straight answers and be able to tick off a few boxes to keep Baxter happy. He figured he had to be due some kind of break by this point. Boyle desperately summoned the energy to pull himself up the last twenty feet up the escarpment. He found it tough going in his weary state and so much steeper than it had looked. His selfish thoughts about tying up the case turned to abject panic about what he'd do when he got there and how he'd ever be able to bring an injured party back down on his own.

He needn't have worried. He thanked the gods his stomach had been empty when he arrived at the body. Virtually unrecognisable as a human being were it not for the outspread arms, the body had been hit from above by a sizeable boulder that still lay partially squashing the pulped remains. From the mangled rifle it looked like this had been the person shooting at them and the memories started arranging themselves in the right order.

He started to push the stone off the body then thought better of it. He hadn't been required to call on too many years of professional experience to work out it had to be a man and then he saw the blood soaked wallet lying a few feet away and came to the thankful conclusion that a forensic analysis would not be necessary to determine the killer's identity. It seemed likely someone else had also made the same connection but had still left this evidence for him to find.

Flipping open the wallet with the end of his pen, he stared in horror and disbelief at the photo identification inside. It was a standard police ID photo. Staring back at him was a fresher faced version of his colleague, Detective Chief Inspector Derek Nimmo.

Chapter 55

Lachie smiled across at the new Lord of Gruinard Island as he expertly piloted them safely back to the mainland. The rib had lost much of its earlier aggression and cruised smoothly and Lachie didn't see any major issues with that. He could barely make out the first signs of smoke from the island and it would be an hour at least before DI Boyle awoke and then Archie had reluctantly promised he would go back over and pick him up later in the day.

Chantal and Helen had been smirking like two mischievous school girls. Right now they were quietly singing an old Annie Lennox song, the one about sisters doing it for themselves, in a wholly unsuccessful attempt to get the baby to sleep.

Lachie had to turn aside and laugh every time he looked at the stunned look on Rocky's face. Both he and Helen had been frantically whispering all the way down to the boat and then out of the blue Lachie saw the big man make what looked like an unprovoked lunge for Helen. Thinking for an awful moment he was going to try and hit her he suddenly realised with amusement that he was trying to give her a bear hug.

The far more experienced fighter in her enabled Helen to easily evade Rocky's clumsy advances and then to everyone's shock she pulled Archie's shotgun on him and everyone stopped still.

'Been enough death today, honey, don't you think?
Let's just leave it at birthday cards for a while eh?'

Epilogue

Boyle sat on the comfortable leather seat and scratched his head in amazement. What was it they said about time speeding up as you got older? More like speeding up then slamming the engine into reverse and running back over you a second time. It had been exactly ten years since the girls had left the island but in some ways it seemed more like ten minutes.

It was late morning, almost lunchtime and yet the crowds were still streaming into the art gallery, his favourite place in the entire world. The place had taken on a new lease of life in the last couple of years, newly invigorated by a healthy flow of cash from a publicity-adverse arts trust and of course the arrival of Picasso's famous Guernica, the first time it had ever left Spain. It made him immensely proud to think that much of this success had been due to the negotiating skills of his remarkable daughter Jenny who'd been appointed curator of the Burrell Collection only two years after graduating from Glasgow School of Art.

He looked over at her, busy talking as ever. Of course she preferred to be known as 'Cat' these days and moved in entirely different circles from him most of the time. He remembered how acutely embarrassed she'd been when he'd enrolled himself as a mature student and sat himself down beside her in the canteen one lunch-time.

Now he had his own art degree but it hadn't helped him one bit. He still couldn't understand her half the time. Just this morning he'd been admiring the famous mural which had transformed the fortunes of the gallery. Jenny had crashed down beside him and tossed a verbal grenade at him which he had been puzzling over for the last few hours.

'Dad?
Don't you think it's a funny coincidence that Guernica is an eight letter word which starts with a 'G' just like Gruinard?'

'Never thought about it love.'

'And they both have a horrible past associated with some of the worst aspects of mankind's war-like nature, our heart of darkness and everything?'

'Go on.'

'And yet both of these things have had such a positive and transformational effect on my life. Weird huh?'

But he would always be grateful they could still spend lots of time sitting here side by side, gazing at the art work, as they'd begun to

371

do shortly before the island had irrevocably changed their lives. And Jenny had been right; Gruinard had somehow changed them all for the better too.

It had been a fiasco for a few months for Boyle and Baxter to sort out. They'd easily pieced together the situation at the Bottoms Up once they'd matched up Nimmo's DNA and so the relationship between him and Steel had become obvious. But they had never made any headway on the true identity of the mysterious kidnapper. The 'army toff' idea had been shelved after Boyle had found reams of irrefutable data proving the guy was on the other side of the world throughout the whole episode.

The crime levels in Glasgow had miraculously plummeted, which the police attributed due to the sudden disappearance of Rocky Bean and rumours of an invincible vigilante still circulated with an inevitable predictability or when the football season was over and there was little else happening in the Not So Mean City.

Not that this had any bearing on Boyle since he'd soaked up as many plaudits as was decently possible before taking early retirement and devoting his time to his family and art.

The girls had closed ranks on the identity of 'the islander' as they called him. The police had found the body of the wee girl but it had seemed as if she'd died of natural causes as the girls had maintained. No other bodies had been recovered and despite wild theories and speculation, no cogent reasons for the abduction to Gruinard had been filed in any police reports to date. Even Jenny had been fiercely protective of her memories of her time on Gruinard and Boyle had eventually put aside the policeman and instead resigned himself to the far more pleasant role of doting father and if she ever brought up the subject of the island then he would listen with only a vague interest.

He sat and looked across proudly at his daughter as she pointed out the finer aspects of a painting to her bronzed and stunning friend. He knew Chantal would never come over and speak to him but she'd acknowledged him with a wink as she'd bowled in earlier with her two youngest kids in tow. Married for about eight years or so, she'd never returned to live in Glasgow. But she'd sent Jenny a postcard from just about every place on the planet worth visiting, each one occupying a place of honour on her bedroom wall with Marie being forbidden to move them even to redecorate her room.

Every year they all got together and had a party. But he'd been informed tonight was going be their very last. They'd all decided it was time for them to move on. From what he'd gleaned from his daughter over the last few years, it seemed they'd each blossomed from their shared experience. Boyle was convinced of this although he couldn't put a finger on exactly why.

He slapped his leg and decided it was time for him to move as well. He'd been about to stand up when he noticed a wee boy standing in front of him looking furtive. He could only have been about seven years old and he held out an envelope.

'Excuse me mister, but are you called Mister Boyle?'

Jim laughed and immediately glanced about the gallery to see who could be trying to wind him up. He saw Jenny still surrounded over on the far side of the huge hall and so he turned back to the boy. He was plainly nervous and his shaking arm was making the envelope quiver.
But he couldn't help himself from having a little sport with the boy. He lifted his eyebrows into his best interrogative stare.

'Who's asking?'

Confusion broke out across the pale face.

'Me sir. I mean, not me. Um.., if you're him then this is for you!'

The envelope was thrust with a more hopeful urgency now. Maintaining his serious tone with great difficulty, Boyle asked the lad to tell him exactly who had given him the envelope as interfering with the mail of another was a serious offence.

'Don't know, mister. He was a big boy!
Maybe a P7, I think, in a baseball jacket.
He gave me a ten pound note and said to
give this to you.'

The boy practically threw it at him so
Boyle accepted the envelope before
commanding him to wait until it was opened.
'I'll give you another tenner if you stand right
there for a wee minute' he offered, wondering at
the same time why he was even interested.

Inside the envelope he found a cheap
postcard and ignoring the usual scenic vista
tourist photo he turned it over, realising for some
daft reason he'd been holding his breath. It had a
stick-on label with a block of computer-printed
text confirming an 8pm restaurant reservation for
one of the swankiest venues in the city, a place
so expensive he'd never been inside ever in his
life.

Boyle read it then did a second take. The
booking for later was in the name of a Mr and
Mrs James Boyle *plus one guest*. He flipped the
card over again and looked more closely at the
garishly coloured photograph. It was of an island.
His brain jangled as he read the bright red text
twice over.

Splashed diagonally across the photo
were four words.

Greetings From The Falklands!

THE END

Also by Alex Breck

The Ridge Walker Thrillers

He Who Pays The Piper
The Piper's Lament
The Piper's Promise
The Loss Report
No Place To Hide

Coming in 2024

21 Days – Countdown To Oblivion

The Lachlan Maclean Scottish Thrillers

The Devil Inside

Coming in 2025

The Devil's Own

www.ingramcontent.com/pod-product-compliance
Lightning Source LLC
Chambersburg PA
CBHW070629180626
46817CB00006B/2087